————————— ★ —————————

"I should have kept an eye on him." She wrung her hands. "He's been acting disoriented lately. I hope nothing's happened to him."

They crossed the brook where watercress and ferns flourished, passed through green catbrier that snared them with curved thorns. Heard crickets and katydids in evening voice. The voices stopped as they approached, then started up again behind them. They moved past stands of mushrooms and toadstools, fluorescent white in the beams of their flashlights and the moonlight.

Finally, they found him, curled up behind a fallen scrub oak tree, his head cushioned by a pad of bright green moss, his feet dug into the stump's rotting wood.

"Lord!" Casey said. "That makes four."

————————— ★ —————————

CYNTHIA RIGGS

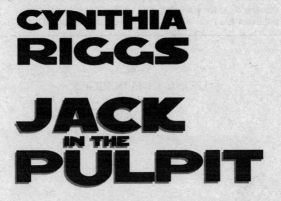

JACK IN THE PULPIT

WORLDWIDE®

TORONTO • NEW YORK • LONDON
AMSTERDAM • PARIS • SYDNEY • HAMBURG
STOCKHOLM • ATHENS • TOKYO • MILAN
MADRID • WARSAW • BUDAPEST • AUCKLAND

FOR
DIONIS COFFIN RIGGS,
POET,
1898–1997

JACK IN THE PULPIT

A Worldwide Mystery/January 2006

First published by St. Martin's Press, LLC.

ISBN 0-373-26553-0

Printed in U.S.A.

Acknowledgments

Thanks to:

Arlene Silva, who urged me to go back to school. And Bret Lott, my first adviser at the Vermont College MFA program. Jonathan Revere, friend, plot doctor, and the quickest wit in the Commonwealth. Rose Treat, the Vineyard's mushroom expert, who went over my mushrooms, characters, and plot— an editor for me as she was for her husband, Larry Treat. Alvida Jones helped me figure out why two seemingly devout ministers would act the way they did.

Lois Remmer and Wendy Hathaway of my writers' group suffered though a half-dozen rewrites. Alvida and Ralph Jones and Ann and Bill Fielder then read and critiqued most of those rewrites. Mary Jo Joiner of the West Tisbury Library promised to buy my books. The Bunch of Grapes, *Publishers Weekly* Book Seller of the Year, stacks my Victoria Trumbull books on the front counter next to the latest Harry Potter.

Bed-and-breakfast guests and West Tisbury villagers have been not only a support but an inspiration for story ideas and characters, both good guys and bad. How could I possibly have created some of the characters I did without their help?

Thank you, Nancy Love, my agent; Ruth Cavin of St. Martin's Press, *the* top editor in the mystery field; and Estelle Laurence, the copy editor of two of my books. She spent some head-scratching hours straightening out my warped time line.

While I've taken a few liberties with actual places, events, and people, my stories are fiction, despite what you read in the Island newspapers.

ONE

"Why don't you go home, Hal? I'll finish the kitchen. The tables and chairs can wait." When she had come into the kitchen and seen Hal Greene's drawn look, Victoria Trumbull, who, at ninety-two, was almost ten years older than the sexton, had put her basket of goldenrod and Queen Anne's lace on the floor beside the sink.

She had stopped by the church parish hall to arrange flowers for Sunday's service. Hal was clearing up after the pancake brunch, folding tables and chairs, and unloading dishes from the dishwasher.

"It's not your heart, is it?" Victoria pulled off her fuzzy tan hat and blue coat and dropped them on one of the tables.

"Stomach cramps," mumbled Hal.

"I hope it wasn't the pancakes." She smiled and ran her gnarled fingers through her hair.

Hal didn't seem to hear her. "I think I'll lie down…in the sanctuary."

Victoria took a stack of plates out of the dishwasher and set them on the counter. She watched Hal with concern.

Hal wrapped his arms around his stomach and bent his knees. "Lie down on a pew…" He straightened up suddenly, his face twisted in a grimace. And with that, he collapsed on the kitchen floor.

Victoria dropped the dishrag into the sink and hurried to

Hal, who was rocking back and forth on the linoleum. She bent over him and put her hand on his forehead. He straightened his legs, kicking off one of his boating shoes as he did.

Victoria skirted around Hal's convulsing body and hustled out through the kitchen door into the Reverend Jackson's small office, which opened off the pine-paneled meeting room. Here, she grabbed the phone off the desk, knocking the base onto the floor in her haste, and punched in 911, her hands shaking so badly she could barely touch the big-print numbers.

"Hurry," she said loudly after she'd identified herself to the communications center. "Please hurry. It's Hal Greene in the West Tisbury church parish hall, and something is terribly wrong."

She snatched a calico-print cushion from the minister's chair, returned to the kitchen, and put the pillow under Hal's head. His eyes were shut tight. He blindly grasped one of the folded checked tablecloths that hung down from the kitchen counter and snatched it off, bringing down a cascade of dishes that had been stacked on top. Glasses and crockery smashed on the floor.

A few long minutes later, Victoria heard the siren on the police Bronco and then Chief Casey O'Neill's booted feet on the stone steps. Casey wrenched open the parish hall door and strode through the pine-paneled meeting room, her coppery hair bouncing on the collar of her blue uniform jacket.

"The ambulance is on the way, Victoria. Is it his heart?"

Victoria shook her head. "Stomach cramps, he said."

Casey bent over the writhing man. "Could be heart."

The pungent smell of fall wafted through the open door, ripe earth and maturing crops. Yellow leaves drifted down from maple trees that arched over Music Street. A slippery confetti of fallen leaves, wet from Friday's rain, littered the brick sidewalk.

Inside on the wall between the kitchen and the meeting room was a wide pass-through with shutters that could be opened to serve refreshments after church, and where dishes were stacked. The shutters were open now.

"Can you hear me, Mr. Greene?" Casey called softly. "The ambulance is on its way."

Hal's eyes were shut tight. He had kicked off his other shoe now. His pressed chinos had ridden up on his legs, exposing gray cashmere socks and hairless shins.

While the chief knelt by Hal trying to comfort him, Victoria hurried out to the Bronco and got a blanket. "It's all I can think to do," she said to Casey, who nodded. Together, they put the blanket on Hal and adjusted the cushion under his head.

"Does this seem like a heart attack to you?" Victoria asked as they attempted to soothe Hal, who was beyond soothing. "I know he's had heart problems in the past."

"I don't know." Casey seemed puzzled. "How old is he?"

"Not that old," Victoria said. "Eighty-four or five."

The chief shook her head and muttered, "I can't believe this Island's definition of 'old.'"

"Hal had volunteered to clean up after the brunch." Opening the closet next to the rest rooms, Victoria brought out a broom and dustpan.

"Leave that for now," Casey said. "Better not clean up yet."

A siren whooped to a stop outside. Victoria heard the iron latch clang and the gate slam open against the picket fence. Footsteps hurried up the brick walkway and bounded up the steps.

"In here, Jennie," Casey called. "In the kitchen." Two medics raced through the door, one with a medical bag. Casey stood up so the EMTs could see her through the open pass-through.

Jennie and the second young woman knelt by Hal, checked his pulse, his breathing, his blood pressure. The EMTs looked as grim as Victoria felt. Hal's convulsive movements were getting weaker and weaker.

The medics and Casey eased Hal onto a wheeled stretcher and pushed it through the parish hall door to the waiting ambulance. Jennie hoisted herself into the driver's seat, and the ambulance took off, siren wailing. Victoria, who had followed Casey out, climbed into the passenger seat of the Bronco, and they shot off to the main road behind the blue-and-white emergency vehicle. They sped past the school, past Whippoorwill Farm, past tall snags of dead red pine. The early afternoon sun glistened on the changing golden brown oak and beech leaves on either side of the road.

By the time the ambulance had gone down the hill into Vineyard Haven, had passed the harbor and the shipyard and the tall fuel tanks, had crossed the bridge that separated Lagoon Pond from the harbor, and had turned into the hospital's emergency entrance, it was too late. Hal had died on the way.

Doc Erickson was on duty in the emergency room. He checked for vital signs and pulled off his stethoscope.

"I'd been treating him for heart problems," he said. "I was afraid of this."

He listened while Casey told him Hal's symptoms. "Not typical of a heart attack. I'll check, of course." He shrugged.

On the way back to the parish hall, Victoria was quiet.

"The church was his family," she said finally. "He and Caroline had no children and after she died he had no other relatives." When they turned onto Old County Road, sunlight dazzled Victoria, and she pulled down the visor. "We played Scrabble together at the senior center only last week."

Casey listened.

"He was seven or eight years younger than me," Victoria continued. "And apparently in nowhere near as good health as we all thought."

"He was with some oil company at one time, wasn't he?"

"A vice president. He retired here about twenty years ago." Victoria sighed. "I suppose I'd better clean up the mess."

"I'll help," said Casey.

Together they swept the broken china and glass into a heap, finished putting the dishes in the cabinets, the tablecloths in a plastic bag to be laundered. Victoria set Hal's shoes to one side.

As they worked, Casey talked into Victoria's silence. "It was this church, as much as anything, that convinced me to accept the police job. Patrick is almost nine now, and I wanted him to have this sense of community. You okay, Victoria?"

Victoria nodded. She turned her deep-set eyes to Casey, listening.

"The day I came for my job interview almost a year ago, I looked in the church windows. I never dreamed the door would be open and that I could simply walk in. In Brockton, the door would have been locked."

Victoria picked up Hal's shoes, brushed them off, then put them down again.

"When I got to the church the town clock struck eleven. I remember it so clearly," said Casey.

"That was the only timepiece villagers needed a hundred years ago," Victoria murmured.

"The maples had turned yellow and the air was clean and blue. I knew right away this was where we belonged." Casey stopped sweeping and leaned on the broom.

Victoria stepped over to the closet next to the rest rooms and brought out a dustpan, which she held so Casey could sweep the mess into it.

"When I walked into the vestibule," Casey continued, "it smelled like old wood and old hymnals." She stopped sweeping. "Hal was a good friend of yours, wasn't he?"

Victoria was tucking a paper napkin back into her pocket.

"Hal was in the church that morning, but I didn't realize it at first." Casey spoke softly.

Victoria sat down on a stool and let Casey talk.

"There were arrangements of chrysanthemums and scarlet maple leaves on either side of the pulpit. I bet they were yours, weren't they, Victoria?"

"Probably so."

"You know that large gilded cross on the wall behind the pulpit?" Casey leaned on the broom.

Victoria sniffed. "That cross was new when you first came. The Reverend Jack Jackson's idea. My grandmother would have called it popery."

"I was brought up Catholic. So when I went down the aisle I instinctively blessed myself and genuflected."

At that, Victoria smiled.

"When I slipped into a pew on the left, I thought how generations of Sunday woolens and silks had polished the wood of that seat sliding in the same way I did."

Casey dumped the contents of the dustpan into one of the trash containers next to the sink. "When I raised my head, I saw this distinguished-looking man holding a bottle of Murphy Oil Soap and a rag. He stared at me as if I'd come from outer space."

"Hal Greene," Victoria said quietly.

"I didn't know who he was then, of course. I thought he was the mayor or something, figured I'd blown my chances of getting the job."

"He thought highly of you." Victoria shifted to a more

comfortable position on the stool. "He often talked about how you've introduced modern police methods."

"Patrick and I go to church regularly now, and I got to know Hal." Casey put the broom and dustpan back in the closet. "You know, Victoria, this is the toughest part of my job, losing someone like him. In Brockton, I didn't really get to know people. Here, we always go to church early because Patrick likes—liked—to see Mr. Greene ring the bell. You know the way Hal climbed the stairs partway to the choir loft and pulled the bell rope?"

Victoria nodded.

"That was a big deal to Patrick. Before the bell began to sound, you could hear the rope rise with a rumble through that smoothed hole in the flooring of the choir loft, rubbing off a dusting of wood."

"I still love hearing the sexton ring the bell for service," Victoria said. "You can hear the rope rise through that hole, then you hear the bell swing in the steeple before it starts to peal."

Casey put the broom and dustpan away. "Such a bright sound. It raises goose bumps when I think of it."

TWO DAYS LATER, the Reverend Milton (Jack) Jackson, somber behind the pulpit in his black robe, conducted the funeral service. Short, dignified, it was a moving tribute to Hal Greene. He'd been a worthy, generous parishioner, the Reverend Jackson said. He had provided handsomely for the church's continuing good works.

TWO

VICTORIA STOOD AT the kitchen window, musing. Morning light filtered through the maples that overhung the fish pond. A few fallen leaves drifted on the pond's still surface. She missed Hal.

The past year had brought changes. Her granddaughter had moved in with her, when? late October or early November, because most of the leaves had already fallen, and Casey had been on the job as police chief for several weeks.

She recalled the night Elizabeth had called, sobbing so moistly into the phone, Victoria could hardly understand her.

"I've left Lockwood," she had said. "I've quit my job. My life is a shambles. Can I stay with you for a couple of weeks, Gram, until I get my head together?"

"Of course," Victoria had said. "I'm surprised you put up with him as long as you did."

"Thanks, Gram." Elizabeth sniffled and blew her nose. "Seven years. What a waste!"

"At least you don't have children to worry about."

"The bastard! He didn't want any."

The next morning, Elizabeth's VW convertible rattled into Victoria's drive, its top gray with mildew and patched with duct tape, the back seat filled with cardboard boxes. Elizabeth's eyes were red and swollen, her usually bright hair was lank and dull.

She slumped into a kitchen chair. "I got the car over on the first ferry, standby."

"You must have driven all night." Victoria poured two cups of tea from the blue-and-white teapot. "Get some rest before you do anything else."

She had settled her granddaughter in the small upstairs bedroom that had been hers when she was a girl, and Elizabeth dropped onto the cherrywood sleigh bed and was asleep before her grandmother left the room. Victoria covered her with a quilt and tiptoed out, closing the door gently behind her.

Instead of staying for only a couple of weeks, Elizabeth found a full-time job and settled in permanently with her grandmother. Victoria found herself taking care of her thirty-two-year-old granddaughter.

Victoria frowned. Now, because of a minor incident just before Hal died, her granddaughter's and her roles had changed. She did not like what the change would mean.

Not quite two weeks ago, Victoria had had a small encounter in the senior center parking lot across the road from Alley's store. She had driven to the center in her green Citation to leave some of her poetry books for Carole Bowen, the director.

She was backing smartly out of her parking space, turning the wheel the way she always did, when she heard a scraping sound and her car stalled. She rolled down the window and looked out. The Meals on Wheels van had parked next to her, much too close, when she was in the senior center talking to Carole, and she had backed into it, leaving what she considered a slight scratch that didn't seem worth bothering about.

However, Manny Smith, the driver, had been filling out forms in his van. He leaped out and ran around to Victoria's window, flailing his arms and shouting.

"It's only a scratch," Victoria said, getting out of the Citation and examining the two-foot-long dent.

"Scratch, hell," Manny shouted. "Look at it, my new van ruined."

"Don't be ridiculous," Victoria said. "It hardly shows."

"You can't control your car any better, lady, you shouldn't be driving."

Victoria reached into the window for her battered leather pocketbook, took out her wallet, and extracted a twenty-dollar bill, which she handed to Manny.

"Here, this should take care of it."

Manny, a pallid young man, turned an unhealthy shade of red, a color that made his white eyebrows, eyelashes, pale hair, and small mustache stand out in sharp contrast.

"Lady, do you know what it costs for a new panel and a paint job?" he sputtered. "Do you?"

"You don't need to shout," Victoria said calmly. "You certainly don't need an entire paint job. Pick up a can of white paint at Alley's. For the twenty dollars, you can get a brush, too. And change." She got back into her car, started it up again, pulled forward to straighten her wheels, put it into reverse, stepped on the gas, and plowed into Manny's van again, this time scraping off part of the elegant paint job, black with gold highlighting, that read, FOOD FIT FOR AN ANGEL.

Two days later, Casey asked Victoria to come by the station house with her granddaughter.

Victoria settled into one of the two wooden chairs in the station and unbuttoned her blue coat. The chief leaned forward across her desk and held out her hand. "Let me have your driver's license, Victoria."

Victoria felt unreal. She had always had a driver's license. She was one of the first licensed drivers on the Island. She'd driven cars since she was twelve years old. Without moving her head, she shifted her eyes from Casey to Elizabeth and back to Casey. "There's some mistake," she said.

"I'm afraid not." Casey continued to hold out her hand.

Victoria turned to Elizabeth, who stared down at her hands, which were clasped between her jeans-clad knees.

"Elizabeth has nothing to do with this," Casey said. "It's time, Victoria. You've been driving for almost eighty years, and there comes a time."

Victoria thought of Jeremiah Silvia driving his truck at twenty miles an hour with a line of cars following him.

"I'm a better driver than most people around here," she said.

"That may be." Casey continued to hold out her hand.

Victoria heard a car go by on the road. Geese honked in the parking space out front. After an uncomfortable silence, she reached into her pocketbook, took out her wallet, removed her driver's license, and handed it to Casey. When she looked up, she caught a glimpse of herself in the glass of a framed painting of Ben Norton feeding geese. She looked like an owl, she thought, deep-set hooded eyes on either side of her beaky nose.

"Manny Smith overreacted," she said finally. "It was only a small scratch."

"It wasn't just Manny, Victoria." Casey opened her desk drawer and dropped the license into it. "There've been other complaints about your driving. His was the last straw. I'll get this framed so you can hang it on your wall."

Victoria felt a wave of hopelessness that her face must have registered.

"I can take you wherever you want to go, Gram." Elizabeth put an arm around Victoria's sloping shoulders.

Victoria looked down at her hands, clasped in her lap.

Two ducks landed on the pond with a splash and a flutter of wings. Someone opened the front door behind Victoria, said "Excuse me," backed out, and shut the door behind him. The phone rang. Casey lifted the receiver, listened, said into it, "Let me call you back," and hung up.

Finally, Casey said to Victoria, who was sitting like a sack of potatoes, "If your granddaughter can't take you where you want to go, when you want to go, I will. That's a promise, Victoria. Shake hands on it."

Victoria held out her hand and they shook.

A week later, Hal died.

THREE

A NOR'EASTER MOVED IN the day after Hal Greene's funeral, gray, raw, and chilly with a fine rain. Elizabeth had put the top back on her convertible, but water leaked in above the windshield. Victoria put a plastic raincoat over her legs.

Elizabeth pulled into Cousin Edna's semicircular driveway and stopped at the kitchen door. Nobody ever used the elegantly carved door that faced a small pond at the back of the house. "I have only a couple of errands, Gram. I shouldn't be more than an hour at most. Can you can put up with her for that long?"

Victoria pushed up the cuff of her turtleneck with her index finger, looked at her watch, and frowned. "If I still had my driver's license…"

Elizabeth laughed. "I don't mind taking you wherever you want to go. Neither does Casey."

"It was just a scratch," Victoria continued. "I don't know why Manny had to make such a fuss over it. He didn't need to involve the police."

"He's a pretty sensitive guy, and he'd just had that sign painted on his Meals on Wheels van."

Victoria made a dismissive sound. "'Food Fit for an Angel.' Ridiculous. I offered to pay him."

"I think that was part of the problem, Gram. He was insulted when you offered him twenty dollars."

Victoria adjusted her tan hat firmly on her hair and slid out of the car. "Make it sooner than an hour, if you possibly can."

Victoria and Edna, Victoria's second cousin by marriage, had little in common, which was why they enjoyed each other's company. Victoria was wiry, almost skinny, and, even shrunk from her prime, she was several inches taller than Edna. Edna was short, stout, and sedentary. Victoria bought clothes at the thrift shop in Vineyard Haven. Edna shopped by mail at Talbots. Every couple of months, Victoria got her white hair cut short at Bert's Barber Shop in Vineyard Haven. Every week Edna had her blue hair rinsed and styled at Paul David's in Edgartown. Edna envied Victoria's enormous patrician nose. Victoria didn't envy anybody anything.

They spent hours together each week, arguing. This time, as always, their argument began with politics, a familiar, comfortable warm-up for bigger and better clashes to come.

"I don't know why you continue to call yourself a Republican," Edna said to Victoria. "You're nothing but a thinly disguised Democrat. The last Republican you voted for was Eisenhower."

"Edna, you've become fossilized," Victoria answered. "Look at you, all your opinions come from that awful man on radio…"

"Rush Limbaugh," said Edna.

"…You're trapped in time like a fly in amber," Victoria finished.

They argued about the Island's younger generation. "Clayton Rogers's son gets an MBA from Harvard and then what…" Edna paused for effect, although Victoria knew "what" perfectly well. "…he takes over his father's carpentry business."

"Shows good sense," said Victoria, as she always did. "Why would he want to live in Boston?"

Edna brought up Victoria's run-in with Manny Smith's van two weeks ago. "You and I shouldn't be driving at our age, Victoria," Edna murmured, knowing Victoria would react. And she did.

"Manny was parked much too close to me," Victoria said hotly. "I was hardly moving. He had no need to shout at me the way he did."

"If you'd hit him only once, it might not have been so bad," Edna said, as she smoothed her hair. "It was when you hit him the second time that he got upset."

"I didn't 'hit' him," Victoria insisted. "He's a pathological exaggerator."

"He's a lovely, sensitive, artistic boy," Cousin Edna said. "He volunteers his time to deliver those meals to shut-ins. You'll be grateful to him, someday."

Victoria thumped her open hand on the table. "Oh, for heaven's sake, Edna."

And concerning the West Tisbury Congregational Church: "The Reverend Milton Jackson has turned out to be a fine minister," said Edna. "So much better than the Reverend John Hutchinson with those long-winded, pompous sermons." She looked slyly at Victoria, who took the bait, as she invariably did.

"Popery," Victoria said, her face flushing slightly. "Short, preachy sermons, full of ghosts and spirits, superstition, and biblical passages." Edna sat back in her rocker with a smirk, patted her tight blue curls, and laced her fingers over her large paunch. Victoria went on. "And why on earth would our congregation encourage him to hold weekly Communion? Weekly!" Edna relished what came next and next after that. "And a life-sized gold-sprayed cross behind the pulpit. If that isn't popery."

Victoria showed signs of winding down, so Edna said, "Jeremiah Silvia carved it."

That got Victoria going again, face quite flushed now. "And the way he treats Jack is shameful."

They called both the Reverend Milton Jackson and the Reverend John Hutchinson "Jack," so anyone listening to Victoria and Edna discussing the two ministers could easily become confused. "The Reverend Jackson has hurt Jack Hutchinson terribly the way he shut him out of the church. After all Jack did during the years he was in the pulpit," said Victoria.

"My Jack," said Edna, "has every reason to want to start his ministry with no interference from your Jack."

Victoria slapped her hand on the table with a thwack. "If your Jack is going to be so damned sanctimonious" (whenever Victoria said "damned," Edna scored a couple of battle points), "damned sanctimonious," Victoria repeated the words and emphasized them, "he should examine his own soul. Jealousy, that's all it is. He's jealous of Jack, and Jack is terribly hurt. Jack has such stature, such respect, such intellect…"

"Balderdash, Victoria," Edna interrupted. "My Jack's been minister only a year and look at the way he's building up attendance—and beneficences. The church is crowded Sundays; people are coming all the way from West Chop."

"Beneficences!" Victoria snorted. "He's nothing but an ambulance chaser." She looked at her watch. "Elizabeth should be here any minute. I've got to get to Vineyard Haven before the bank closes."

The argument fizzled out rapidly, as their arguments usually did. Victoria believed Edna stirred them up to improve her own sluggish circulation.

WHILE VICTORIA and Edna were discussing matters of importance on this blustery day, Casey O'Neill was thinking about her first year as chief. Patrick liked the West Tisbury school and had already made friends there. And now she recognized many of the townspeople, the ones who hung around Alley's store, the ones who went to the West Tisbury church. But this town was not like Brockton, where you weren't expected to know everyone.

She had learned not to say anything disparaging about any of the townspeople. Everyone was related. She had made an offhand comment, half-kidding, to her sergeant, Junior Norton, about Jeremiah Silvia's notoriously slow and wobbly driving. She'd remarked that the turtles crossing the road in front of the police station would get to the other side of the road before Jeremiah did. Jeremiah Silvia, it turned out, was Junior Norton's father's brother-in-law's uncle, and, although Junior laughed, the laugh was a polite one.

The police cruiser was a problem, too. For Island cars, according to the people she had sounded out about a new cruiser, two hundred thousand miles was nicely broken in. Maybe for Islanders. Not for a police cruiser, though. She had asked the finance committee and the selectmen to put a budget item for a new cruiser on the town meeting warrant. The selectmen were not encouraging. Ben Norton, they had said, put well over two hundred thousand miles on his vehicles. Ben Norton, Junior's father, had been West Tisbury's police chief for thirty years.

And the police station! A cute little building, she had to admit, cedar-shingled with a peaked roof. Long ago, even before Victoria's time, the building had been a one-room schoolhouse. But it had only the one room, and that room was half the size of Casey's former office in Brockton.

The structure had six windows with small panes of glass, three on each of the long sides of the building, and a window on either side of the front door, which had never been locked, as far as Casey could tell. When she had asked the selectmen a year ago for a key, they acted surprised. No one had ever locked the police station. There was no need for anyone to break in. The door was always open. Casey added "locks" to her list that included "new cruiser, road signs, drug education, ducks, & geese." She had decided, within a few days of her arrival last year, that West Tisbury's townspeople needed to know what police work entailed, and she planned to set up a training program, so she added "citizen education" to her list.

The windows on the left side of the police station overlooked the Mill Pond, source of the turtles that frequently crossed the road. In fact, someone had put up a temporary sign, SLOW DOWN! TURTLE CROSSING! Casey reluctantly admitted she liked to look at the pond and the shrubbery surrounding it, black alder, willow, and elderberry, each with its own texture and color. Around the pond, late summer's tired green was changing into the subtle colors of the Island's autumn with an occasional flash of bright scarlet sumac. Ducks and Canada geese swam in their separate areas, and occasionally a seagull would splash down. When she was worrying over the wording of some report, she liked to stare out at the birds—as long as they kept their distance. She wanted her reports to be accurate without sounding bureaucratic. Brockton liked bureaucratic wording. West Tisbury did not.

Immediately inside the front door—everything in the police station was immediately inside the front door—was an old rolltop desk that Eric Pinealt, one of the town's carpenters, had refinished for her as a welcome present—and a brand-new computer. Ben Norton had never used a computer. Casey had pushed the desk against the west wall between the windows where she could look out. Junior Norton and her two patrolmen shared the desk across from hers.

There was no privacy in this police station, no room for privacy. No place to interrogate anyone, if you needed to, no lockup, if you needed that. No way to make a private phone call.

Out front, an overgrown multiflora rosebush covered with shriveled rose hips and birds eating the rose hips partially hid the front windows of the police station. The birds' chatter in the rosebush sounded a bit like Brockton's traffic and Casey felt a twinge of homesickness for the city's sparrows and its predictable crime.

Immediately next to the police station, water from the Mill Pond dropped in a smooth glassy sheet over a granite sill, and burbled and chattered over a stony bed that ran under the road into the brook next to the old mill across the road. In summer, the mill was home to the garden club. The brook wandered through patches of watercress, past overhanging swamp azaleas and swamp maples, past ferns and skunk cabbage, mushrooms and toadstools, jack-in-the-pulpit and wild ginger, into the Great Pond, a hand-shaped body of water about two miles long and just as wide.

Islanders seemed to call any water body smaller than the Atlantic a "pond." Casey had even heard someone describing the Azores, where a lot of Vineyarders had their roots, as being "across the pond," meaning the Atlantic Ocean.

Casey had watched some children, eight or nine years old, she guessed, drop sticks into the Mill Pond on the police station side and dash across the road to see the sticks come out in the brook on the garden club side. She scolded the children, told them not to do that, there was too much traffic for that to be safe. They looked at her with incomprehension. Casey knew what the look meant. Their mothers and grandmothers had dropped sticks into the Mill Pond and watched them come out on the other side. Why couldn't they? She imagined Brockton's police chief scolding kids for dropping sticks into a brook and laughed out loud.

When Casey drove up to the station in the two-hundred-thousand-plus-miles cruiser, ducks, geese, and the pair of swans that nested at the sedgy end of the pond hissed and honked around her, stretched their necks, nipped at one another, quacked, and defecated. She parked in the oyster-shell-paved space in front of the police station and opened the cruiser's door. The creatures followed her to the front step with a cacophony of quacks and hisses. They had carved a small muddy bay in the side of the pond. Recently, she noticed, the ducks and geese and swans had been joined by sea-gulls. What next? she wondered. Molly Bettencourt, the animal control officer, fed them and brought them grain. Casey could hardly say—at least not yet—that she thought the ducks and geese and swans and seagulls made the police department look unprofessional , especially when citizens had to shoo them away and dodge droppings. She was city-bred, more accustomed to pigeons in city parks than to wild fowl. Ben Norton, the former chief, had fed the flock for years.

A pair of Muscovy ducks had moved to the police station a few days after Casey had taken the job. She had been too new to protest. The ducks had waddled the quarter mile down the hill past Brandy Brow from Maley's, their tricolored black-and-white-and-red heads bobbing, their orange webbed feet splayed out. Molly Bettencourt had followed them in her station wagon with stick-on letters reading ANIMAL CONTROL OFFICER. The car's transmission growled in first gear, its flashers blinked to warn other drivers of the road hazard ahead—Muscovy ducks emigrating from Maley's to join the flock at the police station.

Ben Norton apparently thought the flock of birds gave the place a relaxed image. Well, it did. There was not much Casey could do about this relaxed image, but that was on her list of things that needed fixing, too.

The closest Casey had ever come to swans and geese before moving to the Island was taking her son Patrick for a ride in the Swan Boat in the Boston Public Gardens. There, some college student had worked the pedals safely to make the swan glide over the water. She'd had no idea then that swans were so mean. She'd gotten a huge bruise on her thigh last spring from a swan attack when she got too close to their nest at the upper end of the pond.

The police station, cute as it was, was barely adequate for modern police work, Casey thought. The town was growing, crime was bound to rise, and as much as she would like to believe her job was public relations and traffic control, she knew she had more than that to worry about. A lot of people in town didn't want to hear about their kids using drugs or about their neighbors' squabbles turning violent. They certainly didn't want to hear about murder. Casey herself, with all her graduate degrees, didn't want to deal with *that*. Ever.

FOUR

ON A BRIGHT sunny morning a week after Hal Greene's funeral, Victoria was in the kitchen washing the breakfast dishes. "Molly has that miserable flu that's going around," she said to Elizabeth. "I don't recall her ever being sick before."

Elizabeth was putting away the cereal. "Why don't we take her some of that soup I made from Sunday's chicken." She took the soup out of the refrigerator and ladled some into an empty cottage cheese container.

A few minutes later as they left the kitchen for Molly's, McCavity, the cat, darted through the door ahead of them, dodged under the wisteria vine, and reappeared shortly with a furry gray object in his mouth.

When Victoria bent down to pat the cat, he dropped the mouse at her feet. The creature scampered under the lilac bush in the turnaround, and as McCavity started after it, Victoria seized him around his middle.

Morning light touched the hills that Victoria could see on the other side of town from her driveway. The trees along Mill Brook and the long grass in Doane's pasture had a golden haze. The hands on the town clock in the church steeple a half mile away glinted. Victoria, whose eyesight was as keen as an eagle's, could almost make out the time from where she stood.

Elizabeth handed her grandmother the container of soup,

undid the hooks that held down the vinyl top of her convertible. "A good day for an open car," she said.

On the way to Molly's, they passed the police station, where Junior Norton was tossing scoops of corn to the ducks and geese.

"That must irritate Chief O'Neill," Elizabeth said. "Using her sergeant's time to feed Molly's birds."

Junior lifted his hand as they passed. "Pretty sporty car, Victoria," he shouted, pronouncing the word "cah."

The mirror surface of the Mill Pond doubled and magnified the edging of shrubbery and reflected early changing colors of sumac and woodbine. Across from the pond, pink geraniums blossomed in window boxes at the old mill, where thĕy would bloom for another month, when frost could be expected.

After they passed the mill, they turned left onto South Road and Elizabeth shifted down at the stop sign on the hill.

The gang sitting on a bench on the porch of Alley's across the road from the senior center nodded as they passed.

"Every time I go past the center, I get mad at Manny all over again," Victoria said.

"I guess he was pretty upset."

By this time, they were passing Maley's Gallery across from the church. Exuberant polyresin nudes danced in Maley's meadow, and in a risqué bas-relief on the side of Maley's barn, Bacchus pursued a maiden, discreetly out of sight of churchgoers and summer tour buses.

"I hate those statues," Elizabeth said, nodding toward Maley's nudes. "Fat white plastic blimps."

"I like them," Victoria said. "I like the way they fling their arms into the air, kick their legs. You can almost see them move. They look like Maley himself."

Elizabeth slowed to take a closer look. "They look like shiny white fat grubs to me."

As they passed the West Tisbury church, the Reverend Jackson was walking around the west side. Victoria waved. "I don't think he saw me," she said, when he didn't wave back. "He wouldn't," she added.

They passed the old Agricultural Hall. Jeremiah Silvia was tacking a sign onto the fence, a notice of the Show of Antique Engines on Saturday and Sunday. "Good car for a day like today," he called out.

"I've got to be sure to put that in my column," Victoria said, scribbling a note on an old envelope. "Antique Engines show. I like the way those old machines chug and puff."

At Tiasquam Repairs, almost on the Chilmark town line, they turned left. Molly lived behind the gas station. Elizabeth parked next to the car with the Animal Control Officer sign, in front of two empty chicken-wire cages.

The shingles on Molly's small house had weathered to a satiny gray. White paint on the trim was peeling in thin strips. Beside the granite back step, dry hollyhock stems slumped under the weight of seed pods. Yellow and orange marigolds and leggy last-of-summer petunias, blue and pink, blossomed in raised beds made of old, white-painted tires with cut-out scalloped rims.

A large black dog in a fenced-in area bounded up to Victoria and Elizabeth, a stick in his mouth. He dropped the stick close to the fence and wagged his tail, tongue hanging out.

"Here you go, Bosco!" Elizabeth reached through the fence and threw the stick for the dog, who dashed to the other side of his enclosure, brought the stick back to Elizabeth, dropped it again, and waited, tongue out, tail wagging.

They knocked and went in the back door, which led to the kitchen then through the dining room into the bedroom.

Molly lay on her back in a narrow spool bed, a patchwork quilt pulled around her face. "Don't get too close, Victoria," she said thickly. "It's a stinking virus, and I feel awful."

"We brought you some soup." Victoria held up the container. "We can heat it for you, if you'd like."

"Thanks," Molly said. "I'd better eat something, though I don't feel like it much. This miserable thing has been going on for almost a week."

"Do you want us to get groceries for you?" Elizabeth asked.

"No thanks. Maddy Hutchinson came by, made a list of things I need. Reverend Jackson brought me some of his chicken soup, too. I've tested every chicken soup recipe in town, I think."

WHILE MOLLY WAS convalescing, the Kneelands' cow somehow got its left rear leg caught in the split-rail fence that surrounded the Kneelands' pasture in Middletown, which was part of West Tisbury and part of Molly's territory as animal control officer. Since Molly was in no condition to get out of bed, Chief O'Neill responded, with Victoria in the passenger seat, riding shotgun.

When they turned onto North Road past the big oak tree, they could hear the cow bellowing like a foghorn before they could see it. The pasture was small, only a couple of acres of tawny mown hay surrounded by a split-rail fence and backed by oak, maple, and beech woods that showed a tinge of color.

Casey parked on the side of the road and Victoria went up quietly to the distressed animal. The cow turned its head, eyes showing white around brown irises, stretched its neck, stuck its tongue out, and lowed, a terrified, melancholy sound.

"I'm no cowboy," Casey said in dismay. "I wish I were back in Brockton. They never taught us how to rope cattle."

"I'll calm her," Victoria said. "Then if you put a line around her there," she pointed, "so she won't hurt herself you can lift her leg back through the fence."

"Lord!" Casey said, and opened the back of the Bronco to get the rope.

Victoria returned to the front end of the cow. She plucked handfuls of choice grass the cow had been trying to reach when it got its leg caught and put the grass under the cow's nose. She patted the animal's velvety snout, talked to it, calmed it. The cow stopped struggling. While she was doing that, Casey lifted the leg back through the fence onto firm ground.

"I can't believe this is happening to me," Casey said. "Molly had better get over the flu soon."

Within a couple of days, Molly seemed to be recovering, and neighbors began to take casseroles to her, West Tisbury's answer to illness, misfortune, and death.

On the day Elizabeth went off-Island to the dentist's, someone left a casserole on Victoria's kitchen table. Elizabeth came home earlier than expected, so they took the casserole, which was just the right size for one person, over to Molly's.

"Wonder who brought it?" Elizabeth said. "That was a nice thing to do." She had changed her skirt and blouse for torn jeans and a sweater.

"Someone from church, probably," Victoria said. "I'm glad they used a foil pan so I don't have to return a dish. Is a name taped on the bottom?"

Elizabeth lifted the pan above her head. "I can see a name on a piece of masking tape, but the name is smeared, and I can't read it. We can ask Jack to say thank you during announcements next Sunday to whoever brought it." Elizabeth stood on her toes and stretched luxuriously. "The minute I get on the ferry to go off-Island I want to be back again."

When Victoria knocked on Molly's back door, Molly answered. Her hair was uncombed, her eyes swollen, her usual red cheeks were pale and chapped. She wore a rumpled flannel wrapper.

"Are you feeling any better?" Victoria asked. "You look terrible."

"Much better. For the past week I could barely get out of bed to go to the john, and I needed to go a lot."

"Someone brought Gram a tuna noodle casserole," Elizabeth told her. "We thought you might like it."

"It looks good," Molly said, lifting the wrapping. "Yesterday was the first time I felt like eating anything solid."

Elizabeth put the casserole into Molly's oven to warm, Victoria set the kitchen table with a plate and utensils, and the two of them went home.

Molly seemed to be recovering rapidly. But within twenty-four hours the flu symptoms came back so fiercely she called Chief O'Neill, who took her to the hospital. Two days later she was dead.

Doc Erickson's nurse called Victoria, told her to come in immediately for a flu shot. Victoria thanked her for calling and said she was busy.

At their next weekly meeting, the Board of Selectmen, after a moment of silence, appointed Gabriel Jernegan to the now vacated position of animal control officer. Victoria volunteered to feed the police station ducks, geese, and swans until Gabe could take over.

FIVE

THE REVEREND MILTON (Jack) JACKSON knocked on Edna Coffin's kitchen door, opened it, and called in, "Anyone home?" He peered over his half-frame spectacles and wiped his feet on the grass mat covering the big flat stone by the doorstep.

"Come in, come in!" Edna was paring apples at the kitchen table. From her seat she could look out at the bird feeder, a colorful display of jays, cardinals, and chickadees. Beyond the feeder, the lawn—actually weeds cut short twice a week this time of year by the neighbor's son, Ricky Rezendes—sloped down to a small pond, one of a chain of ponds along Mill Brook. A swamp maple blazed scarlet at the water's edge, where huckleberry bushes glowed dark red.

"Don't get up, Edna," the Reverend Jackson said. He took off his baseball cap with *USNS Shark* in gold letters on the front, ran a hand over his thin hair, then pulled out a chair, and sat down facing Edna across the kitchen table. "I was driving by on my way to Vineyard Haven and thought I'd see if you needed anything at Cronig's."

The minister settled into Edna's padded wooden chair, unzipped his windbreaker, and leaned across the table. "Apple pie?" he guessed.

"I thought I'd make a pie for Victoria and Elizabeth and that young man who's staying with them. He looks as if he could use some fattening."

"Young man?" Reverend Jackson put his hands into his windbreaker pockets and tipped the chair on its hind legs.

"Don't lean back in the chair," Edna protested, and he lowered the chair to all fours with a thud. "Angelo Santellini, an artist who's been on the Island all summer. He's sold a couple of paintings, enough to keep paying rent to Victoria."

"Are his paintings any good?" The Reverend Jackson took his hands out of his pockets and leaned his elbows on the table.

"Victoria doesn't think so, but you can't argue with sales." Edna finished paring the last apple and began quartering them, cutting out the cores as she went. "By the way, everyone has been commenting on the services you gave for Molly and for Hal Greene." She wiped the paring knife on the corner of a dish towel next to the bowl. "Both so appropriate, so inspirational."

"Lovely people," the Reverend Jackson said. "Hal certainly was a generous person."

Edna sighed. "I suppose you have to approach parishioners to suggest they consider the church in their wills."

"It's part of my responsibility to the church."

"You know you can count on me," Edna said. "Forrester made some wise investments." She got up heavily and carried the bowl of sliced apples to the sink, rinsed them, and sprinkled them with sugar and nutmeg.

"Can I help you with that?" the Reverend Jackson asked, getting up.

"I'm fine, thank you," Edna said.

"I see you prefer nutmeg to cinnamon."

Edna smiled.

The reverend pushed his chair back under the table and picked up his cap.

"How are things between you and Jack Hutchinson?" Edna asked as he paused at the door.

"Not easy." The Reverend Jackson turned. "He was associated with the church for so long he believes no one else can run it the way he did. Well, no one can. We all have our own way of doing things. He should know that."

"He's terribly proud," Edna said. "I'm sure it must be hard on him. It certainly must be for you."

"Not only for me, but for Betty," the Reverend Jackson said, gesturing vaguely in the direction of his house, out of sight across Mill Pond. "Mrs. Hutchinson, Madeline, can't seem to keep from meddling with what is now Betty's turf. The Church Improvement Society, the church fair, the potluck suppers. All the things a minister's wife does."

"Maddy can be imperious," Edna agreed as she sat down again. "She acted as though she were queen bee. I suppose it's almost impossible for her and Jack to back away."

"She's still doing what amounts to pastoral visits," the Reverend Jackson said. "Taking covered dishes to sick or elderly church members, taking them shopping, that sort of thing. I can't fault her for her charity, but Betty finds it hard to be accepted in her new role. People naturally still think of Maddy Hutchinson as the minister's wife." He straightened his cap again. "Enough. Sure there's nothing you need in Vineyard Haven?"

"If you're going to Cronig's anyway, I could use a lemon," Edna said. "Let me give you some money."

"Don't worry about it." The Reverend Jackson waved away any thought of money. "I'll see you on my way back with the lemon."

THE REVEREND HUTCHINSON was, indeed, having a difficult time. He had been minister of the West Tisbury church for twenty years, and he missed the ministry terribly. He had retired only after his seventieth birthday when his legs began giving him trouble. He needed to use a cane when he walked; he could no longer stand at the pulpit.

His house and Maddy's was on a Chilmark hill overlooking the south shore and the Atlantic. He sat by the window in his armchair and stared sightlessly at the smoky gray ocean.

He had loved the West Tisbury church. The simple Quaker-like meetinghouse with its austere white pulpit had suited him well. He was still a dramatic lion of a man, a tall, bulky presence, with his white mane of hair, high forehead, and jutting chin. His voice could still growl and roar, or purr when needed.

He missed the swish of his black robe as, one foot after the other, he scaled the four steps to the pulpit. He missed sitting in the carved wooden armchair where he waited for services to begin. He missed watching his congregation assemble. He had bullied them into silence before the Sunday service, and now they sat, some with heads bowed, some with heads erect, Quaker-like. He bullied them into singing the hymns loud, with joy. Bullied the organist into speeding up the tempo of the glorious old Congregational hymns. Yes, he missed it with a terrible, intemperate ache.

He missed it for Maddy's sake, too. Maddy had organized bake sales, church fairs, exercise classes, sewing groups, senior trips, teen trips. Anything that could be organized. Maddy was the perfect minister's wife. Everyone said so. During the twenty years of their service, Maddy led the temporal church as if she had been born to the role.

During those twenty years no one had ever questioned the fact that Maddy *was* his wife. For the first few years, he and she worried about that question and how they would answer. But no one ever asked.

Before coming to the West Tisbury church, with its congregation of less than a hundred souls, he'd been minister of a three-thousand-member church in Arlington.

His story was a cliché, the Reverend Jack Hutchinson told himself. You would have thought that he knew enough about human feelings and failings to avoid falling for a parishioner.

As he sat by the window overlooking the ocean, he recalled that Sunday, more than twenty years ago. His sermon had felt inspired. No one had coughed during silent prayer. He gave the benediction, eyes closed, his large paw of a right hand held above his shaggy, then sandy, head of hair. While the congregation was singing the closing hymn he strode down the aisle to the front door. He could still feel the way his robe had billowed in a silken cloud behind him. The doors had been thrown open to let in the bright May morning. A wren had caroled, a huge volume of song packed into a tiny bird. He had been high on the exultation that followed a good performance. His robe moved in the balmy breeze. The wren sang.

"Wonderful sermon," Phil Steinbeck had said, shaking Jack's hand. The Steinbecks had defected from the Unitarian church, Jack knew. "Lot of meat to it. You remember my wife Maddy." A faint breath of perfume, then Jack had Maddy's hand in his, a slender hand with long fingers. He remembered the jolt he'd felt, a tingling.

"Thank you so much." She had looked up into his tawny, leonine eyes. The shock of her hands was nothing compared to the magnetism of her eyes, one green, one blue. He had not been able to look away. The line of churchgoers waiting after her froze in time. Her eyes had been moist, and even now he wondered what in his sermon or the readings or the music had moved her so.

She had taken her hand away finally and walked on, and

he accepted the next offered hand. But he continued to feel her fingers, the draw of those strange eyes, smell her perfume.

He had shaken hand after hand. "Thank you," he said over and over. "So good of you to come," he said. "Hope your son is enjoying Dartmouth," he said. "Thank you," he said. "Looking forward to cocktails next Thursday," he said. "Thank you. Thank you." And all the time he had felt her hand.

He had been felled like the great spruce tree behind the church, which had toppled after the gentlest of breezes.

"Darling, a marvelous sermon." His wife Lydia had been last in line. She stood on tiptoe and kissed his cheek. Jack could still feel his sense of having betrayed her.

Even now he could recall the intensity of his feelings, how those feelings had begun to interfere with his reading, his writing, his work. On every page he had seen Maddy, tall, slim. She had worn her chestnut hair in an old-fashioned thick braid wrapped around her head like a crown. Her hair was white now, and she still wore it that way. Somehow the style was not at odds with her elegant carriage, her chic clothing, her strange eyes.

On a Monday morning more than twenty years ago, he had been sitting by himself in a back pew in the sanctuary, letting the creaks and snaps of the building seep into his unconscious, the tick of the clock over his head, the smells of the much-handled hymnals, the feel of the prickly horsehair cushion covered with heavy red damask under him. He had let his mind drift, that long ago Monday, a blankness that soaked up the quiet energy of his great church, a relief from the fervor of reading and writing and praying and worrying about his congregation and the terror he had felt seeping into his soul. Sunlight poured through the stained-glass window onto the pews before him, onto the white cloth covering the table in front of the altar, a pool of ruby, sapphire, emerald, amber.

"I'm so sorry!"

He hadn't heard her come in, her steps muffled to silence by the red carpet, his mind muted by contemplation. He had jerked to awareness and hoisted himself to his feet by the back of the pew in front of him. Maddy materialized, her eyes first, green and blue, then the image that had intruded on every waking minute since he had first seen her.

"I didn't realize anyone was here." She clasped her hands together, then unclasped them and began to twist her wedding and engagement rings on her left hand with the forefinger and thumb of her right hand. "I came to take the flowers." She had spoken breathlessly, words run together. Jack could see her now, twisting the rings, back and forth, round and round, up and down on her finger. She went on hurriedly. "I take them to the hospital." He watched as her long slim finger and thumb twisted her rings. "I take them to Women's and Children in Boston." She stopped. "The hospital."

He, who used his voice like a musical instrument every day of his life, had not been able to say a word. He had reverted to age fourteen, magically transformed by this hypnotic woman.

"Please," he had said finally. "You didn't disturb me. Please go ahead. I was miles away."

She hesitated, caught by an unseen web he had not spun.

He had moved and the spell snapped. "Lydia and I," he said deliberately, "my wife and I appreciate all you and Phil are doing." His words trailed off.

His wife had gone stolidly about church business and home business and children's business. He would find Lydia watching him when he looked up from his reading.

"Jack, darling." When she had first spoken, he felt a pang of annoyance. "I know something is troubling you. Can I do anything to help? Is there anything we can talk about?"

"I'm sorry, Lydia," he had said, putting his book aside and taking his glasses off. "I'm wrestling with a devil and no one can help me but myself. Not even you."

Instead of fizzling out the way he had hoped, the affair that was not an affair—at least not then—got more and more intense.

And Lydia and Phil knew.

Maddy came into the living room with a vase of flowers, and Jack snapped back to the present.

Maddy had kept in touch with friends at the Arlington church. Twenty years later, Lydia still refused a divorce. Lydia was a shadowy presence that came between Jack and Maddy at odd moments, and while Jack tried not to let this presence concern him, it was like a nasty barberry thorn, too small to see, too deep to pry out, festering, paining at odd moments.

"Are you thinking about her?" Maddy asked. "Lydia?"

Jack nodded.

"I can understand her feelings to some extent," Maddy said, as she set the vase on the table. "What I don't understand is why she is so consumed by a life that no longer exists. Why can't she get up off her behind and start a new life? The past is over."

Maddy adjusted the pale fragrant lilies in the vase. "Hardy amaryllis. Aren't they lovely?"

"Yes," said Jack. "Lovely."

Maddy sat across the coffee table from Jack. "I can't understand those two."

Jack knew who she meant.

"When you retired you explained to the church trustees that you would stay on—that both of us would stay on—until the new minister and his wife felt comfortably settled." Maddy stood abruptly. "I'll make us some tea."

Jack sat quietly, staring at the pale flowers on the coffee table.

When Maddy returned with the tea, she continued. "You know all those lists I made up for Betty? I spent hours thinking about what she'd want to know. And she simply rejected all my work." Maddy poured Earl Grey into two fragile cups and passed one over to Jack. "God knows, we tried to be careful not to interfere."

Jack stirred milk into his tea without speaking.

Maddy went on. "We understood that they'd want to set their own style, put their own stamp on the church. I don't know how we could have been any more sensitive to their situation."

BUT THE REVEREND and Mrs. Milton Jackson had wanted nothing from the Reverend (and Mrs.) John Hutchinson. Milton Jackson had asked Jack Hutchinson specifically to stay away from his, the Reverend Jackson's, church. Stay away for at least two years, Jackson had requested. Demanded, really. Take off, travel. You deserve a rest.

Jack Hutchinson's hurt turned into depression. He stopped writing and reading. He had no reason for pastoral calls, no reason to stop at the hospital to visit sick members. Maddy encouraged him to get out of the house a couple of times a week to play checkers with Brewster Harrington-Smith, who lived alone near the Chilmark town line and was getting forgetful.

Jack would stare at the view overlooking Chilmark Pond and the sea for hours. The colors of the Atlantic would change from aquamarine to turquoise to green to violet and he never noticed. Clouds would build up to the south over the ocean, cover the sky, drop rain, dissipate, and he never saw them.

Maddy tried to tempt him with his favorite delicacies and he left them on his plate. She sketched out plans for a visit to the Holy Land, a trip he'd talked about making when they had time. They had time now, but Jack didn't care. She invited his grandchildren to visit, and when they came, Jack, who loved them, stayed in his bedroom, shut the door, shut the children out.

And Maddy worried.

SIX

WHEN JEREMIAH SILVIA drove to Alley's store the week after Molly died and without even getting out of his car began to complain about his stomach, no one paid much attention. Jeremiah tended to be a hypochondriac.

"It's your sweet nature coming out," said Lincoln Sibert.

"Too much bourbon," said Donald Schwartz. Everyone knew Jeremiah didn't touch the stuff.

"You ought to see Doc Erickson," said Sarah Germaine, who was on her way home from the Wampanoag Tribal Headquarters in Aquinnah, where she had a part-time clerical job.

"Seriously, what's good for stomach complaints is a raw egg beaten up with milk and a little powdered sugar," said Lincoln as Jeremiah still didn't get out of his car. "A shot of whiskey helps some."

"Want me to get your mail for you?" asked Sarah with concern. Jeremiah was obviously hurting.

It got so bad that Joe Hanover, the plumber, volunteered to drive him to the hospital. Joe lifted Taffy, his golden retriever, into the back of his pickup truck and brushed dog hairs off the seat with his baseball cap. Lincoln and Sarah helped Jeremiah out of his car and into Joe's truck. Jeremiah sat on the edge of the seat, doubled over.

"Jeez, Jeremiah, it really is pretty bad, hunh?" Joe drove to the hospital as fast and as gently as he could given the condition of the truck's shocks. When he could take his eyes off the curving road, Joe looked over at Jeremiah. The guy was bent over at the waist, his arms crossed over his stomach, his head on his knees.

Every once in a while Jeremiah groaned, and when he did, Joe stepped on the gas. He was up to forty-five on a road designed for twenty-five. He never realized eight miles was so far. He checked the rearview mirror to see how Taffy was doing in the back of the truck. Taffy's tongue was hanging out, her mouth was turned up in a grin, her ears flapped in the wind like golden pennants. She braced herself against the jolting motion of the truck.

When he got to the place where Main Street turned off to the left, he was held up by a line of cars. He jounced the truck onto the sidewalk and passed the cars on the right.

Someone shouted at him. "Where in hell do you think you're going, Joe?" He lifted his left hand in acknowledgment and kept driving. He sped through Five Corners, ignoring the honking horn and squeal of brakes from a car that had already started into the intersection.

He tore past the ArtCliff Diner, scooted around in front of the tractor that was hauling a sailboat across the road from the shipyard. Bob Norton, who was driving the tractor, shook his fist and yelled something at him. He zipped past the oil tanks that rimmed the harbor, didn't even see the early scallopers in Lagoon Pond, some in small boats, some in chest-high yellow waders, their baskets, floating in inner tubes, trailing behind them like pets on a leash. He dodged a bicycle and whisked across the drawbridge, just as Carol Berube was closing the gates to raise the bridge.

"What's your trouble, Joe!" she shouted at him, her voice fading behind him.

He passed the hospital's main entrance and skidded around the curve that led into the parking lot. He pulled into the emergency entrance.

Manny Smith, who worked at the nursing home attached to the hospital and volunteered as the Meals on Wheels driver, brought out a wheelchair, and he and Joe helped Jeremiah into it. Manny waited with Joe while Jeremiah was admitted.

"He's one of my clients," Manny said to Joe, while they waited. "I take him meals three times a week. Nice gent," he said. "I see him in church Sundays."

Manny moved over to the admitting desk, where Doc Erickson was filling out forms. "Do you need me for anything else, Doc?"

"No. Thanks for your help, Manny."

"No problem, Doc." Manny raised his hand in a kind of salute.

"Give me a call when he's ready to come home," Joe said to Doc Erickson. "He left his car up to Alley's."

After keeping Jeremiah overnight, the hospital couldn't find anything the matter and they discharged him. Joe picked him up at the hospital and returned him to his car at Alley's.

"How're you feeling?" Lincoln asked.

"Shaky but okay, I guess," Jeremiah said weakly.

"Call me if you need anything," Sarah said.

Jeremiah started up his car and drove off. The gang on the steps of Alley's store was quiet.

"He doesn't look right." Lincoln watched the car disappear down Brandy Brow.

Sarah nodded.

That afternoon, Fran Kane, the woman who cleaned for Jeremiah, found him on the bathroom floor, dead.

Still later that afternoon, Doc Erickson's nurse called Victoria again. "The doctor insists—insists—that you come in for a flu shot, Victoria."

"Thank you," Victoria said. "That wasn't Jeremiah's trouble, was it?"

"I don't know. But you need to get your flu shot."

September was a rough time for the town's population, everyone agreed. Three deaths in a month. Of course Hal and Jeremiah were no longer young, had to go eventually, but what a shame about Molly. West Tisbury would miss all three. Molly's two boys had come to the Island for her funeral and Victoria had to agree with Edna, Jack gave an eloquent, fitting service.

SEPTEMBER ON Martha's Vineyard is a splendid month. Sumac flares scarlet, the beetlebung trees in Chilmark turn carmine, goldenrod and purple asters line the roadsides, Queen Anne's lace and black-eyed Susans fill the fields. Canada geese that, when Victoria was a girl, made the long trip from the Arctic to Chesapeake Bay, now remain on the Island summer and winter. But they still respond to the primordial call of autumn, flying overhead in tidy Vs, honking as they pass, a practice formation that will circle and land again on the Great Pond. Mitten-fingered sassafras flames orange and yellow among the rough stones in the Indian burial ground in Christiantown. The summer people have gone back to jobs and school.

Victoria and Elizabeth, pruning shears in hand, had cut armfuls of black-eyed Susans to brighten the house. Now Elizabeth was digging up the border, and Victoria, seated in a garden chair, was separating clumps of daffodil bulbs.

"When we finish, do you want to visit Cousin Edna?" Elizabeth removed her leather work gloves and wiped her face on a paper towel. "You haven't seen her for a while."

"It might be nice to take her some of that lemon chicken you made." Victoria looked up from the buckets of bulbs. "Do we have enough, Elizabeth?"

"Definitely. Is that pet seagull of hers still hanging around the bird feeder?"

Victoria nodded. "Part of your gourmet chicken undoubtedly will end up inside that bird." She levered herself out of the white plastic chair and wiped her hands with a clump of dried grass. "That gull chases away the chickadees and finches."

"At least he doesn't eat them the way you-know-who does," Elizabeth said, referring to McCavity, who was dozing on his back under a catnip plant, paws up in the air. "Want me to drop you off while I do errands?"

"Heavens no. Then I'll be at her mercy."

When they got to Cousin Edna's, they knocked on the back door, waited, and finally went into the kitchen. They could see her behind the house pouring birdseed from a plastic bag into the bird feeder outside the kitchen window. Sunlight sparkled and glinted on the pond at the foot of the lawn. Huckleberry bushes, dark red, closed in on either side. Farther back, cedars, scrub oak, and jack pine shaded the undergrowth. The hot sun on the pine released late summer fragrance.

"How's the seagull, Edna?" Victoria called from the kitchen door.

"Frederick. I'm training Frederick to come when I blow a whistle." Cousin Edna tugged the whistle out from the neck of her buttoned beige Talbots' cardigan, where it had been warming between her large breasts. Before Victoria and Elizabeth had time to cover their ears, she blasted the whistle. Small birds fluttered out of the way.

From beyond the cedar tree came a raucous cry. A large

seagull zoomed in at the bird feeder and landed. It extended its long wings, the red spot near the tip of its hooked bill prominent, cocked its head at Edna, beady black eyes menacing. The gull shook itself, settled its feathers, gray on white wings, hunched its shoulders, opened its bill, and let out a mournful reverberating cry.

"You don't mind if I give him some of your chicken, do you?" Cousin Edna flung a piece to the gull without waiting for a reply.

Elizabeth winced and thought of the thyme and lemon and white wine marinade that had gone into the recipe.

Victoria nodded at Frederick. "You'd never imagine something that ungainly on the ground could be so graceful in flight."

Edna tossed it another piece of chicken, then another…and another. Frederick snatched and gulped. Edna laughed, an operatic bellow that rose from her stomach.

"He doesn't even taste it," Elizabeth said, dismayed. "You won't have enough left for your own supper."

"We're on our way to Vineyard Haven." Victoria diplomatically changed the subject. "Do you need anything, Edna?"

"No thanks. Manny Smith said he'd drop off a few things on his route this evening."

Victoria muttered something under her breath.

Cousin Edna looked at her brightly. "You still haven't forgiven Manny for parking the Meals on Wheels van where you could back into it, have you?"

"I don't understand what all the fuss is about," Victoria said. Edna chortled.

VICTORIA'S GARDEN had the earliest blossoms in town. Starting in February, snowdrops carpeted the ground. Drifts of snowdrops piled against the south-facing cellar door, sheltered from the west wind, scattering where the wind or birds dropped seed. Bunches next to the stone wall where Victoria and Jonathan had transplanted them years before.

Then crocuses. Rabbits and squirrels ate the neighbors' crocuses, but not Victoria's. That was McCavity's contribution to the household, keeping down the population of bulb eaters. After the crocuses started to fade, Victoria's flower border turned sunshine yellow with daffodils, then became a riot of crayon-colored tulips, red, yellow, pink, white. Followed by purple iris and white and pink peonies.

The poets and writers who met at Victoria's wrote about her daffodils and irises and peonies. Artists painted them.

When Victoria and Elizabeth had left to go to Cousin Edna's, they saw that Angelo Santellini, Victoria's artist-in-residence, had set up his easel in the west pasture and was painting the border in its autumn browns and scarlets and yellows.

A couple from Schenectady had seen him painting near the Edgartown lighthouse, stepping back from his easel holding his paintbrush at arm's length to capture whatever artists captured by doing that. They bought the painting, on the condition that Angelo paint them and their two children into the scene.

"Don't prostitute yourself!" Elizabeth had been aghast.

"Go ahead," Victoria said. "It might improve the work."

With the sale, Angelo paid for two more weeks in Victoria's attic.

When he had first arrived at Victoria's, Angelo had looked more like a trim and balding gangster than a stockbroker-turned-artist. His chief virtue, Victoria believed, was his large Roman nose, not as large as hers, but certainly patrician. Now, he no longer looked like either a gangster or a stockbroker.

His clothes, face, and hands were splotched with paint. He was careful about where he sat, but, even so, Victoria would find paint blotches on the furniture.

"Angelo is lonely," she said to Elizabeth at breakfast, slicing a banana over her Shredded Wheat. "He's about Casey's age, isn't he?"

Elizabeth looked up from her grapefruit. "You're not matchmaking, are you, Gram?"

"Of course not." Victoria moved her chair back slightly so McCavity could jump into her lap. "I'm simply thinking of introducing two nice young people to each other." She poured milk from the white pitcher over her cereal. "Casey's been too busy to socialize."

"They'll meet each other eventually. Would you like more coffee?"

After breakfast, Victoria called Casey and invited her and her son Patrick to a Saturday night Boston baked bean supper. She also invited Angelo Santellini.

"I'll have to leave early," Casey said. "I need to get Patrick home to bed."

"Thanks," Angelo said. "I'll bring a bottle of red wine."

BREWSTER HARRINGTON-SMITH lived this side of the Chilmark town line. After his wife died, his daughter Lynn urged him to move into the nursing home at the hospital, where her brother Manny worked, but Brewster insisted on staying in the big old house he and Agatha had bought and renovated thirty years ago. As Brewster got more and more frail, Lynn was afraid he was showing symptoms of Alzheimer's. Mrs. Weissbrodt, who lived next door, had given him a ride to Alley's store when she saw him walking along South Road one afternoon. He had seemed confused, she told Lynn later. He thought he was still in Washington heading for the Library of Congress.

Lynn certainly could not have him move in with her and her partner in Cambridge; nor would she consider moving to West Tisbury to be with her father. Manny was no help at all, even though he lived on the Island. Manny's only contact with their father, as far as Lynn knew, was to deliver Meals on Wheels to him three times a week. Her father and Manny had never gotten along. Manny had even dropped the Harrington hyphen from his last name, and went by plain Smith.

Lynn wasn't sure she could arrange to have someone stay with her notoriously difficult father. The problem wasn't his independence, which was understandable, even commendable. It was that he was suspicious of everyone. He had belittled people as long as Lynn could remember, always made her feel inadequate. That was one reason she had left home as soon as she turned seventeen and got a job. Manny, three years younger, left before she did, ran away at fourteen.

Lynn came to the Vineyard on weekends to make sure her father was okay, take him shopping, occasionally to a play. Three days a week, a little before noon, Manny drove up in his white van with MEALS ON WHEELS: FOOD FIT FOR AN AN-GEL, lettered on the side in black-and-gold, dropped off a nice luncheon for his father, and left. The rest of the week, church members brought him covered dishes. The Reverend Milton Jackson stopped by almost every day to talk or read to him, and the Reverend John Hutchinson, the retired minister, played checkers with him a couple of times a week. The Reverend Hutchinson's wife, Maddy, brought elegantly prepared meals garnished with flowers or greens in disposable dishes he didn't have to wash or return. But Lynn worried about the times no one was with him. What if he wandered away from the house? Who would even notice that he was gone?

AT VICTORIA'S, Angelo and Patrick were sprawled on the parlor floor building a tower of Legos from pieces in Victoria's grandmother basket. Casey was wearing her best (and only) dress, printed with blue flowers on a black background. She had debated whether to put on makeup, and decided she would, lipstick and mascara and blusher.

Victoria looked critically at Angelo. "I see you've cleaned off most of the paint. At least on the visible part of you."

Angelo laughed. "Clean clothes, too."

Casey touched a finger to the corner of her mouth to make sure the lipstick hadn't smeared. She watched the Lego construction project from where she sat in the rocking chair, relaxed in front of the fire with a glass of cranberry juice.

"It's not really chilly enough to warrant a fire," Victoria had said as she lighted it. "But a fire is pleasant any time of year."

Sitting on the couch now, Victoria was drinking cranberry juice, too, hers laced with rum. Elizabeth was in the kitchen.

"Do you like being a small-town police chief?" Angelo looked up from the Lego tower at Casey. He propped himself up on his elbows, long legs stretched out.

"It's awkward." She was distracted slightly by his hazel eyes. "Everyone loved Chief Ben Norton. He's related to half the people in town. When he retired, Junior expected to get my job. Now he's my sergeant." She watched Patrick attach a platform to the top of the tower.

"Alien landing strip," Patrick said.

"That's nice, Patrick," Casey acknowledged absently and continued, "I've had to figure out stuff everyone else has known all their lives. Who's related to whom, who won't speak to whom, even where people live. Most of West Tisbury seems to live down sand roads that have no names." She took a sip of cranberry juice, leaned back in the rocker. "One of the best things that happened to me was meeting Victoria. She knows all the stuff it would take me years to learn."

Victoria pushed herself out of the couch. "I'll see if Elizabeth needs any help."

Victoria's Saturday night Boston baked bean suppers were a tradition that she had made into special occasions. Casey, who came from a long line of Bostonians, felt at home with the earthy smell of baking beans, the rich scent of steaming brown bread. Victoria cooked her beans the traditional way, soaking them overnight, boiling them the next morning, and baking them all day with molasses and salt pork in an ancient bean pot. Elizabeth had set the table with silver and Victoria's best china. Patrick and Angelo were engaged in a discussion of Pokémon, and the difference between crayons and pastels, oil paints and watercolors.

Victoria sat at the head of the table with Angelo and Patrick on one side of her. Casey sat across from Angelo and her son, so grown-up acting. Elizabeth served at the other end of the table.

As she pushed beans onto her fork with a piece of buttered brown bread, Casey thought how confident her son had become in the year since they had moved here. The good manners that never seemed to show up at home had emerged at Victoria's table.

She was glad to be able to forget her work, the growing list of things she needed to do for the town. The politics, the delicate balance she had to maintain between law enforcement and neighborliness. She was thinking how little she knew about Victoria's granddaughter Elizabeth and was about to ask about Elizabeth's life when her beeper went off.

"Oh shit," she said, and flushed. "Excuse me, Victoria."

Victoria didn't appear to have heard.

"I need to use your phone," she added. In a few minutes, she returned. "I gotta go, Victoria. I'm sorry. That was the communications center. Mrs. Weissbrodt called to say Brewster Harrington's daughter couldn't come this weekend and Brewster has wandered off. No one's seen him all day. Mrs. W. checked his house and the door's open; no one's home."

"I'll get my coat." Victoria pushed her chair away from the table.

"No, no, Victoria. I'm taking Patrick home. My neighbor will come over and stay with him. I'm not sure how long I'm going to be."

"Do I have to go?" Patrick said. "I want another hot dog."

"'Please,'" Casey corrected.

"With ketchup," Patrick said as Elizabeth put a hot dog on his plate.

"Are you sure you don't need me?" Victoria said.

Casey nodded gravely. "I'm sure."

"Since I won't be going with you," Victoria said, "Patrick is welcome to stay here. He can sleep on the fold-out couch in the woodshed. Angelo might even light the woodstove."

"Can I, Mom?"

"'May I,'" Casey said.

"I'll light the stove now," Angelo said. "Get the room nice and warm." He got up from the table. "If you'll excuse me, Victoria, I'll be back for seconds."

"Thirds," Elizabeth said.

As she put on her coat, Casey heard Angelo gather kindling and wood billets from the entry, where the firewood was stored out of the weather. He marched through the kitchen, through the cookroom, and she heard the door open, his footsteps on the three steps that led down into the woodshed, heard the iron door of the stove clang.

As soon as she got into the Bronco, Casey radioed Sergeant Junior Norton, asked him to call the two patrolmen, Josh Tucker and Elmer West. She stopped at her house, scrubbed her face, and changed into jeans, boots, and flannel jacket.

By the time she reached Brewster's house, it had grown dark. The moon was up, bright, almost full. Mrs. Weissbrodt hovered near the door, where she had turned on the lights.

"I should have kept an eye on him." She wrung her hands. "He's been acting disoriented lately. I hope nothing's happened to him."

Casey, her sergeant, and the two patrolmen fanned out into the pine and oak woods behind Brewster's house, scanning the ground with flashlights, looking for traces of Brewster.

"Mr. Harrington-Smith! Mr. Harrington!"

They dodged pine branches, brushed through the hip-high huckleberry, scuffed through fallen oak leaves. "Brewster! Mr. Harrington!"

They crossed the brook where watercress and ferns flourished, passed through green catbrier that snared them with curved thorns. Heard crickets and katydids in evening voice. The voices stopped as they approached, then started up again behind them. They moved past stands of mushrooms and toadstools, fluorescent white in the beams of their flashlights and the moonlight.

Finally, they found him, curled up behind a fallen scrub oak tree, his head cushioned by a pad of bright green moss, his feet dug into the stump's rotting wood.

"Lord!" Casey said. "That makes four."

SEVEN

"I CAN'T UNDERSTAND IT, Victoria," Casey said as they drove home from the garden club meeting the following Tuesday. "Four deaths in one month. What do you make of that?"

"It does seem odd." Victoria fished a tissue out of her coat pocket and dabbed a drip at the end of her nose. "You can understand Hal and Jeremiah and Brewster. They had elderly problems. But Molly? I can't believe flu is that lethal."

"It can be," Casey said.

She slowed as they passed Uncle Seth's Pond. The water level was high, almost at the road. "Going to have problems again next summer. The beach won't be wide enough to keep toddlers from running into the road. I'll have to close the beach and everyone in town is going to be mad." She shifted gears to get up the hill on the other side of the pond. "Someday someone's going to hit some little kid. Traffic isn't what it was only a couple of years ago when Ben Norton was chief. People already are saying, 'Chief Norton wouldn't have closed Seth's Pond.' You can't win." They drove in silence for a while. Then Casey said, "Speaking of Ben, I have to stop by his house to get some papers signed, Victoria. I know you're reading at the hospital today. I won't be long."

"I'd like the ride." Victoria straightened her quilted blue coat over her knees. "When I was a girl, my dog Jason and I used to walk there to look for boxberries."

Casey turned left onto the Edgartown Road, past Mabel Johnson's yellow house, and turned right onto New Lane.

"Wonder who that is in the Jeep," Casey said. "Do you recognize him, Victoria?"

Victoria turned to look at the Jeep that was pulled off to one side of the road and shook her head.

BEN NORTON, the retired police chief, lived down an unnamed sand road that led to the Great Pond. From his kitchen window he could look over the long, hand-shaped pond to the barrier bar and across to the ocean. Always, always, no matter what the wind direction, no matter how still the day, no matter how brilliant or foggy, he could feel the rumble of pounding surf, a constant obbligato. When he'd gone off to Korea he had been homesick, not for family or his own bed, but for that heartbeat of surf.

The Army was where he got his police training. While he was in the Army, he met and married Rosellyn Schellhammer, a girl from Philadelphia's Main Line, and brought her home to the Island.

Within a few months he realized his marriage was a mistake. Rosellyn had envisioned a different kind of Martha's Vineyard life. She had told him, more often than he wanted to remember, how she had imagined tennis and golf, not too different from the Main Line. Martha's Vineyard meant yachting, cocktail parties, gallery openings, and book signing parties. Socializing with vacationing notables. Garden club teas. Instead, she was stuck at the end of a dirt road where no one came, not even the Jehovah's Witnesses. She told Ben how much she hated the constant drumming of the surf. She couldn't mask it with the TV or stereo because the beating surf wasn't sound exactly, but a rumble that she felt every second of every day. The only time she could remember the rumbling ceasing, she said, was the day before the hurricane. Then it was ominous, a foreboding silence, a terrifying lack of pulse beat.

And then the storm hit.

She'd fling into his face words that he no longer heard. How he had ignored her the day of the hurricane, took care of everyone else in town first.

That was true. He had come to get her in the four-wheel-drive police vehicle only after he made sure everyone else in town was okay. He had taken her and Junior, then a baby, to Victoria Trumbull's, where they would be safe and where she would no longer feel the surf. The sound would be muffled by distance to a low-drawn-out bass note.

She hated the wind that moaned and roared through the scrub oak trees behind their house, she said. She hated the isolation, the raw winters, the foggy springs. She told Ben she hated him.

After six years she departed, leaving behind Junior, who was five. Junior was just like his father, she had said. She hated him too. You can have him, she said to Benjamin Norton.

When she left, Norton, who was not a drinker, drank a bottle of champagne all by himself. He was "shet of her," as his grandmother would have said. He'd had enough bitching and nagging for a lifetime and then some. This, his house overlooking the Great Pond and the sea, was everything life ought to be. Rosellyn had never understood.

In those days he was the police force. West Tisbury crime consisted of teenagers sitting on and breaking the split-rail fence around Parsonage Pond, teenagers smoking and drinking beer on Brandy Brow, teenagers speeding on the Edgartown Road in the moonlight with their car lights out. Some of the disciplinary problems he'd taken care of behind the police station, and the problems never were repeated.

Junior grew up, got an associate degree in the community college on the mainland, and joined the police force, doubling its size to two.

Ben and Junior ate the deer that had fed on the sparse vegetables in his garden during summer. Junior kidded his father about that, fattening animals for slaughter. Together they fished the surf at Quansoo and ate bluefish, spring, summer, and fall. Junior had invented a half dozen recipes for bluefish. They dug clams in the Great Pond when the opening in the barrier bar allowed the tide to flush saltwater into it. They ate oysters they found along the stony shore. They netted crabs. They collected watercress from Mill Brook, mushrooms from the meadow off New Lane, blueberries, huckleberries, wild cherries, and beach plums. Junior was a pretty good cook, Ben had to admit. For three years in a row he'd won blue ribbons at the county fair for his blueberry pie and smoked bluefish.

When the time had come to retire, Chief Norton was in a quandary. The force had grown; crime now consisted of illegal drug use and break-ins and drunk driving and domestic abuse that wives, girlfriends, or, less often, husbands or boyfriends reported.

Junior was not ready to be chief. He lacked something. Chief Norton couldn't put his finger on it. Maybe Junior had not matured yet. Maybe because his mother had abandoned him. That had to be hard on a kid. Ben could never explain, nor would he want to, how inadequate a person his mother had been. Maybe the problem was the way he, Ben, had reared his son in this lonely, womanless house with the eternal drumbeat of Atlantic surf.

Junior was a good cop. But he would not make a good chief yet. Give him a few more years.

When the selectmen advertised the chief's position in off-

Island papers, Chief Norton knew how Junior felt. Another rejection. Junior buried his feelings, but Ben knew.

When the selectmen hired Casey, Ben understood it was going to be tough on Junior and tougher on the new chief. Being accepted by the community was hard enough for ordinary off-Islanders. She, as police chief, was in a worse position. She would need to learn who the troublemakers were, who she could depend on, who needed help, and who didn't.

When she struck up a friendship with Victoria Trumbull, Ben was relieved to see Casey could bend some rules. Granted having a sidekick who was in her nineties was unconventional, but he had been concerned about her emphasis on professionalism. Maybe the time had come for West Tisbury to have professionalism in its police force. He didn't think so, but times had changed.

WHEN CASEY PULLED into Ben Norton's, she saw him scattering scoops of birdseed onto the grass of his front yard from a galvanized garbage pail.

Casey reached into the back of the Bronco for a manila folder. "I brought the papers for you to sign." When she retrieved the folder, she looked at the flurry of birds descending onto the front yard. She laughed. "I can't escape them. Ducks, geese, swans, seagulls, and whatever those are."

"Blue jays," Victoria said and leaned across Casey to greet Ben, who nodded to her.

Ben took the manila folder from Casey. "My pen is inside. You got time for coffee?"

"I do," Casey said. "How about you, Victoria?"

Victoria looked at her watch. "I have to read to the elderly at the hospital, but that's not for another two hours." Victoria held the side of the Bronco and slid off the high seat onto the ground. Casey tensed, ready to help. She needn't have worried. Victoria landed on her feet, straightened her hat, and strode around the front of the vehicle, holding her hand on its hood.

Casey wiped her feet on the mat in the small entry and looked into Ben's living room. She could see a couple of ordinary fat armchairs, a worn couch that faced the Great Pond, a lamp on an undistinguished end table, a braided rag rug that must once have been the gray, brown, and blue wool of worn-out suits and skirts.

Casey stepped through the door and turned into the room, then stopped abruptly. The north wall was covered, floor to ceiling, with a dozen paintings of the view from Ben's window.

She stared at a painting of fishermen in olive-green chest-high waders surf casting into the rushing waters of the opening, a painting of children placing jewel-like stones on the flanks of sand castles, one of gray storm waves breaking furiously on a gray beach with a gray sky overhead.

She drew in her breath. "You did these? They're like nothing I've ever seen."

"Yep," Chief Norton said. "I paint some." He got a can of coffee out of his freezer, measured grounds into the basket, poured water in, and turned on the coffeemaker.

As Casey continued to stare, he said, "I got some paint and canvas from DaRosa's, some brushes and turpentine. Victoria's husband helped some." He opened the cupboard over the coffeemaker and took out three mugs. "What do you want in it?"

"Black," Victoria said.

"Cream and two sugars," Casey said. "Have you shown them anywhere? Like a gallery?"

"Never wanted to." He handed a mug of coffee to Victoria, who'd seated herself in an old platform rocker where she could look at the far stretch of horizon, the sharp indigo line where the sea met the pale sky. Another mug to Casey, who stood with her back to the view, gazing at his paintings.

Ben turned back to Casey. "You got hit with some pretty heavy stuff this first year." He bent over to sign papers with his large flourish and put them back in the folder. "Four deaths in one month. This town doesn't usually have such a high mortality rate. I can't remember a single year when we had even two deaths in one month."

"None of them was in ill health, either," Victoria said. "Except for Molly. And flu isn't exactly ill health."

Casey sat in the fat armchair with her coffee. "By the way, Victoria, have you got your flu shot yet?"

Victoria turned to Ben. "When storms close the opening you must be able to see that."

"The chief is right," Ben said. "Flu shot, Victoria."

THE NEXT DAY Elizabeth was reading a draft of the autobiography Victoria was writing. "Gram, what happened to your father?"

"Father?" Victoria said, slitting a sweepstakes envelope. Elizabeth could see that it said she'd won $10 million.

"My great-grandfather. Your father. You don't even mention him in the first chapter."

"Yes I do," Victoria said, taking the contents out of the envelope. The two of them were sitting at the pine table in the cookroom, a bright warm space. Victoria sat in a bentwood armchair facing the view of town across the fields. Elizabeth could look out the south window at the diminishing woodpile under the Norway maple. We need more wood, she thought. Maybe we can rent another room to pay for it. "All you say is that you remember him when you were three years old," she said to Victoria, returning to the autobiography. "He was going on a business trip."

"Well, that's all there was to it."

"You have to say something more," Elizabeth said.

"There's nothing more to say." Victoria peeled off a sticker that said she accepted the $10 million and placed it in the upper-right-hand corner of an insert. "I remember he picked me up and said good-bye. He was tall and wore a hat. I said all that."

McCavity appeared from some hideaway, walked purposefully to Victoria and leaped into her lap. He turned himself around so he faced out and looked at Elizabeth with yellow eyes.

"Yes, but your father, your own father…" Elizabeth lifted the manuscript page that Victoria had typed, two-fingered, on her portable Skywriter with the dim ribbon. "Didn't your mother say anything about his not coming home? Didn't anyone talk to you about him? Your grandparents? Your aunts?"

"No." Victoria stroked the cat's yellow head. McCavity closed his eyes.

"That's important. Even if they didn't say anything, you should put that in your autobiography," Elizabeth said. "Was he sick? Did he run off with another woman? Was the family alienated from him? The very fact that nobody said anything is significant."

Elizabeth knew from Victoria's expression that continuing was pointless. Victoria's expression was that of a thoroughly stubborn Yankee owl, her hooded eyes peering out from either side of her nose. Nevertheless, Elizabeth tried again.

"Did they try to find him? Did they call the police? Did you hear anyone tell your mother she was lucky to be rid of him? Did anyone mourn? Though it's kind of hard to mourn if someone simply disappears."

"None of that has anything to do with my autobiography," Victoria said, stroking McCavity.

"But…"

The wrinkles of her grandmother's face were set like concrete. Elizabeth sighed. What had happened to her great-grandfather? Ever since she was old enough to wonder about such things, she had wondered why her grandmother and her great-aunts were so silent about their father.

From the little she could put together, she thought her great-grandfather had been an importer of oriental artwork. A long spear, inlaid with mother of pearl, hung over the portraits in the hall. Great-grandfather had brought it back from Japan, Elizabeth had been told since childhood. But one of the cousins said she thought their great-grandfather had never been west of Woburn, Massachusetts. According to one aunt, he was a dope fiend, the result, according to the aunt, who tried to make it sound socially acceptable, of medicine prescribed for some unknown illness. Or was the addiction a result of his oriental contacts? Or shady Woburn associates? Or was he addicted at all?

Victoria sealed the sweepstakes envelope and opened a letter from Madame Zoystra. The envelope was marked "Confidential for Victoria Trumbull."

"A personal letter," Victoria said. "Madame Zoystra says I am about to get a large sum of money."

"For heaven's sake, Gram." Elizabeth was exasperated over the great-grandfather conversation. "How can you be so gullible? That's a bunch of crap. They prey on old ladies. Astrologers and the sweepstakes and the orphaned Native American children."

"I don't send them much money," Victoria said defensively. "Five dollars here and there."

"You ought to give the money to the church instead."

"I'm leaving the church something. That paper your grandfather gave me." McCavity lifted his head, purring.

"The certificate of deposit?" Elizabeth evened up the loose pages of Victoria's manuscript, tapped the stack of papers on the table, and set the pile in front of her grandmother.

"I don't know what the paper is. Your grandfather said it would provide for me in my old age." McCavity shifted so he could dangle his paws over Victoria's knees.

"I don't think you'll ever be old," Elizabeth said. "You're incapable of aging." She pushed her chair back. "I've got to order another cord of wood. We might drive down, talk to Charlie."

"We can stop at Cousin Edna's on the way." Victoria shooed McCavity out of her lap and stood.

"I'm not taking any treats for that seagull. That is one disgusting bird. He doesn't care whether the food is gourmet or rotten. It's all the same to him."

"Cousin Edna thinks he's cute," Victoria said.

"Cute, a seagull? I don't think she's ever watched them squabble over garbage at the dump."

EDNA WAS WORKING ON her bills at the kitchen table when they arrived. From the window they could see the bird feeder. Yellow maple leaves drifted lazily through the clear air onto the lawn.

"How's Frederick?" Victoria said.

"I haven't seen him all day. He's usually here by now. I can't imagine what's happened to him." She beckoned to the chairs around the table. "Have a seat. Can I get you a cup of tea?"

"That would hit the spot." Victoria unbuttoned her coat, took off her fuzzy beige hat, and pulled out one of the chairs.

"Sit still, Cousin Edna," Elizabeth said. "I'll put the teakettle on. Where do you keep the tea?"

Edna pointed toward a rose-painted tin box on the counter. "Thank you, dear." She turned to Victoria. "Maddy stopped by this morning. She brought me some beef stew with mushrooms."

"I guess she wants to keep in touch with her old parishioners," Victoria said.

"As she was leaving, the Reverend Jackson came by." Edna leveled a first attack in her usual argument. "You know how he thinks Maddy and Jack Hutchinson are interfering with his ministry."

"He could hardly criticize Maddy for taking a dish to a neighbor." Color rose to Victoria's cheeks; her mouth turned down.

"Not at all. She's a good cook. She stayed and talked for a few minutes before Jack, the Reverend Jackson, arrived. That was well timed," Edna said. "Wonder if she planned it that way?"

"Edna, *that's* outrageous."

"She hasn't come by here for months," Edna said. "Not since her Jack retired."

Elizabeth set the teapot on a potholder, cups and saucers in front of Cousin Edna.

"Thank you, dear," Edna said, pouring. "Does anyone want milk? Sugar? Lemon?"

"The idea of attributing such motives to Maddy," Victoria said. "I think that's horrid."

"Whatever her motives were, they had an effect." Edna twisted a blue curl around her index finger. "You should have seen Jack's face. Livid."

"Mind if I look around outside?" Elizabeth said. "I'll let you two work this out without me."

"Be careful not to get too close to that marshy area, dear," Edna said. "It's full of snapping turtles, some this big." She made a circle two feet across with both arms.

Elizabeth went out of the kitchen door, down the big stone step at the doorway, and walked across the mowed grass and clover and chickweed and spicy Jill-over-the-ground. She circled around the bird feeder to keep from disturbing the feeding blue jays. Cousin Edna and her grandmother's ongoing battles amused her, but after a while she got tired of the thrusting and parrying.

She breathed in the early autumn smells, felt the hot sun on her back, heard the Canada geese pass overhead. As she strolled toward the marshy spot to see if she could find a two-foot-diameter snapping turtle, she saw something white in the huckleberry undergrowth, a piece of blown paper, probably. She detoured to pick it up. It was large, not paper, she saw as she got closer. Plastic? A milk jug? Some people were really careless about the way they disposed of stuff. Another step, and she saw what it was. A dead seagull. Frederick. She picked him up with a tissue, his limp head dangling from his body, and started back to the house. On Cousin Edna's back porch she found an old copy of the *Island Enquirer,* laid Frederick's corpse on it, and took the corpse into the house.

"What on earth…" Edna said, interrupting the latest riposte. "For heaven's sake. What happened?"

"He is some big bird," Elizabeth said, admiring the glossy white feathers, the gray wing feathers, the black-and-white tail feathers. A thin membrane covered Frederick's eyes.

"I wonder what happened? He was a young bird, not more than a year and a half, I should think." Cousin Edna turned Frederick over and poked into his feathered armor with her pencil. Bird lice scurried for cover. "Nothing seems to have attacked him, a raccoon or skunk or hawk." She stroked the stiff body. "I can't think of a predator that would tangle with a young gull. And he hadn't seemed sick. He was such a beautiful creature."

"Maybe he ate something that didn't agree with him," Victoria said.

"Not likely." Elizabeth laughed. "They have cast-iron stomachs."

"The last thing I fed him was bluefish," Cousin Edna said. "You'd think fish would be just right for him."

"Where did you get the bluefish?" Elizabeth asked.

"The Reverend Jack Jackson brought it to me last week, a fish Junior Norton caught at Quansoo near the opening. Junior even scaled and filleted the fish." Edna stared at the dead gull. "What beautiful birds they are. Engineered for perfect flight." She spread the tight, glossy feathers.

"Hadn't you better be careful about handling Frederick?" Victoria murmured. "Birds have all sorts of diseases."

Edna nodded and continued to stroke the dead bird. "I don't care for bluefish—it's too oily for me. But I didn't want to offend Jack. He's quite a good cook, you know. I put the fish in the refrigerator and forgot about it until I smelled it." She got up from the table, went to the sink, and washed her hands. "I didn't think overripe bluefish would hurt Frederick. I certainly didn't think it would kill him."

"Is there any fish left?" Elizabeth said.

"I doubt it." Edna dried her hands on a dish towel. "You know his appetite."

"Was it cooked?" Victoria said.

"No. Jack had rolled the fillet around a mushroom stuffing, held together with toothpicks. He told me to cook the fish for about a half hour." She came back to the table and sat down again. "I took the toothpicks out before I gave the fish to Frederick, so I don't think one of them could have stuck in his craw."

"Would you like me to bury him?" Elizabeth asked, picking up Frederick, the newspaper, and the bird lice.

"I suppose we should," Cousin Edna said, looking away. "That would be nice. Thank you, dear."

"I saw a shovel on the back porch. Shall I bury him near the bird feeder?"

Cousin Edna nodded.

"I can't believe even badly spoiled fish would kill a seagull," Victoria said.

"It wasn't even spoiled, just fishy smelling." Edna tapped her fingernails on the table. "I can't believe that would have killed my poor Frederick."

EIGHT

"GRAM, THAT WASN'T Lockwood again, was it?" Elizabeth had come into the cookroom from a wastewater committee meeting just as Victoria was hanging up the phone.

"He wanted to say hello, that's all." Victoria avoided Elizabeth's eyes by shuffling papers on the table in front of her.

"Hello, hell," Elizabeth said. "He's a certifiable maniac, a menace." She unzipped her sweater, tugged it off, and flung it into the captain's chair by the door. The sweater slid onto the floor. "Did he say where he was calling from?"

"I assume he was calling from Washington."

"You can't assume anything with him," Elizabeth said. "He may well be here on the Island. With his job, you never know where he is." Elizabeth went to the sink, filled the electric teakettle, and plugged it into the wall socket. "Can't you hang up on him when he calls?"

"He's not *my* ex-husband," Victoria said. "Lockwood and I always got along." McCavity, in Victoria's lap, stretched his front legs and yawned hugely, fangs exposed.

"Ouch!" Victoria winced as he kneaded his paws on her thighs and tucked them back under him.

"He's dangerous, Gram, honestly, he is." Elizabeth rinsed out the blue china teapot, put in two scoops of tea, and added the now-boiling water from the kettle.

"I think you're overreacting, Elizabeth."

"Do you think I'm overreacting when the neighbors call the cops and I end up in the hospital?" Elizabeth felt her voice get higher and louder. "You call that overreacting?" She brought two mugs down from the shelf and slammed them on the counter.

"I didn't know that," Victoria said quietly. "I had no idea he'd been violent."

"I'm sorry, Gram. I never told anyone, I was too embarrassed."

McCavity jumped down from Victoria's lap, sniffed the cat food he had rejected earlier, went to the west door, and looked up at Elizabeth.

"That cat!" Elizabeth opened the door, and when McCavity paused on the sill, she gave him a shove with her foot. "Scat!" she said and slammed the door.

"Every time Lockwood and you came to visit," Victoria said, "I felt as if I was near a volcano about to erupt."

"That's exactly what living with him was like. And now he's stalking me. We're divorced and yet he's still stalking me." Elizabeth's hands shook as she poured tea and passed a mug to her grandmother. "He's going to show up here any day, believe me. Thank goodness every room in this house has at least two doors." She picked up her mug of tea, put it down again without drinking. "I'm a piece of property, that's all I am to him. He wants his property back no matter what he has to do."

"He wouldn't do anything foolish," Victoria said, half closing her eyes as she sipped the steaming tea.

"Yes he would. He's crazy, Gram, and he's driving me crazy. I wish you wouldn't talk to him." Elizabeth was close to tears. "You're letting him think he has a chance to get back into this family. Well, he doesn't. I feel as if you're against me, too, encouraging him the way you are."

"Elizabeth, I've known Lockwood for years, even before you married him. He's obviously troubled. He needed someone to talk to. We didn't talk about you. He asked about my writing and about the garden. He talked about a new recipe he's trying. He's lonely."

"Bullshit." Elizabeth found a wadded-up paper towel in her jeans pocket and wiped her nose.

"He seemed perfectly normal."

"He seemed perfectly normal when I married him. Most of the time I was married to him he could act normal. But, believe me, he's not."

"At least he was a good cook," Victoria said, changing the subject. "I remember some of the meals he served and how artistic they were. Cold potato soup with blue borage flowers and a sprinkling of bacon." She looked over her tea mug at Elizabeth. "And he really did support you in some of your adventures."

Elizabeth got up from the table, went into the kitchen, picked up her sweater from the floor, folded it, and put it on the seat of the captain's chair. She set McCavity's dish in the sink and sat at the table again. She held her tea mug in both hands and made circles on the tablecloth with the bottom of it.

"He has a lot of good points, Gram." She looked at the circles she was making. "But that doesn't mean he's not a creep. Please don't encourage him. Don't talk to him when he calls. I know you do." She looked up at her grandmother, and their intense dark eyes met, Victoria's questioning, Elizabeth's agonized. "He's looking for an opening to come storming back into my life."

LOCKWOOD WOLFRICH HAD not called Victoria from Washington. He had called her from the campground off the Vineyard Haven-Edgartown Road, five miles away. He had been living there in a camping trailer for three weeks. Nor was this the first time he had called. He had called regularly, to chat with Victoria. Whenever Elizabeth had answered the phone, he had either hung up or had disguised his voice, apologizing for dialing a wrong number. Once he had asked her, in his disguised voice, about the availability of long-term rentals. He liked thinking about that. She tried to be so accommodating. If she had known who he was, her voice would have turned to ice water and she'd have hung up (the bitch). Before he'd decided to come to the Vineyard he'd tried calling her and she had hung up on him. When he'd called back to tell her how rude that was, she had apparently set the phone receiver on the desk and left it there, unlistened to. He'd talked into the phone for a good ten minutes before he realized she wasn't there. She hadn't said a word, and he had thought he was finally getting through to her. He'd dialed again and gotten only a busy signal. She needed to be taught a lesson.

Elizabeth was nothing like her grandmother. He had always gotten along with Victoria, one of the few women in his life he respected. He still considered that he was part of the family. He couldn't understand why Elizabeth had turned out to be such a bitch when her grandmother was the opposite.

Lockwood had taken a leave of absence from his job with the Agency in Washington, where he was a Russian expert. His job had changed somewhat since the breakup of the Soviet Union. It used to be primarily intelligence gathering, translating Russian newspaper articles, scanning scientific and technical journals. Now he was compiling statistics on oil production in Russia and what used to be the Soviet bloc countries. Recently, the Russians were having technical problems with an oil pipeline, and he had been following and reporting on that.

Elizabeth had walked out on him for no reason. By rights, he should be thinking about retiring some day to the Trumbull homestead on Martha's Vineyard. For the years they had been married, the Vineyard had been part of his life, too, part of his plans to move to the Island when he retired. After all he had put into the marriage, he, by rights, should be planning for his retirement to the Vineyard house. He should be spending his vacations there, working in the garden, working on the house, walking on the beach. What right did that bitch have to deprive him of the retirement he had counted on? The house was Victoria's after all, and Victoria still seemed to consider him her grandson-in-law. He would be pleased to take care of her when she needed a caretaker.

At least he had kept the house in McLean, Virginia, even though the bitch's lawyer had drawn up papers saying it was hers. Let her try to force him out. He'd bought himself a 357-magnum handgun in case she wanted to make an issue of it, and he had the gun with him now. He had changed all the locks on the McLean house. He knew her well enough to know she was not going to argue with him. If she wanted to come back, he'd welcome her. She walked out. He didn't.

The day after Elizabeth had left him, he'd driven from Washington to Woods Hole and had taken his car over on the noon ferry to the Vineyard, pretty sure she'd run home to her grandmother.

She had. Elizabeth's battered car was parked at the end of the driveway.

"Elizabeth is asleep," said Victoria, after greeting him cautiously. "She drove all night."

"She walked out on me," Lockwood said. "She simply left me."

"Have you had lunch?"

"Not yet."

Victoria made grilled cheese sandwiches and they ate at the cookroom table. She avoided talking about the subject that was on her mind, saving it until after their meal.

They were doing the dishes, Victoria washing, Lockwood drying. The window above the kitchen sink overlooked the fish pond.

He opened the cabinet and put away the glasses he'd wiped. "As I was saying, Elizabeth left. No excuse whatsoever."

Victoria was quiet for a long time. She continued to scrub the cast-iron skillet in which she had cooked this morning's bacon. She wiped it with a damp sponge and hung it over the stove. She rinsed out the sponge and wiped the sink, took out the drain basket, which had celery leaves and onion skins in it, and emptied it into the compost bucket under the sink.

"Lockwood," she said, finally looking straight at him with those deep-set eyes, "I refuse to take sides. Find yourself another woman and forget Elizabeth." Before he could reply, the telephone rang, and they never finished the conversation.

LOCKWOOD HAD often thought about that conversation in the past year. Elizabeth had married him, for better or worse, and despite the rough times—she was responsible for more rough times than he was—she owed it to him, and to herself, of course, to stay in the marriage she had contracted.

He had come to the Island to keep an eye on her. He bought a used four-wheel-drive Jeep that looked like every other vehicle on the Vineyard. Even if she noticed car makes, which he knew she didn't, she would never associate him with this. He had grown a beard, let his hair get shaggy, put on weight. If he was careful, she would never recognize him. And he knew how to be careful. He could never disguise his height, six foot five, but he didn't intend to get close enough for her to identify him by height.

Day after day he had parked by the side of New Lane watching the driveway, noting her schedule. Her schedule was erratic; you could never depend on her. However, he knew in general when she went for the mail, when she went for groceries, always to Cronig's, almost never to the Edgartown A&P. He knew when she took Victoria and her weekly column to the *Island Enquirer*.

During the time he had parked by the side of New Lane, the police sergeant—he thought it was Chief Ben Norton's son Junior—passed by him and waved. He didn't think Junior recognized him. It had been a long time, after all. Even if Junior had some reason for checking his license plate, Lockwood didn't think the name would mean anything to him. Elizabeth had dropped her legitimate last name, *his* last name, Wolfrich, and had taken the name Trumbull, which was her mother's maiden name.

Lockwood was quite sure Elizabeth had no idea he was anywhere within five hundred miles. The Jeep was camouflaged by bushes and small trees that grew along the lane, but he could see the house through gaps in the dense growth. Watching Elizabeth, unknowing, so unself-conscious, gave him a great deal of satisfaction. He often thought about where this would end. In a confrontation of some kind, probably. He would make her understand she needed help, psychiatric help, and make her understand how he had always been there to help her, and still was there, watching over her, despite the fact that she had walked out on him. He would be there for her when she finally came to her senses. He had bought a pair of handcuffs at a police supply house in D.C. in case she needed to be restrained—for her own good, of course.

FOR THREE WEEKS, whenever Junior Norton drove down New Lane to visit his father Ben, he had been aware of the Jeep and driver parked by the side of the road half-hidden by shrubbery. Each time he passed the man he'd raised the fingers of his left hand from the steering wheel in a kind of salute and the man did the same.

He'd reported the parked Jeep to Casey the first day he'd seen it. The man wasn't doing anything wrong that they could see. They decided to wait. After a couple of weeks, Junior brought it up again.

"He's a bearded guy," Junior said. "Late thirties, heavyset. He looks vaguely familiar, but I don't recognize him."

"Any complaints about him?" Casey was sitting at the computer behind her desk. "Do you have any reason to question him?"

"No," Junior said, pulling out the chair at the desk across from hers, shared by him and the two patrolmen. "Not that many people drive down New Lane, so he's not really bothering anyone on the road. He's parked with all four tires off the pavement like he should, and he seems to be listening to his radio or something, just sitting there." Junior shifted his beeper to a more comfortable position on his belt. "But something about him just doesn't feel right."

"You might check out his license plate." Casey closed down her computer and stood. "I've got to pick up Victoria. She's writing a paper for the Kippers on 'Law Enforcement in West Tisbury, Then and Now.'" Casey shut the door so she could reach her jacket hanging on a hook inside the small closet. "Be nice to have enough space so we wouldn't have to perform acrobatics just to get a coat from the closet," she muttered. She was about to go outside when she turned back to Junior.

"What do you know about the Kippers, anyway?" She held

her jacket in one hand, the doorknob in the other. "Victoria has been going through files in Town Hall and looking up stuff in the library for her talk."

Junior glanced up from his desk, where he'd been sorting last year's yard sale permits. "It's a literary club," he said. "A couple of years ago it had its hundredth birthday. Got written up in *Yankee Magazine*." He tapped the stack of permits on the desktop to straighten it, tugged a rubber band out of his desk drawer, and put it around the cards.

"How did it get the name?" Casey shrugged into her jacket, hunching her shoulders because there wasn't room enough between her desk and the door to stretch out her arms.

"It stands for 'Knowledge Is Power,'" Junior said. "The club has twenty-four members. Each member prepares a paper every other year, and on alternate years serves tea and cucumber and watercress sandwiches with the crusts cut off."

Casey lifted her hair out from under her collar. "Victoria's really serious about her law enforcement paper."

Junior chortled. "Now she's got a legitimate excuse to ride with you, you'll never get rid of her."

"Actually, she's been a big help to me," Casey said defensively.

On the few occasions Victoria was not riding with her, Casey missed her keenly. "We really need a map of West Tisbury," she said to Junior, "a map that shows the town's roads. I know you and your dad know every one of them, as does Victoria, but I still don't. Neither does the fire chief."

"Good idea." Junior made a note. "I'll bring that up at the selectmen's meeting."

"I believe that's my job," Casey said tersely, hand still on the doorknob.

"Oops, sorry." Junior got up from the desk, put the stack

of permits in the bottom of a file drawer, and slid it shut. "I think Victoria is trying to shock the club ladies who expect to hear a paper on who really wrote Shakespeare." He looked up from the desk. "She going to talk about police scanners and firearms?"

Casey laughed. "There's nothing wrong with Victoria's mind. I'd love to go to that meeting and hear her law enforcement paper, about the druggies and alcoholics of West Tisbury, the club ladies' grandchildren. They would prefer to pretend the sordid side of the Island doesn't exist." She started out the door but turned to Junior. "Sorry I snapped at you about the selectmen's meeting. I'm overly sensitive."

"Not to worry," Junior said. "Say, before you go, what do you think about giving Victoria an honorary badge and cap to wear to the Kippers' meeting?"

"Great idea," Casey said.

"WAIT ONE, JUNIOR." Casey had answered the call on her radio. She and Victoria were at the West Tisbury side of the airport checking out an accident involving a bicyclist and a dog on the bike path. The bicyclist was sitting beside his bike, the wheel bent at an ugly angle. The dog was lying on his side, panting. Victoria had gone to the dog with the first aid kit she had put together for her rides with Casey. The bicyclist was scowling.

Casey knelt beside the man. "Are you hurt? Do you need the ambulance?"

He stood up, dusted off the back of his skintight spandex bike pants, and pointed angrily at his bicycle, an expensive model. "I thought they had leash laws here. I'm not hurt, but someone's going to pay for that."

"We'll get the animal control officer here right away," Casey said. "She'll...he'll take care of the dog. And the dog's owner." Casey still found it hard to believe Molly was gone. She radioed Junior. "Would you get Gabe Jernegan here, Junior? I'm at the airport gate and the bike path."

The radio spit out static, and Casey adjusted the squelch. Junior's voice came through. "I checked the license plate of the car parked off New Lane with the motor vehicle department."

"Let me get back to you," Casey radioed. "I've got my hands full right now with this bicyclist and dog."

AFTER CASEY HAD taken care of the bike rider and the paperwork, after Gabe Jernegan had caged the dog in the back of his truck, and after Casey and Victoria were in the Bronco heading back to town, Casey called Junior on the radio.

"The motor vehicle department says the Jeep is registered to a Lockwood Wolfrich, McLean, Virginia," Junior reported.

Victoria made a strange choking noise.

"Doesn't mean anything to me," Casey said.

"I have a feeling I know him, but I can't put my finger on where I know him from," said Junior.

Casey hung up the mike and looked at Victoria, concerned. "What was that all about?"

"Lockwood Wolfrich is Elizabeth's ex-husband. He called this morning from Washington. I thought it was Washington."

"Oh no, Victoria." Casey shook her head. "He's been around for about three weeks, staking out your place from New Lane." She turned onto the Edgartown-West Tisbury Road. "Was he abusive to Elizabeth?"

"That's why she divorced him. He's always seemed like such a good person, intelligent, well educated. I can't believe he would do anything like that." She looked at Casey. "He and

I always got along. Surely, Elizabeth must have exaggerated the situation."

"I doubt if she exaggerated. We've been making excuses for wife beaters too long."

"I can't think of Lockwood as a 'wife beater.'"

They had reached Victoria's house. Casey turned into the drive. "I'm dropping you off now instead of having you ride with me. You need to tell Elizabeth what's happening. That her ex is parked in New Lane and has been for some time. He's probably figuring out her schedule. She may be in danger."

Casey looked at Victoria's profile, the regal nose lifted slightly, her left eye with its drooping eyelid looking straight ahead, her downturned mouth determined, the network of wrinkles working through a curious mixture of delight at this new challenge, concern at what it meant. Victoria can handle it, Casey thought. I hope I can be like her at seventy-two, let alone ninety-two.

NINE

"I KNEW IT, I just knew it!" Elizabeth dumped bread dough out of the wooden mixing bowl onto a floured breadboard on the counter. "Didn't I tell you he was stalking me? I asked you not to talk to him, didn't I?" She pounded the dough with both fists, flipped it over and beat it some more. "What in hell am I going to do?" She burst into tears.

Victoria tore a paper towel from the dispenser and handed it to Elizabeth, who shook the flour off her hands, blotted her eyes, blew her nose, and put the crumpled paper towel in her jeans pocket.

"Casey said she wants to talk with you," Victoria said. "She's had special training in this sort of thing."

"I'm sorry I've gotten you into this mess." Elizabeth threw her arms around her grandmother.

Victoria patted her granddaughter. "Casey said police methods have changed over the past ten years."

"When I called the police, even four years ago, they told me, 'Kiss and make up,'" Elizabeth said. "When I tried to press assault charges they advised me against it. Now Lockwood doesn't have a record, he's got the house in McLean, and he's convinced, completely, totally convinced, he's the misunderstood good guy. And everyone, even my own sister, thinks, 'Poor Lockwood.'" Elizabeth kneaded the bread dough. "'Poor Lockwood,' baloney!"

"Casey agrees with you. Lockwood may be dangerous. Casey said if he shows up, call 911, and get to a safe house, a place he wouldn't know about."

"Where? He probably knows every place I'm likely to go to."

"Ben Norton's. Casey suggested that."

WHILE VICTORIA and Elizabeth were discussing the Lockwood situation, Junior Norton pulled up in front of the Jeep parked on New Lane. He got out, shut the cruiser door, adjusted his navy blue baseball cap with "West Tisbury Police" stitched in gold letters, hitched up his gun belt, and strode back to the Jeep. Professional cop, he thought. Chief Casey O'Neill would approve.

"Mr. Wolfrich," he said, when Lockwood rolled down the window. "Do you need any assistance, sir?"

Lockwood grinned, teeth yellow against his brown tweed beard. He moved his heavy horn-rimmed glasses higher on his nose, holding the earpiece with his thumb and third finger. He peered at Junior's name tag. "You're Ben Norton's boy, aren't you?…I see you looked up my license plate. Very clever." His voice was deep and authoritative. This creep, Junior thought, is hoping to knock me down a peg or two. And he's not that much older than me.

"Do you need any assistance, sir?"

"Assistance," Lockwood repeated. "Let me see." He looked steadily at Junior, his green eyes, flecked with dark red spots, brilliantly lit behind his thick lenses by the afternoon sun. "No, I don't think so, thank you. I assume there's no law against my parking here." He gestured toward Victoria's house. "Nice view." The view of the house was almost hidden by a growth of bright yellow wild cherry, gaudy red euonymus, and viburnum.

"Yes, sir," Junior said. "There's no law against your parking here, sir. But it is unusual."

"'Unusual,'" Lockwood repeated, imitating Junior's voice and inflection. "'Unusual.' I don't know about that. I'm bird-watching." He nodded toward the house. "That's what I'm doing here, bird-watching." He bared his teeth in a grin. "Nothing unusual about bird-watching, is there?"

"No, sir, Mr. Wolfrich," Junior said. "In case you decide you would like our assistance, sir, we'll be around."

"Well." Lockwood drew out the word as if he were playing in a western shoot-'em-up. "That's mighty nice of you, boy."

Junior felt the blood rush to his face. He tipped his baseball cap and strode back to the cruiser, feeling Lockwood's green eyes with red flecks staring at his back.

"CHRIST," JUNIOR SAID to Casey when he got back to the station. "The bastard really pissed me off. Arrogant, insulting, son of a bitch. 'Boy.' There's something familiar about that guy, but I can't place him. What about arresting him for loitering?"

"Afraid not. You did what you could. I'll get Josh or Elmer to spend whatever time they have available parked where Wolfrich can see the cruiser." She got up from her desk and gathered a stack of papers from the counter. "Also, I talked to your dad, asked him if Elizabeth could stay with him if necessary."

"He'd probably like that," Junior said. "He's got plenty of room. He misses police work and I think he's lonely."

LATER THAT AFTERNOON Victoria was typing her weekly column for the *Island Enquirer* at the cookroom table. Elizabeth had put the bread in the oven and its aroma filled the kitchen and cookroom.

There was a knock at the door and Elizabeth opened it to

Winthrop Lodge, who rented the small shack he chose to call a cottage behind Victoria's house. Winthrop was wearing his maroon beret with a silver dolphin pin on its side. He pulled out a chair and sat, facing Victoria.

"It's getting chilly at night," he said. "I lit the cottage stove last night."

"All you need to warm that little place are matchsticks," Victoria said.

Winthrop laughed.

Elizabeth was scrubbing her bread-making dishes. "Don't burn the place down," she advised over her shoulder.

"I've been so busy all summer I haven't had a chance to chat with you." Winthrop took off his beret and brushed it with his hand. "Are you mentioning anything about the recent deaths in your column, Mrs. Trumbull? Strange. Four of them, and within such a short time."

Victoria stopped typing, two forefingers poised above the typewriter. "I wrote about what each of them meant to the community. I said how much we miss them." She paused. "All of them left sizable bequests to the church. I mentioned that. Except for Molly Bettencourt, who didn't have a lot of money. I didn't say that, of course."

"They were all elderly, weren't they?" Winthrop straightened his dolphin pin. "Excuse me, Mrs. Trumbull, I shouldn't have said elderly. They were all younger than you, weren't they?"

"All elderly except Molly," Victoria still held her two fingers above the typewriter. "It is strange. We didn't expect any of them to die. Hal was healthy. Jeremiah Silvia complained a lot, but he was healthy, too. Brewster was forgetful; he was tedious, certainly. Everyone expected him to keep going for ten years at least."

Elizabeth finished with the dishes and joined her grandmother and Winthrop. "That beret looks good on you, Winthrop," she said. "I like the dolphin."

"Thanks," Winthrop said. "Kirk gave the pin to me. I don't believe you've met him." He put on his hat, smoothed the back of it, and stood up. "I'd better get up to Alley's for my mail."

Footsteps clattered down the front stairs, tramped through the front hall. Dishes in the dining room breakfront rattled. Angelo Santellini appeared, a broad, merry grin, his face daubed with paint, his T-shirt a palette of smeared colors, his hands a dirty greenish-brown.

"Angelo, don't touch anything," Victoria said, alarmed.

Winthrop took his hat off again and looked with interest at Angelo. "I'm Winthrop Lodge," he said. "I live in the cottage out back." He held out his hand.

"Shack," said Elizabeth.

"Don't shake hands with him unless you want a paint job," Victoria said. "You could frame that T-shirt, Angelo, and sell it. It's better than some of your paintings."

Angelo looked fondly at Victoria and laughed. "Hey, Elizabeth, something smells marvelous."

Elizabeth had taken the bread out of the oven and was emptying the loaves onto wire racks. "The most fragrant smell on earth," she said. "What are you working on now, Angelo?"

"I thought I'd drive to Quansoo and paint the ocean. I want to show a strip of beach with sandpipers running along the swash line." Angelo ripped a paper towel off the roll under the cabinet where the mugs were kept and wiped his hands.

Elizabeth reached under the sink for a can of heavy-duty hand cleaner and handed it to him. "You need more than a paper towel to get that off."

Victoria said, "It'll be windy at the beach today."

"I can shelter behind the dunes." Angelo pried the lid off

the can of cleaner, leaving a smear of paint on it, scooped out a dollop of the jelly-like stuff, and worked it into his hands.

"I was planning to take a walk there, myself," Winthrop said from the cookroom, where he was standing next to the table, gazing through his thick eyelashes at Angelo. "Would you mind company? We can go in my car. I noticed you had trouble starting yours."

"Great." Angelo put the lid back on the hand cleaner and dropped the paper towel in the rubbish can.

"Don't get too much paint on the beach," Victoria said.

AFTER THEY LEFT, Victoria sat at her typewriter for a long time, gazing at the church in the distance and stroking McCavity's soft fur. The afternoon light muted the sharp outlines of the spire, blended it into the sky. The trees beyond the brook showed a misty haze of yellow, orange, red, and green. No wonder artists loved the soft light. She could hear the Canada geese wheeling overhead, even with the windows closed.

What could she do about Lockwood? She had not taken Elizabeth seriously, she realized. She had always assumed there was equal blame for arguments. She hadn't understood how serious the situation was. She had not supported her granddaughter the way she should have. Her inclination would have been to invite Lockwood over for coffee, talk to him, reason with him. Casey, however, had warned her to stay away from him, it was a police matter, let the professionals take care of it. Batterers were often not reasonable, Casey said. But Casey could not dedicate police time to watching a man who probably was doing nothing more than feeling resentful of Elizabeth and sorry for himself. They do take a look when they drive by, though.

Victoria sighed and looked out of the window at the view.

And why four deaths? Ben Norton had said he had never known so many townspeople to die within such a short time. It certainly was strange.

"Almost ready, Gram?" Elizabeth held Victoria's blue coat open. "It's cool out, windy."

"I guess so." Victoria rolled the paper out of her typewriter, preoccupied.

"Are you okay? I can wait. I'm not in a hurry."

"No, I'm ready, I was thinking about Hal and Molly and Jeremiah and Brewster." Victoria looked thoughtful.

"You must miss them," Elizabeth said sympathetically. "Especially Hal."

"There was nothing between Hal and me," Victoria said sharply, looking up at Elizabeth. "He was not my 'gentleman friend.' I wish you'd stop telling people that."

She shooed McCavity out of her lap and got up stiffly from the typewriter. McCavity stared at Elizabeth reproachfully, leaped into the wastebasket, curled into a bread-dough-shaped lump, one leg sticking up in the air, and began to wash himself.

Elizabeth laughed and helped Victoria into her coat. "I feel a lot better with the police keeping an eye on Lockwood. At least we know where he is."

"He's staying at the campground," Victoria said. "Casey had one of her men follow him." She shuffled papers on the table. "Where did I put my copy for the column?"

"Here," Elizabeth said. "In your pocketbook."

THE EDITORIAL OFFICES of the *Island Enquirer* were in Edgartown, eight miles from Victoria's. The road was once a path Wampanoag runners had beaten down between Great Harbor, now Edgartown, and Takemmy, now West Tisbury.

On their way to Edgartown with Victoria's column, they saw a heavy gray fog bank above the scrub oak to their right, rolling in from the ocean over the great ponds that lined the south shore. Scrub oak, the leaves turning a rich brown, and scrub pine, a velvety dark green, stretched as far as they could see on either side. Huckleberry and sweet fern edged the road. A hawk circled high above them. As they drove into the hollows, the air was cooler, and smelled of ripe, lush vegetation returning to the soil. As they came out of the hollows, the scent of hot pine wafted to them in waves.

At one time the area was called the Great Plains. Victoria remembered when her sea captain grandfather drove them in the horse-drawn truck wagon to pick blueberries on the plains. How large her blueberry bucket seemed, although her grandfather had said, "the little pail for the child." She recalled how long it took to fill that pail, how the berries covered the metal bottom, blue, red, green. She remembered Aunt picking leaves out of Victoria's little bucket and pouring berries from her own big one into Victoria's so the task didn't seem so endless. She remembered the smell of sun-warmed pine, the sound of chewinks rustling in the undergrowth.

Victoria talked about this to Elizabeth as the road crossed the ancient glacial drainage channels that led to the ponds, swales deep enough to hide oncoming cars. She told Elizabeth how Mack, the horse, struggled up the hill out of Deep Bottom, how her aunt and her grandmother and little Victoria would get out of the truck wagon to ease the strain on Mack and walk beside him on the sandy, rutted road. The road had been paved for eighty years, now.

THE *ISLAND ENQUIRER* occupied an entire gray-shingled building on Summer Street in Edgartown, a corner building surrounded by a white-painted picket fence. In June the fence was festooned with pink roses. Now a few late blossoms adorned the shiny dark green leaves, their perfume intense in the late summer air.

"Want me to take the column in for you?" Elizabeth realized immediately she shouldn't have asked. Without deigning to answer, Victoria opened the convertible door on her side, eased herself out of the low car, and strode into the *Enquirer* office. Elizabeth watched her, walking like the ten-year-old tomboy she still thought she was, more than eight decades after the fact. Elizabeth's mother, Amelia, had grown up and aged; she, Elizabeth, had grown up and aged; yet their mother and grandmother never believed the aging process applied to her.

Victoria took longer than usual. Elizabeth had almost finished reading the editorial page of last week's *Enquirer* when Victoria came out.

"Sorry it took so long. I wanted to look something up in the morgue," she said.

"Did you find what you needed?"

"No. I'll have to go to Town Hall."

"We can go now. It's not five yet." Elizabeth pulled the convertible away from the curb. "What were you looking for?"

"Death statistics for the past couple of decades."

"You're not comfortable about those four deaths, are you? It does seem like too much of a coincidence. But, aside from Lockwood, I can't think of anyone crazy enough to kill three old men and the animal control officer." She turned right onto Cook Street at the Federated Church. They drove past tidy white houses with freshly painted black shutters, perfectly repaired white picket fences, all with rose vines with sweet-scented fall roses. Red and pink geraniums filled window boxes.

Whenever they came this way Elizabeth calculated how much it must cost to keep each house, each picket fence, each rose vine in such perfect condition. She thought of their own struggle to keep Victoria's house repaired, thought of the mortgage payments. The house was like another member of the family. It had been in the family since it was built two hundred and fifty years before.

Time collapsed in a disorienting way around the house and its inhabitants. Victoria told the story over and over about how her grandfather—Elizabeth's great-great-grandfather—had been scolded by his great-aunt Rebecca for climbing the pear tree when he was a little boy. Aunt Rebecca had been a teenager during the Revolutionary War. One glimpse of Aunt Rebecca, seen through the eyes of a seven-year-old pear tree climber, passed down through two centuries, to be passed again from Elizabeth to her grandchildren, who would repeat the story of Aunt Rebecca scolding their great-great-great-great-grandfather for climbing the pear tree.

Each generation had built onto the house, added wings, removed or added partitions, modernized it to accommodate changing tastes. Elizabeth's grandfather, Jonathan, had installed electricity with Victoria's help, fishing wires through the tough old oak that framed the house.

Victoria had said she planned to fix the roof with the money she was going to win from the Publishers' Clearing House sweepstakes. Clayton Rogers's son, the one with the MBA from Harvard, would climb up on the roof and fix it.

They returned from Edgartown, and Elizabeth parked her convertible under the Norway maple. Winthrop and Angelo pulled up next to her. "How did the painting go?" Victoria asked.

A yellow maple leaf drifted onto Elizabeth's car. McCavity, who had been sitting by the side of the drive, leaped onto the hood, pounced on the leaf, batted it off, placed his front paws on the windshield, and peered at the two women inside, his soft underbelly fur pressed flat against the glass.

"The painting went fabulously well." Angelo bounded out of his side of the car.

"Lovely colors." Victoria cocked her head. "I can tell from your pants."

"You didn't get paint on my upholstery, did you?" Winthrop said, coming around the front of the car.

"Not a lot." Angelo looked at the seat. "Here, I'll wipe it off with turpentine."

Winthrop snatched the paint-smeared cloth out of Angelo's hand.

Angelo grinned and shrugged. "We brought you a present," he said to Victoria. "Someone left a basket of mushrooms near the creek."

Winthrop opened the trunk of his car. "Whoever picked them must have forgotten the basket. It was in the shade of the bridge."

The path to the beach led across a shaky wooden foot-bridge that spanned Crab Creek, into the dunes, and ended at the ocean. The arrow-straight creek emptied into Tisbury Great Pond.

"We used to pick mushrooms there when I was a child," Victoria said. "At that time the entire area was a sheep pasture, the grass was short, and mushrooms grew everywhere. I haven't seen any there lately, now the pasture is overgrown." She opened the car door and held on to it while she pulled herself out. "Wonder where they found them?"

Angelo held the basket out to her with a pleased expression.

"That looks like one of my baskets." Victoria looked inside, then up at Angelo. "These aren't field mushrooms, Angelo. I think these are the poisonous kind." She picked up one of them. "Field mushrooms, the edible kind, have pinkish or brown gills underneath. Look at these. The gills are white."

"Are you sure?" Angelo said. "Why would anyone have picked them, then?"

"They probably didn't recognize them. A lot of mushrooms look alike. This morning I was reading Jessica Dell's annual letter to the editor in a back issue of the *Enquirer* warning readers to 'beware of the deadly amanita.' Death's angel. They sprout in the warm wet woods, on lawns, in children's play areas, around pine trees." Victoria put the mushroom back in the basket. "Every year around the end of August, she warns readers about poisonous mushrooms. Jessica's on call at the hospital whenever they suspect mushroom poisoning. The hospital asks her to identify bits and pieces from stomach contents or leftover scraps from a meal." She turned the basket. "This does look exactly like mine."

"It is yours," Elizabeth said. "I put that piece of twine on the handle so we could hang the basket from a hook in the cookroom." She looked from Angelo to Winthrop to Victoria. "That's weird. Did either of you take the basket?"

Both Angelo and Winthrop shook their heads no.

"How on earth?" Elizabeth said.

"Where did the mushrooms come from?" Victoria pondered. "I don't think there's a pine tree within a mile of the creek."

The road to Quansoo was two and a half miles long, a sand road that was the despair of Chief O'Neill because a dozen identical, unmarked roads led off it to who-knew-whose houses. Year-round residents could direct emergency vehicles to the correct road. Summer renters usually could not.

Where the Quansoo Road branched off South Road tall beech trees and oaks arched overhead. As the road got closer to the sea, the trees became more and more stunted, salt shorn from wind-borne spray. A half mile from the ocean the trees gave way to scrubby bayberry, wild rose, beach goldenrod, and poison ivy, species that tolerated salty storm winds.

Winthrop lifted his dark eyebrows. "How did your basket get there? And why? Why poisonous mushrooms? And why should anyone leave a basket of mushrooms by the bridge?"

"I suppose it will sort itself out," Victoria said. "I have a phone call to make."

TEN

CASEY WAS ON HER WAY home from the hospital with Victoria, who had been reading to the elderly. Victoria was quiet.

"We'll stop for a treat, okay, Victoria?" Casey looked over at her sidekick with concern. "We'll get some coffee and pastry at the Black Dog on State Road, okay?"

Victoria nodded, her eyes straight ahead, her mouth turned down.

Casey parked the Bronco and they went in the side door.

"You hold our seats, Victoria. I'll get the coffee. How about lemon curd?"

Victoria nodded again. Her eyelids drooped, even her nose seemed to sag. Her wrinkles were a pen-and-ink sketch of melancholy.

"A rough time at the hospital?" Casey said.

"It's as if they've been thrown away," Victoria said finally. "They sit there all day, waiting to die. They're always glad to see me, although it's not me they're glad to see. It doesn't matter who I am or what I read. I could read a treatise on economics, and it would all be the same." She unbuttoned her blue coat. Casey held it so Victoria could work her arms out. "I give them a break from the routine of sitting there." She looked up at Casey. "The nurses are kind and caring. The place is clean. They have everything they need physically, but…"

"You'll never be there with them." Casey understood why

Victoria was so down. "Elizabeth will make sure you never go there. I will too."

Casey went to the counter, hitching up her gun belt as she walked. Victoria needed something special today. She poured two mugs of hazelnut coffee from the urn and put cream and two sugars into her own. She paused before she emptied the second sugar packet and thought how she ought to cut out the second sugar. She bought a lemon curd from the young woman behind the counter, asked for two plates. She picked out a plastic knife from the utensil container.

Casey sat down and cut the lemon curd into two pieces with the plastic knife and put half on a plate for Victoria. They sat quietly, sipping coffee and eating pastry.

"Would you mind stopping at Jessica Dell's on the way home, Casey?" Victoria asked.

Casey looked up from her plate.

"It's in Oak Bluffs," Victoria continued, "only a couple of miles out of our way. I called her, said we might come by."

"Sure," Casey said, her mouth full. "She's the mushroom expert?"

"Yes."

"I ought to meet her, anyway," Casey said. "Who knows when you might need a mushroom expert."

"Mushroom poisoning is more common on the Island than you would think." Victoria took a paper napkin out of the black metal holder and wiped a spill of coffee from the table, its rough surface slicked by layers of polyurethane.

"I didn't have much experience with mushroom poisoning in Brockton," Casey said. "It never occurred to me that the Vineyard might harbor killer mushrooms."

Victoria wadded up the paper napkin. "Amanitas are common in late August and September—this time of year."

"I take it you have a reason for wanting to see Jessica now." Casey stirred her coffee.

"It's a thought," Victoria said. "I wanted to ask Jessica about symptoms of mushroom poisoning."

"Hal and the others?"

Victoria nodded, wiped powdered sugar off her mouth with a clean napkin. "Edna Coffin's seagull died the other day. He'd eaten a bluefish stuffed with mushrooms someone gave her that she didn't want. She fed it to the seagull, and he died."

"Hmmm." Casey drew out the exclamation. "Are you suggesting what I think you are?"

"I don't know what I'm suggesting, Casey. Remember how Ben Norton said he'd never known of so many deaths at one time in West Tisbury? I looked up death records at the courthouse in Edgartown for all six towns. There's never been anything like this. Maybe back in the 1918 flu epidemic."

"Flu shot, Victoria?" Casey went on before Victoria could respond. "You have a point. I can think of only three explanations." She held up her left hand and counted off fingers with her right. "First, the four deaths are what they seem to be, a coincidence. Coincidences do happen. Second, the four deaths might be the result of some accident common to all four, or maybe to only one, two, or three of the four. The third—" She paused, dropped her hands, and took a last sip of coffee. "Third—I really don't want to think about it. Murder." She brushed powdered sugar from her lap. "Why, though? Who on earth would have it in for those four? What do they have in common?"

Casey stood up, rubbed her boots on the backs of her trouser legs. "I want to believe it's like the hundred-year storm, a coincidence that won't happen for another hundred years. Why during my watch, though?"

She picked up the mugs, plates, napkins, and plastic knife.

"Don't throw that away," Victoria said, holding her hand out for the knife. "We can still use it."

Casey laughed. She wiped off the serrated edge and gave it to Victoria. The rest she took back to the counter and dropped the paper napkins into the trash container.

"Something else," Victoria said when Casey returned.

Casey sat again. "Yes?"

"Angelo, the artist in the attic, and Winthrop, who rents the field house, found a basket of mine—definitely mine—next to the bridge at Quansoo." Victoria stopped. Casey waited. "It was full of mushrooms. Amanitas."

Casey looked thoughtfully at Victoria. There was a long silence while their eyes met and held.

"Did Angelo and Winthrop take the basket to the beach? Did they pick the mushrooms, thinking they were edible?"

"They were as surprised as I was. They brought the mushrooms home, thinking they were bringing me something special." She looked at Casey. "Strangest of all, how did my basket get there?"

"I'll be interested in hearing what Jessica has to say. Here, let me hold your coat," she said when she saw Victoria struggling with it.

"Thank you," Victoria said. "My sleeves ride up."

JESSICA'S HOUSE WAS down an unmarked, unnamed sand road that ended at the shore of Sengekontacket Pond.

They drove through pines and russet-leaved oaks, came to an open meadow with pale grasses moving in the breeze like waves on the ocean. Around the edge of the meadow were masses of goldenrod and purple asters. As they got closer, they could see dozens of butterflies feeding on the asters. Sengekontacket Pond spread out beyond the meadow.

"How on earth do you pronounce it?" Casey said.

"Sen-jah-kon-TACK-it," Victoria said. "Accent on the next to the last syllable. That's what Leonard Vanderhoop told me. He was a Wampanoag."

"Sengekontacket, Chappaquiddick, Quansoo, Quenames, Wampanoag. I feel as if I live in Indian territory sometimes."

"Turn left here," Victoria said. "Her house is at the end of this road."

Jessica's house was on a slight rise overlooking the large shallow tidal pond. A low finger of land projected into the pond on the right, Felix Neck Wildlife Sanctuary. Trees in the sanctuary were turning, the regal dark reds and browns of the oaks, the splash of scarlet swamp maples, orange, yellow touches among the dark green pines.

Vineyard autumns are not usually spectacular; the colors tend to be muted. But occasional bright hints of color accent the Island's subtle fall tapestry.

Water birds were feeding in the shallows of the pond. Something startled them, and they rose in a single body, circled, swooped, and settled back on the water.

"I suppose I ought to learn what all these birds are," Casey said. "I can recognize pigeons and sparrows. That's about all. Swans, now. And ducks and geese." The bruise on her thigh from the swan attack had faded long ago, but she could still feel a lump through her uniform trousers.

As they pulled into Jessica's drive, they saw cars on Beach Road on the other side of the pond a half mile away. The road was built on a thin strip of sand, a barrier bar that separated the pond from Nantucket Sound. The bar formed one of the Island's most beautiful public beaches. Beyond the road, a fishing boat headed out toward Georges Bank, once one of the richest fisheries in the world, now almost a ghost place.

"COME IN, come in!"

Jessica Dell, not much younger than Victoria, Casey guessed, probably in her eighties, was so tiny Casey thought she was a child at first. Jessica peered at them through thick glasses, her face lit up in a pixie-like grin.

They went into her small entry, and she shut the door behind them. From the entry, they could see into the living room, where the expanse of windows looked out over a panoramic view of the pond, the beach, and the sound.

"Jessica," Victoria said, coming to the point at once. "This is the time of year for poisonous mushrooms, isn't it?"

"All kinds of mushrooms," Jessica said. "Sit down. You'll want to face the view, I know." She indicated a chintz-covered armchair and a chintz-covered sofa. "Mushrooms like the warm moist weather this time of year. You need to watch out for amanitas, though. People don't realize how common they are."

"What do they look like?" Casey asked, settling into the corner of the sofa. She shifted the green-and-pink cushion out from behind her.

"Here, I'll show you photos." Jessica fetched several framed photos of mushrooms from the other side of the living room. "I won a prize for this photo of a group of amanitas. They're beautiful. And deadly. They look a great deal like the common field mushrooms that the old-timers harvested. The difference is underneath."

She put the framed photos on an end table, picked up the top one, and pointed to the undersides of the mushrooms in the picture. "The common field mushrooms have pink or tan or brownish gills; amanitas have white gills. You see here?"

She moved her finger around the picture indicating the gills. "Where they come out of the ground, you see?" She pointed to the stalk. "The stem is slightly swollen, like this."

Jessica showed them a second photo of amanitas and a third. "Now let's look at common field mushrooms."

She set aside the top three pictures and lifted up the fourth, a photo of a group of mushrooms in a grassy area. "You see?" Jessica said. "Pink or tan gills and a straight stem. These are field mushrooms." She started to pick up the stack of framed photos.

Casey immediately got to her feet, took the photos from Jessica, and carried them to the side of the room where the pictures had been hanging.

"Thank you," Jessica said after Casey had rehung them. "Can I make tea for either of you?"

"No thanks," said Casey. "We just had coffee and pastry." She waited until Jessica settled herself on the couch and then sat at the other end, where she could look at the view.

"If someone were to eat an amanita, what would the symptoms be?" Victoria's hands were on the arms of the chair. Giant pink peonies bloomed in chintzy splendor beneath her fingers.

"I don't advise eating one." Jessica settled a pillow behind her on the couch. Even with the pillow, her feet didn't quite reach the floor. "They are supposed to have a pleasant taste— I wouldn't know, of course. The toxin is not destroyed by cooking, and the amanita is poisonous to most animals, too. The symptoms don't show up for almost twenty-four hours, and, by then, the toxin has done tremendous damage, destroying liver and kidney function. By the time someone recognizes the symptoms, it's often too late. Not much can be done. A very painful death."

Victoria and Casey stared at Jessica. Both sat rigidly. Victoria clutched the arms of her chair.

"After the symptoms first appear—nausea, vomiting, severe diarrhea"—Jessica peered at Casey, then at Victoria—"the victim usually is in such agony he—or she—goes to the hospital. Often, the symptoms disappear after the first onslaught."

Casey and Victoria watched the tiny woman without moving. Casey sat forward slightly.

"I've known cases where the patient is discharged from the hospital because the symptoms disappear," Jessica continued, "only to collapse and die a day or so later."

Victoria looked from Jessica to Casey.

"Could someone eat amanitas by mistake?" Casey leaned forward, clasped her hands, and put them between her knees.

"Easily. That's what usually happens," Jessica said. "Just a couple of years ago, a Vietnamese family here on the Vineyard picked amanitas, thinking they were the same species they ate in Vietnam. It was a classic case of the symptoms appearing, severe enough to make the family members go to the hospital. The hospital suspected amanita poisoning and called me. I identified the mushrooms, the hospital tried to treat all five, but one of the men, when the symptoms disappeared, refused further treatment. He died."

Casey and Victoria were silent for a few minutes. Then Casey asked, "If someone were to try to poison someone else, would amanita be a logical choice?"

"It would be a choice, certainly, but a nasty one. It's not a nice death." Jessica peered at Casey.

"If the mushrooms were cooked up in some dish, say a tuna noodle casserole, would that be enough to kill someone?" Victoria leaned forward.

"Yes, anything like that. Any dish where you would think of using mushrooms. Amanita poisoning is fatal in only about fifty percent of the cases of ingestion. It would be most effective against someone who is in frail health, children, the elderly."

"The two young men who are staying with me found a basket of mushrooms under the bridge at Quansoo." Victoria opened her pocketbook and brought out an orange Halloween napkin. "This is one of the mushrooms."

Jessica took the napkin next to the window and examined the mushroom. "Yes," she said. "That's an amanita. One of the most deadly species." She returned to her chair. "Do you want this back again?"

"No thanks." Victoria closed the flap on her old leather pocketbook. "Where would someone have found the amanitas, a whole basket full of them?"

"They have a symbiotic relationship with pine trees, so you would find them around pines." Jessica took the Halloween napkin with its deadly mushroom over to the fireplace and stuffed it under the fire that was laid, ready for a match. "That would include a lot of places on the Vineyard, in a yard, in the forest, anywhere there are pine trees. Or even where the pines have been cut down."

"Would you be apt to find a lot of them in one place?" Casey asked.

"That depends. I would guess you would find three or four in one place. You said there was a whole basket full? How large a basket?"

"Enough to hold a couple of quarts," Victoria said.

"I would guess, then, that someone had to go to several places to find that many." Jessica went over to a large built-in bookcase. "Let me lend you a mushroom field guide," she said. "You can give it to me at church next Sunday so you don't have to come all the way out here."

"Thanks, Jessica."

Most of the way back to West Tisbury, Chief O'Neill and Victoria were quiet. Casey concentrated on her driving.

"Curiouser and curiouser," Casey said finally.

Victoria spoke. "It's worse than that." She clasped and unclasped her hands. She looked down at her feet, at her sturdy shoes, one with a hole cut out for her sore toe. Finally she said, "I killed Molly."

"What!?" The Bronco swerved.

"I gave Molly a tuna noodle casserole." Victoria sat quietly for several minutes more, her hands now held in her lap. Casey stared straight ahead at the road. They were coming up on the blinker, the only traffic light on the Vineyard, and she switched on the left-turn signal, slowed the Bronco.

"She was almost over the flu. She didn't die of flu complications. The tuna noodle casserole killed her." Victoria gazed at Casey, who took her eyes off the road briefly to look back at Victoria.

"What are you saying, Victoria? What tuna noodle casserole?" Casey waited for a car to pass and turned onto the airport road.

"Someone left it on my kitchen table one day when Elizabeth was off-Island," Victoria said. "She came home early, so we took it to Molly. There was only enough for one."

"Why on God's green earth would anyone poison you?"

"Molly doesn't fit the pattern," Victoria said, hands busy again, clasping and unclasping. "I do. Three elderly people died. If Elizabeth hadn't come home early, if I had eaten the casserole, if I hadn't given it to Molly, I'd have been the fourth elderly person."

"Lord," Casey said. "But why?" They passed the state forest on the left, the airport on the right. The straight road ended at the West Tisbury-Edgartown Road.

"We have to figure that out." Victoria looked ahead at the intersection. A blue pickup truck flashed by. "If Edna Coffin had eaten that stuffed bluefish, she'd have been number five."

"We don't know the bluefish was poisoned. Where did Edna get it?"

Victoria looked at Casey. "Milton Jackson."

"You mean the Reverend Milton Jackson? The new minister?"

"Watch your driving," Victoria said, bracing herself.

"Victoria, this is too bizarre." Casey steered the Bronco back onto the road. "No minister is going to go around poisoning people. I mean, ministers don't do that."

"I wouldn't put it past that Jack Jackson," Victoria said.

ELEVEN

LATER THAT EVENING, the Reverend Jack Jackson was preparing supper. He flung a peeled potato into a bowl of water with a splash and turned to his wife, who was sitting on the deacon's bench on the other side of the kitchen. "Do *you* think I'm being unreasonable?"

"No, dearie. Not at all," Betty replied. "The trustees are not supporting you the way they should. A new minister doesn't copy the old one. He needs to set his own tone."

Jack returned to the potatoes. From the window over the sink he could see the police station on the opposite side of the pond, and if he looked to the left of the police station, he could see a corner of Edna Coffin's house through the changing maple trees at the head of the pond.

Betty was working on her braided rug. The afternoon sun streamed through the west window behind her and cast a long moving shadow of her braiding onto the blue painted wood floor, a steady turning and twisting of the strips into the fabric of the rug. Colored strips were spread around her on the bench and on the floor.

Jack noticed wool from an old black blazer, a favorite jacket he had worn until the collar and cuffs had frayed—a jacket he would still be wearing if Betty hadn't insisted he give it up.

Betty and Jack looked much alike. She was in her early fifties, short and pleasantly plump, her rosy face framed by a halo of wispy graying hair. Her comfortable grandmotherly appearance implied freshly baked gingerbread cookies—although she and Jack had no grandchildren or children, and Jack, not she, did all the cooking.

"I gather Jack Hutchinson has sunk into a depression and Maddy is upset about it," the Reverend Jackson said. "I find it difficult to conjure up the Christian sympathy I should feel for those two."

"I'm sorry they're taking it so hard, I really am. But we can't sacrifice your ministry for the hurt feelings of one rather vain man and his controlling wife."

Betty moved the rug-making material off her lap, got up, went to the laundry room next to the kitchen, took a needle, spool of thread, and a pair of nail scissors out of her sewing basket, and returned. "By the way, would you like me to do anything special for the children's service next month? The third Sunday, isn't it?"

"I thought I might ask the eight- to ten-year-old Sunday school children to give a short program before the regular adult service," Jack said. "Perhaps you could work with them, help them pick out a hymn, an appropriate Bible reading, that sort of thing."

"The congregation would enjoy that, I know." Betty moved the rug back into her lap. "I'd like to ask Patrick O'Neill, the police chief's son, to do the reading. He's a sweet boy, quite bright, reads very well for his age."

"Good idea. I'd like to get Chief O'Neill more involved with the church." Jack scooped the potato peels out of the sink and put them in a plastic basket on the side of the counter. "Did I tell you that Edna Coffin said Victoria Trumbull thinks I'm jealous of Jack Hutchinson?"

"You know that's ridiculous, dearie." Betty pursed her lips and concentrated on folding a strip of fabric, twisting the cut edges to the inside of the fold. "I know better than anyone how hard you've had to struggle to overcome your tendency toward jealousy." She rolled the folded black strip of fabric into a ball and set it to one side on the bench. "I remember how annoyed you were with Ralph Ordway when we first met. You were so upset with me, I was a tiny bit frightened."

"I hardly think wanting the former minister out of my way shows I'm jealous." He scowled.

"No, dearie. I didn't mean to imply that you're jealous of Jack Hutchinson."

"You certainly did. You're bringing up an incident that happened almost thirty years ago." He took a stick of butter out of the refrigerator and vigorously greased the baking dish with the unwrapped end of it. "Ralph Ordway was an ass."

"You're right, of course. I was lucky you came along when you did, although I don't think Ralph Ordway would have stayed in my life much longer anyway."

After several minutes of silence broken only by the soft sound of Betty tugging and twisting the rug braid, Jack said, "It's not as if I excommunicated them." He dropped the last of the peeled potatoes into a large bowl of water and squeezed lemon juice over them. "I asked Hutchinson to stay away from the church for two years. Two years isn't forever. I said they should take advantage of this time. Travel. See the world. Wouldn't you think they would want to do that?"

"Money is certainly no problem. They, of all people, ought to understand how you feel. Remember that big to-do when they were asked to leave the Arlington church?"

"How can I forget? I was taking that graduate course in cults at the seminary the spring before it all happened. You were working at Filene's Basement, I recall." Jack dried his hands on a dish towel and put the bowl of potatoes into the refrigerator. "Baked bluefish for dinner. Junior Norton brought me some more fillets."

"Junior has been so generous. I love bluefish, especially when it's fresh like that." She threaded a needle and stitched the end of the balled-up black strip onto the loose black end of the braid. She snipped the thread with the nail scissors. "I always thought Maddy manipulated Jack Hutchinson. The affair was traumatic for Lydia and the children."

"For the church, too. The congregation almost split up because of them." He leaned down, opened the drawer at the bottom of the stove, and took out the lid to the glass baking dish. "The other day I stopped by Edna's, and who should be there but Maddy."

"What did she have to say?"

"She was polite, as always. She didn't say anything beyond pleasantries, gave me that irritating smile of hers."

"Knowing her, she probably timed her visit to Edna deliberately to irritate you," Betty said. "I know it's awful to feel the way I do about them, but she is such a meddler and he is so arrogant with his sermons referring to Greek classics no one's ever heard of. We're all supposed to be impressed with his mental gyrations." She picked up the braid that tailed off the embryonic rug and continued to work the black blazer strip against a light blue strip from an old suit of hers and a cream-colored strip from a worn-out blanket. "It's going to be pretty, don't you think?" She held it up for his approval.

Jack nodded.

The Jacksons had moved into the parsonage, a small white clapboard building a half mile from the church and two houses away from the cemetery, when he became full-time minister. He and Betty had summered on the Island, and over the years he had occasionally substituted for the Reverend Jack Hutchinson.

The parsonage was on a slight rise overlooking the Mill Pond. From the house they could see two horses, one white, one brown, grazing in the field next to them. The field and the horses belonged to a family that lived off Old County Road, and every day the two daughters of the house, one about eleven, one about thirteen, came on their bicycles to feed and ride the horses.

"It's such a shame we've lost those four wonderful people," Betty said. "The three men, Hal, Jeremiah, and Brewster, left quite a bit of money to the church, didn't they?"

"Yes, they did, all of them. Only a month before Brewster died, he changed his will to leave almost everything to the church." Jack took the bluefish fillets out of the refrigerator and laid them on the breadboard. "He left something to Linda, of course, but she seems to feel that, as his daughter, she should have been left more." He straightened out the pieces of fish on the board and went back to the refrigerator for a bowl of stuffing. "He cut Mandred out of his will entirely."

"That's too bad." Betty pursed her mouth and twisted the braid. "Brewster and his son never did get along. Such a pity."

"Mandred was pathetically grateful when I took him under my wing." Jack spooned bread stuffing into the centers of the fish pieces and rolled the fillets around the stuffing.

"I should think he would be grateful. It's been only a short time, but you have been like the father Brewster never was to him." She tugged out more of the cream-colored strip from the ball of fabric and moved the braid so she could work more easily.

"I encouraged him to get involved with community activities," Jack said. "He's quite a loner. Works as chef at the nursing home, helps out at the hospital. I suggested he volunteer for the job running the Meals on Wheels van. Give him a chance to get out and meet people, help them." Jack stuck toothpicks in the rolled-up fillets and dipped them into cracker crumbs.

"He's really taken to that. You have such creative ideas."

Jack smiled faintly. He arranged the fillets on the glass baking dish, sprinkled paprika on them, and set the lid on top.

"That fish looks nice, dearie." She braided. Right over left, left over right.

"Kill two birds with one stone," Jack said. "Gets him out, and gave him the opportunity to make his peace with his father before he died—I don't know that he did, but the opportunity was there." He opened the oven door and slid the baking dish of fillets into the oven. "Now Linda is telling everyone that when her father was ailing, I put pressure on him to change his will." He slammed the oven door, and the salt and pepper containers on the back of the stove fell over.

"How dreadful of her. Even with the stress of her father's sudden death, that's an ugly thing to say. From what I understand, she and her father weren't close, either." Right over left, left over right. "Of course, a parent's death is always a great loss, even if you're not close."

"During his last few months she came to the Island every weekend to see him, but really, the church was his main support," Jack said.

"I'm sure he looked forward to your visits, especially when you read to him. That was sweet of you."

Jack picked up the salt and pepper containers and put them on the back of the stove again. "That's what a minister is supposed to do. We did talk about his making a bequest to the church, of course. It came up quite naturally."

"I'm sure it did," Betty said. "It seems to me that's one of your many great strengths, encouraging well-to-do parishioners to make bequests to the church." She tugged more of the folded strips off their rolls and continued to braid. "Jack Hutchinson fell far short of you in that respect, building up beneficences for the church."

"I do seem to have a knack for that." While Jack washed his hands, he looked out at the pond with its sprinkling of ducks and geese. "Edna was telling me the other day that Forrester had made some wise investments, and she has rewritten her will to the church's benefit."

"What about Victoria Trumbull?" Betty said. "She's not wealthy, but all these elderly people seem to have a little something."

"Victoria is close to Jack and Maddy. I've always felt awkward around her."

"Yes, I know what you mean," Betty said. "She's so well thought of in the community, but she's really a snob. You know how I've been hoping to join the Kippers, that women's literary group? Victoria is their oldest member, both in terms of her age and her seniority. She has refused to sponsor me for membership."

"Refused?"

"Maybe refused is too strong a word. She simply hasn't done anything about it."

"They *are* restricted to only twenty-four members," Jack said. "You'll have to wait until someone dies to join. No one ever quits the Kippers."

"Victoria is doing a paper next month on law enforcement." Betty's eyes were on her steady braiding. "I'd like to hear that. Maybe I can get someone to invite me as guest." She tugged out more of the fabric strips. "That fish is going to be nice. There's nothing quite like fresh fish. Didn't you use the pickled mushroom mixture of Hal Greene's? Chopped mushrooms in olive oil with garlic, isn't it?"

"I wanted to try this Pepperidge Farm recipe. Last time Junior brought me fish, I took a fillet to Edna Coffin stuffed with Hal's mushrooms. I ought to stop by and call on her, see how she liked it." He opened the oven door to check on the placement of the baking dish. "Actually, I'm not terribly fond of mushrooms myself," he said.

"I'VE NEVER SEEN anything like the way food flies back and forth from one household to another in this town," Casey said to Victoria later that evening when they were leaving the Zoning Board meeting at Town Hall. "Fresh-caught fish, home-grown tomatoes, zucchini, casseroles, venison, bread, soup. You could live off things that get left on your kitchen table."

"Or die."

"Victoria, you are being terrible." Casey turned on her blinker to make a right turn at the foot of Brandy Brow.

"Who do you suppose left me the tuna noodle casserole that killed Molly?"

"Stop blaming yourself. For all we know, nothing was wrong with that casserole. By the way, you made a really good point about the zoning bylaw, how the developer needs to obey it or the town needs to change it."

The Bronco's headlights reflected from the eyes of some creature by the side of the road, two bright spots.

"Skunk," Victoria said. "I wish they'd learn not to cross the road when a car is coming."

"So does the animal control officer." Casey slowed as they passed the Mill Pond.

After a moment Victoria said, "I can't, for the life of me,

figure out how my basket found its way to the Quansoo Bridge. Full of amanitas. Death's angels. Who took my basket? Who picked the mushrooms that were in it? And why?"

"This whole thing really bugs you, doesn't it?" Casey said. "Actually, how many mushroom dishes are involved? Your tuna noodle casserole…"

"It wasn't mine," Victoria said.

"…the tuna noodle casserole, the bluefish stuffed with mushrooms that Jack Jackson gave to Edna Coffin, your basket of mushrooms. We have no idea what Hal Greene had eaten in the day or so before he died, or Brewster Harrington-Smith, or Jeremiah Sylvia, and we have nothing to indicate all four deaths were not from natural causes. Nothing." Casey turned right into Victoria's drive, and the Bronco jounced over the deep ruts.

"Ungh! Ungh!" Victoria said as she jounced. "I've got to get someone to fix this road."

"We don't know, for sure, that the mushroom stuffing or the tuna noodle casserole poisoned anyone," Casey said, steering around the deepest holes. "In fact, the more I think about it, there's no indication of foul play. Flu can be a killer, Victoria."

"Don't tell me again to get a shot."

"All we have are four deaths, an unusual number in a short time, but all easily explained. The seagull's death probably has no connection." She pulled up next to the side door that opened into the kitchen and killed the engine. "I think we need to drop this, Victoria."

"Someone took my basket and filled it with poisonous mushrooms. How do you explain that? And if you think about it, every one of the four deaths plus the seagull's death could be explained by mushroom poisoning. That would be more logical than four natural deaths—plus a seagull—in a row."

She opened the Bronco's door. "Would you like to stop in for a cup of tea? I think Angelo is home."

"I'd better not," Casey said. "I honestly don't think Angelo is my type, Victoria. Mrs. Bradshaw is staying with Patrick until I get back, and I don't want to impose on her. Besides, I have to check my e-mail at the station house."

"You knew, didn't you, that three of the four left sizable amounts of money to the church?" Victoria said before she made a move to get out of the vehicle. "If I'd eaten the tuna noodle casserole and died, I'd have been the fourth. In my will, I'm signing over to the church some paper my husband Jonathan left me. Elizabeth thinks it's worth quite a lot of money. If Edna had eaten the bluefish Jack Jackson gave her, she'd have been number five. She talked all the time about how much money she was leaving the church."

"If you're saying what I think you're saying, it sounds as if you're accusing Jack Jackson of murdering church members to get beneficences for the church, is that right?"

"I don't mean to have it sound so bald," Victoria said. "If it were any minister other than Jack Jackson, I would not believe it myself. But that man is a jealous, hypocritical snipe."

"'Snipe'?"

"You know what I mean. Minister or not, I want to look into those deaths."

"Well, don't, Victoria. If there's a killer loose, he or she could be dangerous. We have nothing concrete, no documentation, no way of knowing whether Brewster, Hal, and Jeremiah even ate any mushrooms." Casey started up the Bronco again. "I don't mean to dismiss this, Victoria, but I've got other stuff I have to do." She glanced at Victoria, whose nose was lifted slightly. "Stay out of it, Victoria. I'm serious."

"I DON'T ESPECIALLY like Jack Jackson, either," Elizabeth said once Victoria was back in the house, sitting in front of the fire in the parlor. "But a murderer? Come on, Gram."

"He has been pushing this beneficence business so hard I'm sick of it. I've changed my mind about leaving that paper to the church."

Elizabeth set down a tray with drinks and crackers and cheese on the glass-topped coffee table. "If you suspect Jack Jackson of murdering people to get their money, you'd better not tell him you're disinheriting the church until after you get Naomi to change your will," Elizabeth said. "You'd better not tell Cousin Edna, either. She's like the operator on an old-time party-line telephone."

Victoria was sitting on the couch, an old one with carved wooden scrolls and flowers along the back. McCavity stalked into the room and without a pause landed in Victoria's lap, almost spilling her drink. He turned around to face the fire, dangled his paws over the front of Victoria's knees, and closed his eyes.

"I wish we could find out whether Hal and Jeremiah and Brewster ate something with mushrooms before they died." Victoria stroked McCavity. "Jack could easily have given them a covered dish of some kind. He thinks he's such a good cook. He could have taken something to all three of them, and they'd never have been the least bit suspicious." She sipped her drink. McCavity lifted his head, eyes still closed. "He might have left the tuna noodle casserole for me. Everyone on the Island knew you were going off-Island that day. I wrote it up in my column."

Elizabeth got up and knelt by the fireplace. She pushed the smoldering logs to the back with the tongs, and put a fresh log on the fire.

"He visited Brewster several times a week," Victoria said.

"Since Hal was church sexton they saw each other practically every day. He could have given Hal mushrooms. He probably paid ministerial visits to Jeremiah, too. We know he gave Cousin Edna that poisoned stuffed bluefish." She took a sip of her drink and winced as McCavity kneaded his claws into her knees.

"We don't know the fish was poisoned." Elizabeth sat down again. "Even assuming he intended to murder elderly parishioners, that's too obvious. If you're planning to poison someone, you don't tell everybody in the world you're giving them poisoned food."

"He'll have some innocent-sounding excuse or other," Victoria said. "Junior gave him the bluefish, according to Cousin Edna. You just wait. He'll say someone gave him the mushrooms. He'll say he was planning to use them for himself. If we ever find out the bluefish was laced with amanitas, he'll be all properly aghast, profuse expressions of contrition."

"What does Casey have to say about all this?"

"Casey says she's not going to do anything unless she has something more concrete to go on. We've got to find out whether any of them ate mushrooms or not."

"We can hardly disinter people based on nothing," Elizabeth said. "Surely you're not thinking of digging them up?"

Victoria disengaged McCavity's claws from her knees and put her glass on the coffee table with a clink. "You know what we can do?" she said. "We can dig up Cousin Edna's seagull and gut him. Take his stomach contents to Jessica."

"Yuck! Frederick?"

"Not 'yuck' at all," Victoria said. "It's perfectly feasible. If you dig him up, I'll dissect him. I used to pluck and clean chickens for my grandmother when I was a little girl, after she'd chopped off their heads."

"For Pete's sake, I'm trying to eat." Elizabeth laid her cracker on the tray.

"What do you think those nicely wrapped pieces of chicken breast you buy at Cronig's used to be?" Victoria said. "Done up on a yellow Styrofoam tray all wrapped in plastic. Someone chopped off their heads."

"Gram!"

"The hospital is always calling Jessica to analyze stomach contents when they suspect mushroom poisoning," Victoria continued. "If you won't go with me, I'm sure Casey will."

"Okay, okay. First thing tomorrow, I'll dig up Frederick's corpse."

The log flared into new flame. The fire hissed and snapped. McCavity purred. The west wind rattled the window frame and rippled the sheer curtains.

Elizabeth watched the billowing curtains. "I'd better put up the storm windows before it turns cold." She turned back to her grandmother. "If you suspect the Reverend Jack Jackson, how are you going to disinter Frederick without having Cousin Edna tell him and everyone else in the world why you're doing it?"

"I'll think of something."

TWELVE

VICTORIA HAD the breakfast things already on the cookroom table before Elizabeth came downstairs the next morning. She'd put a vase of purple asters and goldenrod in the center of the table and had set out cereal bowls and grapefruit halves. Elizabeth came in to the aroma of freshly brewed coffee. Victoria was sitting in the bentwood armchair where she could see the church across the field, her yellow coffee mug next to her, a bowl of Shredded Wheat in front of her.

"I'll invite her to lunch," Victoria said without preamble.

"What?" Elizabeth was still muzzy from sleep. "Who? What are you talking about? What lunch?" She poured herself a cup of coffee from the pot on the counter next to the east door. Black-eyed Susans had overrun the little kitchen herb garden, and they reflected brilliant golden sunshine in the glass panes of the open east door. A leaf drifted down from the maple tree. A duck skidded to a landing on the pond.

"Cousin Edna. You can drive us to the Red Cat for lunch. That way, you'll have time to exhume Frederick."

Elizabeth plopped into a caned side chair next to the cookroom table. "Not that again." When she looked up, she saw a gleam in her grandmother's eyes. "Maybe we could talk about it after I've eaten."

But Victoria was wound up. "Cousin Edna probably isn't up yet." She looked at her watch. "It's already seven-thirty."

Elizabeth groaned. "It's still the middle of the night."

"I'll wait until eight-thirty to call her."

"Make it nine."

"I'll call her at nine, then, and invite her to have lunch with me. You can drive us. Or maybe the Black Dog—their service is nice and slow."

"And I'm supposed to drive you into Middletown to the Red Cat or to Vineyard Haven to the Black Dog, come back to Cousin Edna's and dig up her flower beds to disinter Frederick?"

"You won't be digging up her flower beds. You buried him only the day before yesterday."

"And having dug him up, I'm supposed to bring him home, bird lice and all, and then go pick you two up, and Cousin Edna won't know a thing?"

"Exactly," Victoria said. "If you'll lay out the carving knife and some newspapers on the picnic table, the one by the shed, so it's not in plain sight, I'll perform the autopsy. I'll need some plastic bags for his innards." Victoria cut a nick in the top of a banana, broke it off, and peeled the skin partway down. She began to slice the banana over her Shredded Wheat.

"What does Casey have to say about this?" Elizabeth sat, semicomatose, in her chair with her untouched breakfast in front of her.

"She doesn't know. She wants documentation, hard evidence, that kind of police thing. So we'll get it for her."

"My God," Elizabeth said. "Out of Lockwood's arms into this! Have you and Cousin Edna ever, ever gone out to lunch together?"

"No." Victoria poured milk over her cereal.

"Don't you think she's going to be suspicious when you suddenly, right out of the blue, ask her to go to lunch with you? She's not dumb."

"I'll think of something." Victoria reached for the phone. "I'll call Jessica so she can be ready."

ELIZABETH DROPPED the two, her grandmother and Cousin Edna, at the Black Dog Tavern on the Vineyard Haven waterfront, and settled them at a table by the window where they could watch the ferries coming and going. She'd brought a bottle of Chicama Vineyard's white Zinfandel for a special treat. She didn't think Victoria's surgical skills would suffer, and she thought it wouldn't hurt to anesthetize Cousin Edna. Vineyard Haven was one of four dry towns on the Island; you could bring your own wine and spirits with you but couldn't buy any on site.

"Bye," Elizabeth said brightly, wiggling her fingers at the two women. Victoria was deceptively placid, a faint smile on her face, a flush of color on her cheeks. She's being too obvious, Elizabeth thought. Cousin Edna is bound to suspect we're up to something. "I'll pick you up at one-thirty; that'll give you almost two hours."

Victoria's smile broadened.

Elizabeth walked quickly to her convertible, backed out of the Black Dog parking place, and drove, as fast as she dared, up-Island to West Tisbury, turning left onto Old County Road, and pulled into Cousin Edna's half-circle drive. She looked at her watch. The drive from the Black Dog had taken fifteen minutes.

She had brought her own spade, her leather gardening gloves, and a white plastic garbage bag. She pushed through the prickly overgrown shrubbery at the side of Cousin Edna's house and headed to the back lawn. Birds fluttered up from the feeder as she approached. She put on the gloves, opened the plastic bag, and thrust the blade of the shovel into the earth next to the feeder where she had buried Frederick.

"Hi! Whatcha doing?"

Elizabeth started, knocking the shovel over, and turned with her hands in the air.

Ricky Rezendes, the kid who cut Cousin Edna's grass, stood with his hands in his back pockets. "I didn't mean to scare you."

"Don't you have school today?" Elizabeth asked crossly. Adrenaline was pumping through her.

"Nope. Teachers' meeting." He was a short, chubby twelve-year-old with red hair and freckles, coloring he got from his mother. "Planting stuff for Mrs. Coffin?" A week ago, two days ago, even, Elizabeth had thought he was cute. Now he looked like an imp, straight out of the fiery pit. Somewhere in the back of her mind she thought she remembered the word "imp" had something to do with grafting feathers onto birds. Appropriate, she thought.

"What are you doing here?" she said. She picked up the shovel and held it with both gloved hands. She paced to calm her nerves.

"Cutting Mrs. Coffin's grass, of course, silly," he answered.

"This isn't your usual day, is it?"

"How come you're acting so funny?" Ricky asked. "Are you digging up a body or something?"

"Yes, as a matter of fact." Elizabeth stopped pacing. "A body."

"No kidding?" Ricky's eyes were wide.

"It's a secret. Can you keep a secret?"

"Cross my heart." Ricky motioned to his chest.

"Better not tell. You tell and Beelzebub will get you." She looked directly at him and scowled. "Beelzebub is the King of the Flies, you know."

"Wow," Ricky said. "I didn't know that."

"All right, you can turn around with your back to me and close your eyes, or you can help me."

"Wow," Ricky said again, excitement written across his face. "What'll it be?"

"I've never seen a dead body."

"Close your eyes? Or help?" Elizabeth said.

"I don't have to touch it, do I? I don't have to look if I don't want to, do I?"

"Are you chicken or something?" Elizabeth said.

"What do you want me to do?"

"You hold the body bag open so I can shovel it in."

"Has he been dead a long time?"

"Yes," Elizabeth said. "That's why I need a shovel. Probably almost turned to liquid by now. That's how come I'm invoking the King of the Flies."

"I don't feel good." The freckles across Ricky's nose had turned an ugly shade of green.

"You're not going to get sick, are you?" Elizabeth asked, with some satisfaction. "You're not going to be much help if you get sick on me."

"I just remembered I forgot something," Ricky said. "Wait for me. I'll be right back to help."

"Yeah, sure," Elizabeth said.

The instant he was out of sight, Elizabeth dug the shovel into the soft earth next to the feeder, stepped on the top to push it deep into the ground, and disinterred the gull. She shook off as much dirt as she could. Frederick's corpse looked almost as fresh as the day she had found him, the white feathers glossy, the red spot on his bill bright. She noticed some small thing crawling around his head, a little red worm she didn't want to look at. She dropped the corpse into the plastic garbage bag, and set it to one side while she filled in the hole and smoothed it over.

She looked at her watch. The exchange with Ricky and the exhumation had taken almost forty-five minutes. She had barely enough time to get home and set up the autopsy table before she had to go to pick up the two ladies from the Black Dog.

"THAT WAS LOVELY," Cousin Edna said. "Such a nice idea. We'll have to do it again." Elizabeth had come into the Black Dog, and Victoria and Cousin Edna had risen from the table.

"Yes, indeed," said Victoria.

"Let me pay." Cousin Edna reached into her pocketbook.

"No, no, Edna, my treat." Victoria reached into hers.

"I'll treat you both," Elizabeth said, hauling a MasterCard out of her jeans pocket and handing it to the waitress.

"You've been gardening." Edna looked at Elizabeth's grubby hands.

"Let's split the tip," Victoria interrupted.

There was a scuffling while Victoria and Edna found the right bills and change in their pocketbooks, Victoria's worn brown leather, Edna's a Nantucket basket with a scrimshaw whale decoration.

"Glad you both had a good time," said Elizabeth, once they had taken care of the bill and the tip. They went out the front door of the Black Dog, down the short alley that led from the harbor to the parking area.

On the way to West Tisbury, the talk was about the food at the Black Dog, the waitress and whether she had come from off-Island or not, whom she was related to if she came from the Vineyard. Whom she resembled, in any case.

When they got to Cousin Edna's, Elizabeth held the car door open and offered her arm to the older woman, who took it and moved heavily up the steps to the kitchen door. She turned around and waved to Victoria.

"Don't forget, the Kippers' meeting is here, next week, dear." She disappeared inside.

"How could I forget?" Victoria said, once Elizabeth had shut the door to the back seat and had come around to the driver's side. "I'm the one giving the paper."

As soon as Elizabeth got back into the driver's seat, started the car, put it in gear, and pulled out of Cousin Edna's drive, Victoria said, "Did you get the body?"

"All set." Elizabeth looked both ways down Old County Road. "Ricky Rezendes came by. Scared the dickens out of me. When I told him I was digging up a body, he got sick and went home."

"While I'm dissecting the corpse, would you call Jessica and ask her if we can come over? Tell her what we're doing."

"'You,' not 'we.' I don't want credit for this."

Victoria changed from her going-to-town plaid suit into her worn gray corduroy pants and the turtleneck shirt printed with pink rosebuds, pulled on her navy fleece jacket, and went outside to the picnic table. Elizabeth could hear the crunch of bones as Victoria cut into the gull. Why did the sound seem so ghastly? Elizabeth didn't mind picking apart a roasting chicken for soup. Frederick was different. She shuddered.

"All set." Victoria came through the kitchen door with several plastic sandwich bags full of repulsive-looking entrails. "I buried Frederick's remains. I didn't put him on the compost heap because his feathers won't decompose." She put the sealed bags on the counter near the sink and washed her hands, scrubbing her nails with a brush.

"Jessica said fine, we can take the evidence to her right now," Elizabeth said. "She has some kind of portable lab she sets up in the kitchen, and she said it should be pretty simple to tell whether or not amanitas are involved."

"Let's go," Victoria said.

THEY JOUNCED DOWN the dirt road leading to Jessica's house, Victoria clenching the plastic bags of entrails. They drove past the open field with its border of goldenrod and purple asters, backed by the reflected sky-blue waters of Sengekontacket. A V of Canada geese circled and landed on the pond's glassy surface. The reflected sky broke into shards of blue, ripples moved outward.

Jessica greeted them at the door of her house, which overlooked the pond.

"How beautiful it is," Victoria said.

"What a view." From where Elizabeth stood she could look over the pond, the barrier bar, and could see Nantucket Sound dotted with sailboats on this perfect early fall day. She could make out the mainland across the sound, a white line of beach, houses, trees.

"It's unusually clear today," Jessica said, once they'd entered the house. "The old-timers called a day like this a 'weather breeder.' We'll have a good storm tomorrow or the day after. You don't often see houses so clearly on the mainland."

"It's like a mirage," Elizabeth said. "The mainland seems to have lifted up off the horizon. You can see sky between it and the water."

Victoria handed her sealed plastic bags to Jessica. "The gull's been dead for two or three days. I put his stomach, intact, in this bag"—she handed it to Jessica—"his entrails in this one." She turned over a second bag. "And this has his liver, heart, and gizzard. Is that all you need?"

"That should be enough. Come with me into the kitchen, Victoria. I've set up a little lab."

Elizabeth sat on the chintz sofa. "If you don't mind, I'll stay here and look at the view." She could see the weirdly shimmering mainland hovering above the sound. She could see a water tower, factory chimneys, even a tall broadcasting antenna. The images were so clear she might have been a quarter mile away, rather than five miles. As she watched, the land reattached itself to the water, and the strip of sky between water and land disappeared. Then the land floated up into the sky again and suddenly seemed to turn upside down, still as clear as a sharp photograph. The water tower, the antenna, the houses, pointed down into the water of the sound. Like something out of *Arabian Nights*. An oasis in the desert suspended in the air. She had never seen anything like it before. A mirage, she supposed. An optical illusion caused by heated layers of air.

She half listened to the two women, Jessica, who was certainly in her eighties, and Victoria, in her nineties, discussing the contents of the stomach of the dead gull.

"You see this, Victoria," she heard Jessica say. "You said it was bluefish and mushrooms." Elizabeth heard a scraping noise as if Jessica were moving something with a scalpel on a glass dish. "This is a piece of mushroom."

"It doesn't look too badly decomposed," said Victoria. "Or even digested." Elizabeth heard Victoria move a kitchen stool next to the sink, heard the stool creak as she sat.

"I'll separate the mushroom pieces from the fish and we can run some tests," Jessica said. "He'd have had to digest some of the mushroom, if it was amanita, to get it into his system. The amanita affects the liver and kidneys."

"You said it usually took a couple of days to take effect, didn't you?" Victoria said.

"With humans, yes. I've never analyzed a seagull before." The two were quiet while the scratching and scraping went on. "Now this is his liver," Jessica said. "Look at this, Victoria. You see these blotches?"

"These? The greenish-gray spots?"

"Yes. I don't think that's normal. I've never seen a seagull's liver, but it doesn't look right to me."

"You think that might have been what killed him?"

"Quite possibly. Again, I'm used to dealing with humans, not gulls." More scratching, scraping, rustling.

The strip of mainland righted itself again, antenna and water tower pointing up into the sky, and while Elizabeth watched the mirage, the land rose in the air like some elongated hot air balloon. The strip of sky between land and water widened. The land is taking off, Elizabeth thought. Floating, drifting away to some far destination.

"I'll grind up these undigested mushroom bits," Jessica said. Elizabeth winced. "Add some acid to dissolve them." She heard sloshing noises as Jessica presumably shook up a test tube of mushroom bits and some reagent. "Now I'll add a little of this."

"Ha!" Victoria said. "Look at that color change. Like magic."

"Magic it is," Jessica said. "Amanita."

THIRTEEN

FOR SOME TIME Elizabeth had been meaning to organize the books in Victoria's library. Today, the storm Jessica had predicted hit, a blustery nor'easter, perfect for book sorting. The day was still mild enough, though, so she wouldn't freeze in the unheated library, especially if she lighted a fire in the fireplace.

The rain pockmarked the fish pond to the east, pelted against the small windowpanes, ran down the glass in coalescing streams. Elizabeth could look through the library door and through the dining room windows and see the yellow leaves of the maple drop to the ground under the weight of the rain, laying a soggy yellow carpet. It was hard to tell where the drive left off and the lawn began.

She laid the fire in the library, brought in kindling, brittle sticks her grandmother had gathered from under the maple trees and stored in brown paper grocery bags. She felt a moment's guilt as she brought in one of the bags. She was always hassling her grandmother about how trashy the paper bags of sticks looked in the entry. Yet on a wet day like this she was glad to have the kindling.

She would put poetry books next to the east window, travel and history books along the inside west wall next to the door that led into the dark front hall. Now the weather was cooler, she and Victoria kept all four hall doors closed, the grand front entrance and the doors that led into the parlor, the library, and the dining room. When Victoria hosted the Kippers' meetings, members entered through the front door. Otherwise, it was seldom used.

Why did they put so many doors in houses back then? she wondered.

The room was full of furniture. No one had ever, ever thrown anything out, and as long as Elizabeth could remember, the library, a beautifully proportioned room, had been used as a junk room. Here was a tiny chair that had belonged to her great-great-grandmother, who had shortened its legs because she was so small. One of many objections to great-great-grandfather's off-Island bride, besides the fact that she came from off-Island and his mother had already selected a local woman for her son's wife, was that she was not statuesque like the Trumbulls.

Elizabeth carried some of the furniture up to the attic. She made three trips with chairs and tables, until, the library less cluttered, she had more room there in which to sort books.

The northeast wind blew a sheet of rain against the front windows, rattled the windowpanes, and moved the sheer curtains. Yellow leaves plastered against the panes. The fire flared briefly, then resumed a quiet hum.

Elizabeth culled out poetry books from every room in the house, including the downstairs bathroom, and carried them to the library, where she stacked them. The room above the library had been Aunt Rebecca's room, two hundred years ago. It, too, had stacks of books that Elizabeth took down to the library.

Her grandmother appeared suddenly in the dining room door, wearing her blue-quilted coat and tan hat and causing Elizabeth to start and drop the book she was holding.

"I didn't mean to frighten you," Victoria said. "The library has needed attention for some time. The Augean stable." She smiled. "Casey and I are going to read over my talk and then have lunch at the Red Cat. Do you need me to do anything before I go?"

"No, thanks." Elizabeth sat on the floor again, surrounded by books. The room had the musty smell of an old bookstore. Crumbs of dried golden brown paper had sifted over the oriental-patterned maroon rug. The fire flickered.

Victoria turned at the sound of a car splashing on the rutted drive. From the door where her grandmother stood, Elizabeth could see the Bronco.

After her grandmother left, Elizabeth cleared off the shelves where she planned to put poetry. It was incredible how many books this house held. She got a damp cloth and oil soap from the kitchen and wiped the shelves. The clean scent of the soap cut the musty dry-book smell. She looked around her at the heaps and piles and jumble of books on the floor. What have I gotten myself into? she thought. Gram is right. It's a Herculean labor.

The sound of the rain on the windows, the sound of the fire, the smell of books, the smell of early autumn, wood smoke from the fireplace, mingled together in the pleasant morning of sorting and piling books, occasionally flipping through them. Time folded into itself. She could imagine past generations fingering the same books. Here was an autographed copy of Robert Frost's poetry. One of two volumes of *Uncle Tom's Cabin*. A first edition? What treasures this house held. A book on the exploration of the Grand Canyon. She riffled through them. The morning shifted into early afternoon. She forgot lunch.

She wiped the shelves dry with a soft piece of old towel, its loops worn thin. She might as well start putting books on the shelves. The heat from the fireplace had warmed the room. She took off her heavy wool sweater and laid it on the couch. The leaking stuffing of the couch added to the library's feeling of decay.

Here was a thick leather-bound book, *The Works of Josephus,* stamped in gold leaf. Elizabeth picked it up. On the spine was a golden bust of Josephus, she supposed, with intricate curlicues and leaves twined around the bust. An ornate interwoven design was embossed into the leather cover. Intrigued, she opened it. The endpapers had a feathery pattern in shades of blue and cream and maroon. How beautifully books used to be made, she thought. A steel engraving in the front of the book, protected by a tissue page, was of the biblical Rebecca, Aunt Rebecca's namesake, being helped off a kneeling camel by Isaac. Two palm trees in the background shaded skin tents. A handmaiden sat sidesaddle on her camel behind Rebecca.

Enchanting, Elizabeth thought. She turned the pages. Who is Josephus? I've never seen this book before. Published 1860. "Embellished with elegant engravings," it said, and the engravings certainly were elegant. "Translated from the original Greek." Elizabeth gingerly turned the brittle pages, lost in the accounts of the history of the Jewish wars. Time passed. Elizabeth thumbed through the book looking for pictures, the way she used to do when she was a child. Between pages 164 and 165 she found an envelope, a place marker, she assumed.

She held the envelope in her left hand while she read, at the bottom of page 164 and the top of page 165, "Alexandra, the shrewdist woman in the world, Hyreanus's daughter, begged of him that he would not go out, nor trust himself to those barbarians, who now were come to make an attempt on him openly." She turned the envelope over. It was old, of thin, yellowed paper, addressed to her great-great grandfather, Victoria's grandfather, whom she had lived with when she was a child. The envelope had no stamp on it and looked as if it had never been opened. She wondered if she should wait for Victoria before she opened it, and had decided her curiosity was too great to wait, when she heard a car splashing through the puddles in the drive.

That's funny, she thought. She looked at her watch. Two o'clock. The chief must be bringing Victoria home early, for some reason. Elizabeth stood up, glanced through the door and through the dining room window. A Jeep, looking like almost every other Island car, had stopped in the drive near the kitchen entry. She waited to see who the visitor might be. Then she recalled with a jolt that Casey had told her that Lockwood was driving an old Jeep.

She stood at the dining room door, transfixed. The driver opened the door on his side and got out, a tall, portly, bearded man. It took her an instant to recognize that it was Lockwood. When she had last seen him, only a year ago, he had been slender and clean-shaven. When he came around the front of the Jeep toward the kitchen door, his walk recalled to her the familiar terror she had felt when she had lived with him. This was the way he had walked when he was angry with her. He was holding something in his left hand that glinted in the diffuse light of the rainy day, something dangling from a short chain. Handcuffs? Surely not handcuffs?

Elizabeth felt a rush of adrenaline. She had to get out of here, she thought, and quickly. She closed the book on the letter and laid it on the library table. She snatched her sweater from the couch. By habit she put the screen in front of the open fire. Where had she left her rain jacket? Damn, in the kitchen, over the back of a kitchen chair. She shut the door from the dining room so he wouldn't see her when he came into the house. She could hear his boots scraping on the stone steps outside the entry. A gust of wind shook the window, slatted the rain against it. The fire flared and hissed.

In seconds he would open the entry door, walk across the brick floor, open the kitchen door. Then he would be in the house and getting away would be difficult. He was strong, he was quick, he was crafty. She knew. She had tried everything she could think of to keep his anger at bay. She had believed, for years, that she was to blame for his sudden bursts of anger. She had tried to change herself into the woman he wanted her to be, a woman who would not rouse that fearful anger in a man she thought she loved.

She had to get out of this house immediately, forget the rain jacket. She heard him open the outside entry door, heard his scraping footsteps on the brick, heard him knock on the kitchen door, heard him call, "Elizabeth? Elizabeth! I know you're there."

She eased open the door leading into the front hall and slipped into the gloomy, chilly half-dark, shutting the door behind her silently. The front door was to her right, opening into a small covered entry with a second, main door that led outside. She tiptoed to the first door, carefully turned the white porcelain knob so it would not make a sound, lifted the door on its hinges slightly to keep it from squeaking, silently shutting it behind her.

Behind her she heard him open the kitchen door. "Elizabeth? Elizabeth! I know you're there. Why don't you come out?"

Her scalp prickled. The voice was so familiar, even though he was no longer part of her life. She felt hypnotically drawn, like a bird to a snake. She had the eerie feeling that she must respond to him. She was in the small entry, less than five feet from the front yard.

Once she got across the open front yard, across the road beyond, she would be safe, she thought, or at least safer. The outer front door was the only door in the house that was ever locked, and only because the north wind would blow it open otherwise. Her hands were shaking so badly she could not move the brass slider at first. She pushed her knee against the door to relieve the friction and finally she felt the brass bar ease back.

She turned the knob quietly, and the door opened with a shriek of protesting unoiled hinges. She was outside on the front steps. Rain slashed at her face and neck, and she didn't notice. She shut the door firmly, praying it would not blow open right away, that it would hold against this northeast wind. She hoped Lockwood hadn't heard the shriek of hinges over the sound of wind and rain.

She knew the methodical way his mind worked. She would have a minute, maybe two, while he looked around downstairs, before he went upstairs, which she thought he would do before he checked the library.

She could hear his deep voice, muted by the three doors between them, could even make out the words. "Elizabeth? Elizabeth! I know you're there. You'd better come with me."

Elizabeth crossed the front lawn on a crouched run to the side, where she would be partially concealed by a huge, over-grown trumpet vine and overhanging forsythia bushes. She hoped he wouldn't look through the parlor windows. Not yet. He could still get at her. She moved quickly under the dripping vines and shrubbery, where she was protected slightly from the direct rain and was out of the wind.

She could imagine Lockwood opening the door from the dining room into the front hall. She prayed he would not notice the main front door had been unlatched. As long as he didn't notice, he would probably go up the front stairs to the study, where she usually worked on her computer. That would give her another minute or two to cross the road, duck behind the tall pines around the house, which was empty now that the summer people had gone. If Lockwood looked out the front windows in the upstairs hall, he would see her. But she had to chance it.

In which direction should she go? She could head toward the police station to the left. She wasn't sure anyone was there now, though. Casey and Victoria had probably finished lunch and would be working on Victoria's talk at Casey's house. The police station was only a quarter mile down the road, but there was no way she could conceal herself between here and there. There were only open fields or fenced house yards between them.

Once Lockwood found she was not in the house, he would probably head in the direction of the police station, looking both ways first. She had to keep hidden, and stay to the right. The house across the road was almost concealed by the pines the owner had planted years before.

Behind the house, Elizabeth could work her way, under cover, to a small valley at the eastern edge of Victoria's land. She would have to cross the road again to get back to Victoria's side, onto a dirt road that followed the small valley, almost impassable except to four-wheel-drive vehicles. The dirt road met New Lane at the back of Victoria's property. She could hide in the thick brush alongside the lane and follow the lane to Ben Norton's. She would be under cover except for a couple of open fields until she reached his house, a mile down the paved road, another mile on a dirt road.

She waited for a lull in the storm, then dashed across the road and ducked under the pine trees, which hid her from the road. The wet resinous pine needles lashed across her face. The wind tossed the branches, sent showers of water onto her head, sighed in the tops of the pines, made a mournful sound like people chattering. Water trickled down the back of her neck inside her sweater.

She crouched under the lower branches of the trees while she caught her breath, calmed a bit, decided what to do. She watched the drive to see whether Lockwood's Jeep was leaving. If he left, she might go back into the house. Otherwise, she probably should start working her way to Ben's.

Elizabeth was chilled and edgy. Her clothing was soaked. The rain poured steadily without letup. The pine trees didn't offer as much shelter as she'd hoped. Fortunately, the temperature was bearable, chilly and raw, but not bitter cold. Would he position himself in the house to watch for her? She couldn't guess.

FROM HIS SPOT ON New Lane, Lockwood had seen Victoria and Chief O'Neill leave. The man who rented the shack was gone and so was the artist. Elizabeth's car was still parked under the Norway maple, so she was home. He had not seen her go out. This was a good time to talk with her, without Victoria's interference. A rainy day when she would think twice about going outdoors.

He started up the Jeep, shifted into gear, and, looking behind him, eased onto the pavement. Where the lane met the Edgartown Road, he turned right, and right again into Victoria's drive. Yes, Elizabeth's car was still there. He parked in front of the kitchen entry in such a way that her car was blocked. That would ensure that she couldn't drive away, he thought. Not that she would. Surely she would be reasonable after this long a time.

If she wanted a confrontation, he was prepared for that. He

had taken the handcuffs out of the glove compartment and was dangling them from one hand in a relaxed, nonthreatening sort of way. He could understand she might be upset if she saw him holding them as if he meant to use them on her. This way it looked casual, as if they were something he simply wanted to show her. But there certainly was no need for that. Once he started reasoning with her, she would come to her senses. He had let her play single girl for a while now, and it was time for her to come home. He'd kept track on his calendar, week after week.

When he retired, they would come and live with Victoria. He had always respected Elizabeth's grandmother. He was in a financial position to help her when she began to need some support.

He could smell wood smoke when he went up the stone steps to the covered entry. The rain was pouring down, a good day for her to be inside, probably working on her computer upstairs. She must have lit a fire in the downstairs parlor, probably before Victoria left.

He wiped his feet on the braided rope mat by the door, walked across the bricks in the entry, and called her name. No answer. She probably hadn't heard him. He opened the door and called in. Still no answer. Well, he was pretty sure she was home. He looked to his left into the dining room, didn't see her, hadn't expected to. To make sure, he would check the cookroom and woodshed.

He had been in the house several times since he'd been on-Island, always when he knew they were not there. Knowing that he was looking at the bitch's things when she had no idea he was around gave him a great deal of satisfaction. He had gone into the bathroom, seen her clean laundry folded on top of the dryer. He could have taken some of her lingerie; he knew she was so careless she would never miss it. But he didn't, and that gave him pleasure, too, that he had not taken anything of hers.

He had checked out the rooms to see which one she was sleeping in now, and he was sure, knowing her, that she didn't suspect anyone might be looking through her belongings. She had what was practically a fetish about privacy. One time, before she had left him, he had read her diary, read passages about himself he thought were offensive, challenged her on those passages she had written about him, and she had flown into a rage. She had claimed later her reaction was not rage; it was outrage that he had looked over her private diary.

That was one of the times he had had to control her, keep her from hurting herself and him. He had apologized later, of course. He hadn't meant to hurt her, but she made him do it.

He liked sitting in the rocking chair in her room, reading the notes she made along the margins of the crossword puzzles by her bedside, looking over her diary (not much of interest there), looking through her clothes (not much of interest there, either). He thought about leaving some kind of memento, so she would know someone had been there but decided not to, and that gave him pleasure, too, that he had not left a clue.

Today was the day he would talk to her. He turned to his right and walked across the varnished wide floorboards in the kitchen. This was his home, too, as much as hers. He should be free to come and go as he chose, shouldn't have to knock on the door and wait for someone to invite him in. He felt the usual irritation with the bitch rise in his throat, a burning sour bubble.

He had to be careful—he knew it was not good for his health to get riled up about her; he needed to control himself, to deal with her in a reasonable way, even if she was not reasonable. He put his hand on the kitchen table in the center of the room. She had moved that table down from the study where he remembered it used to be, had it refinished so it was no longer painted black but was stained and waxed natural wood.

He had to give her credit, she had good taste. She had fixed up the kitchen with a new stove, new dishwasher. Where was she getting all the money? He felt the sour bubble rise in his throat again. Control, he told himself, use control. He knew his anger might surface if he encountered her when he had that feeling of injustice. His righteous anger would overcome all his best intentions.

He called her name again. He looked in the bathroom. She might be there. He looked in the woodshed, which she had turned into a sort of garden room. She always had been a gardener. And he had helped her and still would, if she would come to her senses.

Not in the back of the house. He would move toward the front, close off any possibility of her running away from him. Of course there was the front door. Somehow he didn't think she would use it. The front door was for grand occasions. Habit was pretty hard to break. He couldn't see her sneaking away from him, anyway. She had a lot of failings, but sneakiness was not one. No, she probably would not use the front door.

He went into the dining room, a long room Victoria's husband had made by taking out a partition between a small birthing room and the original small, dark dining room. It was bright with afternoon light, even on this rainy day. She was not in this room. Nor was she in the bedroom off the dining room. Nor in the parlor.

He noticed she had rearranged the furniture slightly, had a couple of comfortable easy chairs where before there had been only the formal caned wooden chairs. Funny, the fire was not lighted, although he knew he had smelled wood smoke. He would check the library after he'd gone upstairs. The last time he had been in the library, it was full of junk, no room to even turn around. The fireplace had been unusable, closed off with a metal panel. No, it was unlikely that she was there.

He opened the door into the dark front hall, the hall with the camphor sea chest and portraits of Victoria's ancestors. He went up the curving front stairs, the treads painted like a green carpet. He went into her study. She had taken up the computer after she left him, a skill he had not had time to master.

When they got back together, he would make sure he knew as much about computers as she. He knew her limitations. She undoubtedly didn't know as much as she thought she did.

Where was she hiding?

FOURTEEN

SHE COULD NOT CROUCH there much longer. She was chilled and shivering. Lockwood might decide to wait for her in the house, but if she stayed out in the rain much longer, she was likely to get hypothermia. Keeping low, she crept under the pine trees toward the back of the summer people's house. She could not chance being seen from her grandmother's windows. She would duck behind the hedge at the back of the house and follow that until she came to the small dip in the road where no one could see her from her grandmother's.

The chill was seeping through her wet clothes. She had better move. She kept the summer house between her and her grandmother's until she reached the hedge, which she had assumed was privet or viburnum. Instead, the bushes were thickly knitted multiflora rose with wicked thorns. There was no way she could get through them. She would have to move in front of the bushes in plain view.

Her brown-and-black Iceland-patterned sweater had turned a dark nondescript color now it was soaked, and luckily would be difficult to see. Almost like camouflage, she thought. She took a deep breath to stem her shivering. As slowly as she dared, she crept toward the hedge on hands and knees, looking over her shoulder to check when she was out of sight of Victoria's windows. Rapid movement would be seen too easily, she thought. She didn't want to chance Lockwood's watching her from the attic window.

The rain poured down incessantly. The rose hedge seemed endless. Elizabeth clenched her teeth to stop the shivering, but that made it worse. She thought briefly that this whole escape scene was ludicrous; there was no need to be so stealthy. Then she remembered how Lockwood had looked when she saw him through the dining room windows. She thought of the handcuffs he was holding so casually. Why?

Yes, she had good reason to get away from him. She could not imagine how his mind was working this out, and she was not sure she wanted to know.

She reached the end of the rose hedge, where the land dipped into the gentle swale. She stood upright. She was stiff from crouching. She could not be seen from the house, but if he decided to look for her from his car, she was visible from the road. She stumbled to the marshy bottom of the dip, crossed the road again, running, and was back on Victoria's side. The sandy track along the bottom of the hollow eventually met up with New Lane. As she ran, her shivering eased. She went through stretches when her shivering stopped altogether, then suddenly it would start up again, and she would shake with wet chill and fear.

She was badly out of shape and could run only a short distance before her breath burned her lungs and she had to slow to a walk. Her mind began to shut out everything but reaching Ben Norton's house, shut out the rain, the weight of the wet wool sweater, her wet hair dripping into her eyes, her hands—wrinkled and white from soaking in rain-wet grass— her hot wet tears that ran down her cheeks and cooled. Every part of her body was giving up its warmth. At Ben Norton's she would be safe, safe and dry and warm. Lockwood receded into some small part of her mind. All she knew was that she had to reach Ben Norton's.

The bottom of the swale dipped out of sight of the road. She could not be seen unless someone drove down this sandy, unused track, and that seemed unlikely. The middle of the track was lush with thorny locust saplings, foot-high cedar trees, goldenrod with heavy, wet blossom heads, and poverty grass. No car had driven this way for ages. Before the road had been paved, this was the shortcut to Ben's. She stopped to catch her breath, bent down, put her hands on her knees, let her wet hair swing heavily into her face, felt the rain enfolding her. For a brief moment she was aware of the rich autumn colors, enhanced by rain. The pasture rose gently to her right, touched with scarlet sumac. When she turned her head to her left, she saw the dark green pine and dark brown oaks. She took in the fleeting image of beauty, felt a wave of new energy, and started running again.

SHE'S PLAYING her little game, Lockwood thought. He had gone through the entire house methodically, found the fire burning in the library fireplace, found the front door unlatched. He went to the door, looked around, decided she had probably crossed the road behind—what was their name, Milford?—behind the Milfords' summer house. Sneaky bitch, he thought. No need for him to go out into that messy weather. He would get in his Jeep and go to the police station. If he didn't see her along the way, he would try the other direction, toward Edgartown. If he still didn't see her, he would drive to the end of New Lane.

She couldn't have gone far. Unless she was hiding under some wet bushes, he would meet up with her. Eventually, she would return. He might come back to the house and wait in the library. That would surprise her. She wouldn't expect to see him sitting in that cleaned-out library, sipping a cocktail, enjoying the fire. Of course, if Victoria came back first, he and Victoria would have a nice talk, like old times. Victoria was all right.

He locked the front door. That way, she would have to come around to the side, where he could see her when she came in.

He got back into his Jeep, turned left out of the drive, looked both ways to see if she might be within sight. The police station was only a quarter mile down the road. He drove up to it, didn't see anyone around. He wondered if they still kept the door of the police station unlocked. He pulled into the small parking area, went up to the front door, tried it. It opened. No one was there. The police department had been under new management for almost a year, he thought, but everything was the same as it had been when Junior's father was chief.

He returned to the Jeep. A swarm of ducks and geese gathered around him, quacking. He pushed them aside with his foot and got back into the Jeep. He backtracked past Victoria's house, past the Milfords' summer place, slowed so he could look more closely. He considered whether getting out into the rain to find her tracks was worth the effort. He decided it wasn't. She undoubtedly had passed that way, next to the hedge. Then where? He drove down into the small hollow, looked on both sides of the road, went up the other side.

No, not likely she had come this far. Probably not this way, either. He turned the Jeep around, slowed when he came to the swale, stopped. He saw the overgrown road and considered whether he should attempt to drive on it. That seemed a likely place for her to go. He smiled to himself. Knowing how her mind worked gave him great satisfaction.

No, he wouldn't go along that road, even though he had four-wheel drive and he was fairly sure she had gone that way. He would cut her off where the road intersected New Lane. He calculated how much lead time she had and figured that she would arrive at the lane just about the same time he did.

Actually, this was quite enjoyable, he thought. He was warm and dry, had a vehicle, and was in no hurry. If he didn't catch up with her today, there was always tomorrow and tomorrow and tomorrow. He smiled to himself. He liked that. *Macbeth.* He accelerated to get up the other side of the dip, passed Victoria's house, looked at the yard to see if any new cars had shown up, then turned left onto New Lane. He knew the lane well, since he had driven it so many times recently. He often drove to where it became the Tiah's Cove Road and then branched off in several directions to unknown places. He was quite sure he would find her along the lane before she had time to go off onto one of the mazelike tracks.

AHEAD OF HER, Elizabeth could see where the sandy road ended at the lane. She ran the last hundred feet, stopped to catch her breath in the shelter of a prickly cedar tree, and looked both ways for him. She heard a car engine around the bend of the lane. Did she have time to cross the road, get into the shelter of the brush on the other side?

She decided to chance it and darted across, dodging through huckleberry and briers, through long ropes of wild honeysuckle, through poison ivy. She was not making much progress, and she heard the car rounding the bend. She would be seen unless she did something quickly. Elizabeth threw herself on the ground facing out toward the road next to a brushy thicket. She quickly scooped herself a nest of soggy leaves, piled them around her wet head.

From here, she could see the Jeep, and a sudden surge of fear hit her so that she almost vomited. He had outguessed her. He had known what she would do. Her only hope was that he would not see her in the rain and wet leaves. The Jeep was moving slowly. His windshield wipers made a swish-slat, swish-slat sound that cleared a small patch of glass. She prayed that the windshield was murky enough to fog his view. She put her head down into the leaf mold and froze. She tried not to breathe.

The Jeep was going slower and slower. Elizabeth curbed her urge to look. Her nose was flattened into the pungent wet earthy leaves. She wondered, as she burrowed her face into the mold, would she remember this smell as the smell of sanctuary, of safety? Or would it, from now on, mean terror, capture?

The Jeep stopped. She could imagine Lockwood looking out both windows, leaning over, wiping the fog from the insides of the glass with the palm of his hand. He probably had binoculars. She knew she had to remain still even if he got out of the car and walked toward where she was lying in plain sight.

After an eternity, the Jeep started up again and moved slowly past her. She had to control herself, stay where she was until he went to the end of the road and came back. She was shivering again, shaking so badly she was sure the vibrations of her body were signaling her fear to every living creature around.

Her hearing, sharper than she had ever known it, picked up the sound of the Jeep's engine around the curve by the Morgans' house, followed its echoes in the dip in the road, heard the downshifting of gears as the Jeep came to the end of the pavement where the four dirt roads branched off. Which one would he follow? Or would he try any? He was probably puzzled. Maybe he would assume she had doubled back toward home when she saw him leave the drive. She would have to stay where she was. He would be driving back past her in a few minutes. He must know she couldn't have gone as far as the end of the paved road.

She was probably more difficult to see now. The rain had flattened the leaves she had scuffed around her, a few more leaves had dropped onto her back. If she could stay where she was for another ten or fifteen minutes, even if he looked closely, he would see only a slightly raised lump.

Her mind raced. She tried to recall the symptoms of hypothermia. Shivering first, she knew. The body trying to warm itself. After that came disorientation, a sense of drifting, loss of judgment. She would have to conserve body heat as much as she could. She could not allow herself to become disoriented. The wet leaves under her insulated her somewhat from the cold ground. Water trapped by the wool sweater was warm next to her body. She would be okay for the fifteen minutes she needed.

She could hear the Jeep returning, closer and closer, the engine racing as it went down the slight incline into the swale, the windshield wipers swishing back and forth, swish-slat, swish-slat. On a day like today, the shadows were so diffuse, it would be difficult to make out shapes. She hoped that would help conceal her. Lockwood slowed, stopped, almost as if he were teasing her, telling her he knew she was there. She remained motionless. She heard him shift into gear, and the Jeep started up again. She must stay where she was for several minutes longer. He might be tricking her into showing herself. By now, she didn't even know if she *could* move.

Once she was reasonably sure he was gone, she got up slowly and stiffly, brushed off the wet leaves that clung to her. She had better stay away from the road in case he did come back. She jogged along a faint animal trail within sight of the road until she began to warm up slightly, and her breath came in short hurting gasps. She walked, she jogged, she walked, she jogged, until she came to the end of the paved road, where the four dirt roads branched off. She took the second one from the right, stayed in the right-hand rut, thinking she would hear any car that came this way long enough ahead of time so she could hide again. The road branched, and she took the right fork. It branched again, and she took the left fork.

This was familiar territory. As a girl, she had walked along this road dozens of times with Junior's cousin, had ridden with Junior's grandfather in the back of his pickup truck when he took water in open pails to the cows down by the pond.

For the first time since she had seen Lockwood drive up to the house, Elizabeth's fear began to ebb. Still, she ran when she caught her breath, walked when she lost it. Finally, she could see Ben's house through the rain that continued to pour down in silvery sheets, on a rise looking over a sweep of the Great Pond, backed by the woods that had hidden her.

The house rose out of the steaming rain. A sanctuary. She stumbled up the big granite stone step in front of Ben's house, fell, and thumped the flat of her hand on his door. She was spent. Totally spent. Next to her face she could see raindrops plink into a hollowed-out spot on the granite step. She concentrated on the plinking raindrops, nothing else. She would stay here, draped like a sodden scarecrow, over Ben Norton's stone step through all eternity.

The door opened. "Jesus Christ," Ben said. "Who the hell?"

She couldn't lift her head. She couldn't speak. The sound of his concern brought salt tears, which ran over the bridge of her nose, onto the downhill side of her face, and mingled with the fresh raindrops in the hollow in the stone step.

He knelt beside her.

"Elizabeth?" he said.

She moaned.

"I'm taking you inside." He stooped, draped her right arm over his neck, his left arm around her waist, and half carried her inside to the living room with his paintings on the north wall, the south wall facing the ocean. A fire sizzled in the stone fireplace.

She smelled turpentine. *He's painting,* she thought, *I've interrupted his painting.* Ben put her down on the ancient braided rug in front of the fire where she lay curled, her prune-wrinkled hands between her legs. She had started shivering uncontrollably again. He came back with a thick bath towel and rubbed her hair, her neck. He took off her heavy dripping sweater and dressed her, like a baby, in his wool flannel jacket that he put over her thin wet shirt. A few minutes later he came back with a pillow, which he put under her head, and a down sleeping bag, which he laid on top of her.

"Tea'll be another minute," he said.

She hadn't said a word, had kept her teeth clenched tightly, her mouth shut, her jaw set in a hard line to control the shivering. He put a mug of hot tea with milk next to her. The steam carried the bracing aroma of rum. She tried to sit up and found she was too weak.

He lifted her head, held the mug to her mouth, and she sipped. He'd put sugar in the tea, which she usually hated. Now it tasted like the elixir of life. He held the mug for her until she had finished every drop. Then she slumped back on the braided rug, her head on the cedar-scented pillow, the silky sleeping bag over her, the fire humming on the hearth.

Ben tucked the sides of sleeping bag under her. "Lock-wood?" he asked.

"Yes," she murmured and fell asleep.

FIFTEEN

WHEN VICTORIA and Casey pulled into the drive, Lockwood's Jeep blocked their way.

"Wait here, Victoria." Casey opened her door and stepped out into the rain. "I'd better see what's going on."

Victoria opened the door on her side and got out. "I know how to handle Lockwood." She pulled her hat over her forehead, stepped around a puddle, and hurried into the entry, where she stopped long enough to shake rainwater off her coat. Lockwood was sitting in the cookroom reading last Sunday's *Boston Globe*. He put it down with an elaborately casual gesture.

"Fancy meeting you here, Victoria," he said. "I don't believe I've met the chief of police."

Victoria stood at the cookroom door, at the top of the step. Casey, behind Victoria, started to say something, but Victoria interrupted her. "Where is Elizabeth?" she asked Lockwood, looking straight into his red-flecked green eyes.

"I don't believe she's here," Lockwood said. "I looked." He took off his glasses. "It's nice to see you, Victoria. You're looking well. Haven't seen you for quite a while." He fished a red bandanna handkerchief out of his right pants pocket, shifting slightly in the chair to get at it, wiped his glasses, put them back on.

"Where is Elizabeth?" Victoria glared at him from the

cookroom step. Her hands were by her sides, her feet spread apart slightly, her knees bent, almost like a boxer about to deliver that first punch.

"You know I can't keep track of your granddaughter," Lockwood said. "I never could."

"Don't be smart with me, Lockwood. She was here when I left and her car is still here, blocked in by yours." Victoria straightened her knees and pulled herself up to her full height.

Lockwood grinned, his teeth a yellow slash in the middle of his beard. "It's a little mystery, isn't it? While we're waiting to solve it, why don't you introduce me to your police chief and we can discuss it."

Casey stepped in front of Victoria. "Mr. Wolfrich, sir, I am Chief O'Neill. The owner of this house wants you to leave. You may leave on your own, sir, or I can call in my officers to remove you."

"You're giving me an order, are you? Is that what Victoria wants?" Lockwood remained seated. "A macho lady cop. That's good. What this town needs. Shape things up."

"Sir, I'm asking you to leave."

"I suppose you can make me leave, can't you? Victoria, are you going to allow this lady cop to order me out of your house?" He sat back in the armchair. "Seems to me that's your decision, not hers."

"You'd better leave." Victoria stepped to one side of the door.

"Come, now, Victoria," he said.

Casey unhooked her radio from her belt and keyed the mike. "Junior, send West and Tucker to the Trumbull house, on the double."

"Lady copper playing hardball with the boys." Lockwood stood up. "Victoria, I'm disappointed in you. I never thought you'd cave in to pressure."

He had scarcely finished speaking when the cruiser pulled up in Victoria's drive, blue lights flashing. Patrolmen Josh Tucker and Elmer West, in yellow rain slickers, opened the driver and passenger doors and both stepped out, over and around puddles on either side.

"You win this time, lady cop." Lockwood watched the two policemen come up to the kitchen door. He took his green waterproof jacket off the back of the chair, grinned at Victoria and Casey, brushing past them as he moved toward the door. Tucker and West stopped at the door. Josh Tucker was a compact five foot eight with close-cropped dark hair. Elmer West was wire-thin, sandy-haired, and a couple of inches taller. Lockwood confronted them, an intimidating figure who towered a half-foot over them, a bulky six foot five.

"I'm leaving, boys." Lockwood put his right hand on Tucker's muscular shoulder. Tucker flinched. "Don't get yourselves into a tizzy."

After Lockwood had left, trailed by the two police officers, Casey said, "I'm calling Ben Norton. I hope that's where Elizabeth went." She took the phone off its bracket on the wall and dialed. "It's Chief O'Neill, Ben. Did Elizabeth get there okay?" She nodded to Victoria. "Okay if she stays with you tonight until we can get a restraining order against the guy?" She nodded again to Victoria. "Great. Thanks."

"I must say, that's a relief." Victoria took off her blue coat, hung it over the top of the kitchen door, and sat in her usual chair. "I thought I could reason with Lockwood."

"He's probably gotten worse with time." Casey hung up the phone. "He's undoubtedly been mulling over what he thinks is the injustice of Elizabeth leaving him. Denying completely that she had good reason." Casey moved toward the door. "Will you be all right by yourself tonight, Victoria?"

"Heavens, yes. I'm not alone, really. Angelo is upstairs in the attic, and Winthrop is in the shack out back."

"I don't think Lockwood will bother you. I suspect he'll try to figure out where Elizabeth has gone. Even if he decides Ben Norton's is a logical safe house, which I don't think he will, she's in the hands of a trained cop."

Casey started to open the door when Victoria said, "Before you go, I need to ask you something." Casey stepped back into the kitchen. "First," Victoria continued, "do you think it likely that Lockwood took my basket, filled it with mushrooms, and left it at Quansoo?"

"That's possible, I suppose," Casey said. "Let's go back into your breakfast room and sit down."

Victoria scowled. "Cookroom. This used to be the summer cookroom."

Casey waited until Victoria sat before she pulled out her own chair. "First of all, Victoria, like everybody else, you never lock your doors. He may well have come in here while you were out of the house. But then, almost anyone on this Island could have come in, too. It's time people in this town started to lock doors and windows."

Victoria scowled. "Forty-five doors and fifty-two windows?"

"Everybody on this Island walks into everybody else's house, leaves stuff, takes stuff. I've never seen anything like it." Casey tapped her fingers on the table. "You come home and here's your granddaughter's creepy ex-husband making himself at home, reading your paper, even. What nerve!" She put her elbows on the red-checked tablecloth. "How do you expect the police force to look out for you if you don't take the simplest precautions?"

"We don't have crooks around here." Victoria glared at Casey, her lower lip stuck out, her eyes hooded.

"No, just murderers," Casey said. "And wife beaters."

"If Lockwood took the basket and picked the mushrooms, why? Does anyone besides me suspect that four people and a seagull were murdered with mushrooms?" Victoria's scowl deepened. "Even you think I'm being melodramatic. Yet you expect me to lock all forty-five doors to keep murderers and robbers out?"

Casey laughed suddenly. "Come on, Victoria. Peace."

"As far as anyone knows, three elderly men died of heart attacks, and a youngish woman died of flu complications." Victoria's mouth turned down.

"You're right. I'm not convinced that those were anything other than normal deaths and coincidence."

"You will be when you hear the second thing I've got."

Casey waited.

"Jessica positively identified amanita mushrooms in the contents of the seagull's stomach."

Casey whistled and sat back in her chair. "Why did you wait until now to tell me?"

"You said we needed proof that those deaths were murders. Is that enough for you to go on now? To exhume four people? Doc Erickson is coroner, isn't he?" Victoria asked. "Or is it Doc Jeffers?"

"Erickson. I'll talk to him. Tell him what you found. Do you still have the evidence?"

"I put it in the freezer."

"I'll see if he thinks Molly's death might warrant further investigation." Casey stood again. "I gotta go, Victoria. I must admit, it looks as if you're on to something. I'll call Doc Erickson as soon as I get back to the police station."

LOCKWOOD DROVE BACK to the campground in the pelting rain. When the Jeep went through a puddle, it sent a sheet of water to one side or the other or both. His windshield wipers went swish-slat, swish-salt. His car radio, set to WFCC, a classical music station broadcasting from Cape Cod, played the William Tell Overture, the fifth or sixth time he'd heard it since he started listening to the station. He pulled off Barnes Road into the campground and parked at his camping site, next to his tent trailer.

Good day for staying inside, he thought. He stepped from his Jeep, across a puddle, a few feet up the path, and opened the narrow metal door of his trailer, unsnapping the canvas flap at the top. He went up and shut the door after him, resnapped the flap from the inside. The rain drummed on the canvas roof. He'd make himself a pot of coffee, prop himself up on cushions on the bunk on the right side of the trailer, and read one of the reports on the Russian oil pipeline he'd brought along. Get his mind off the bitch.

The inside of his tent trailer had a double bunk on the right, a table with two seats that could be made into a single bed on the left, and straight ahead, as you entered, a two-burner stove and a small sink with a container of water suspended over it. Under the sink and stove was a small portable cooler. The trailer could be folded in on itself: bunk, table, stove, sink, all collapsed into a small, low, canvas-topped trailer he could hook onto the back of his Jeep.

Lockwood knew exactly how long it took him to set up the trailer, four minutes from the time he undid the trailer hitch and taillight wires and manhandled the trailer into a level spot. It took him three minutes to break camp. He had tried to streamline the operation, get the times down still more, but four minutes for setup, three minutes for breakdown, seemed to be the limit.

Where could she have gone? She probably had a friend she

had visited. If he thought about it, he could figure out who it might be. He was sure he knew most of them. She wasn't that outgoing. During the time she was with him, she had lost touch with most of her friends. She had him and her work, and that was it. He didn't blame her acquaintances for drifting away. She could be cold one minute, manic the next. He had been the only one to stick by her, and that wasn't always easy.

He read a few pages of the report, which was dense with mathematical equations. Sometimes he liked to work out the equations like puzzles, but he didn't feel like doing that now. That damned bitch was on his mind more than he cared to admit. He would find her. She couldn't hide from him indefinitely.

He smiled to himself when he thought of the encounter with Victoria and the police chief. Casey thought she was such hot stuff. Well, he would knock her down a peg or two. He had his ways. He had time. He thought of his visits to Victoria's house when no one was home. Now he was a bit bothered that no one knew he'd been there. It would be satisfying to think they were worrying about some imaginary prowler inside their house. His house, too, he thought, with irritation. No, no, mustn't let himself get upset about anything the bitch did.

He thought about the time a week or so ago when he'd taken the basket from the cookroom. That must have puzzled them. He had wanted to make sure the basket eventually got back to them so they would worry about that, too. Worry about who had taken it, and why? And who had brought it back, and why? He laughed out loud and went back to his report.

After another couple of pages his mind wandered again. That foolish, simpering Cousin Edna. Throughout the years, he'd sent her cards, printed cards that read, "Happy Easter to My Dear Cousin," or "Happy Mother's Day, Cousin," the sappier the better. He kept in touch that way, good idea to build up sympathy for the poor misunderstood husband of Elizabeth, a woman who certainly could be trying.

Cousin Edna had told him, when he called recently, that it was a wonder that he had put up with Elizabeth as long as he had. "She has a mind of her own" is what Edna had said. He laughed out loud again, had to blot his eyes, in fact, when he thought about Cousin Edna telling him how Victoria suspected that someone had poisoned her seagull.

When he'd first arrived on the Island, he'd noticed mushrooms growing under the pine trees all around the campground. He'd looked them up on the Internet on the computer at the Vineyard Haven library, where no one knew him, found they were death's angels, amanitas, and stored that bit of knowledge away for future use. There was almost no knowledge you couldn't use eventually, he thought.

His coffee had finished perking on the propane stove. The smell filled the tent, the rich aroma of a dark Colombian brew. He poured himself a cup, added some of the half-and-half he kept in his cooler, three spoonfuls of sugar, and sat back on his bunk, boots off, feet up on the sleeping bag. Really living, he thought. Hunting for a human bitch, no hurry about it, living in ease while he contemplated the next move. Waiting at the campground where the pine trees sighed in the wind, where poisonous mushrooms grew near the roots of the pines. He sipped the coffee, opened the report again.

And again, his mind went back to Cousin Edna and how she thought she knew everything that was going on in West Tisbury. Keep talking, Cousin Edna, he murmured to himself. Little do you know.

ELIZABETH WOKE UP with a start. It took her a couple of seconds before she remembered she was on Ben Norton's living room floor, in front of a lazily burning fire, warm and cozy under a sleeping bag scented by long-ago campfires and pine woods, her head cradled in fragrant pillows. She was aware of the pungent smell of turpentine, a smell she thought she would associate with safety for the rest of her life.

"Chief O'Neill called." Ben was painting at his easel set up by the window and must have seen her open her eyes. "She wanted to make sure you got here."

"What time is it?" Elizabeth said, sitting up.

"About five. You've been asleep a couple of hours."

"I've got to get home," Elizabeth said. "Victoria needs me."

"No, she doesn't," said Ben. "You're staying here tonight. Victoria can look out for herself." He dipped his brush into a glass jar of murky turpentine, wiped it off on an old piece of sheeting, and put it, brush end up, in a pineapple juice can. "You're staying here until we get rid of your ex."

"I can't!" Elizabeth ran her hands through her tangled hair, dry now, and got to her feet. Her jeans were still slightly damp, but her shirt and underclothes had dried. Ben had put her shoes and socks next to the fire, and they were almost dry. She tucked her shirt into her damp jeans.

"You don't have any choice," Ben said. "Might as well make the most of it." He walked over to the kitchen. "Coffee or tea? Lemon Zinger, if you want."

"Oh hell. I'm sorry to have landed on you like this."

Ben laughed. "Junior and Casey probably set the whole thing up, between them. Said I needed company." He filled the teakettle with water, put it on the stove, struck a big, strike-anywhere match on a flat beach stone next to the stove, and turned on the burner, which lighted with a pop.

"Lemon Zinger, then. Did Casey tell you about my ex stalking me?"

"Yep."

"What should I do?"

"If it were up to me," Ben said, "I'd probably take the guy out and beat the devil out of him, show him what it's like. Give him a taste of his own medicine."

"He's a couple of inches taller than you and outweighs you by fifty pounds." Elizabeth gathered up the pillows and folded the sleeping bag.

"From what I can tell, he's in no kind of shape," Ben said. "I'm not the chief, however. And I doubt if Chief O'Neill plans to beat up on him. She's got enough training; she probably could. She's on this 'professional police force' kick." He adjusted the heat under the teakettle. "I remember when you and Lockwood visited summers. I didn't like him then, either."

The teakettle made a bubbling sound, and Ben took two heavy china mugs off the shelf above the stove, put a Salada tea bag in one, a Lemon Zinger in the other, turned off the heat, and poured hot water into the mugs. "The chief will probably get you to take out a restraining order. If he shows up she can arrest him. Want honey in your tea?" Elizabeth shook her head. "Restraining orders aren't a hundred percent effective, but they're better than nothing."

"Where's this all going to end?" Elizabeth went over to the armchair that faced the rain-shrouded view, and sat down, holding her mug in both hands. "Do you think I'm going to have to worry about the guy stalking me with handcuffs for the rest of my life?"

Ben set the paintbrush he was cleaning down on the table deliberately. "Handcuffs?" he said.

Elizabeth looked at the partially completed painting on his easel. "You really are good." She turned her head first to one side, then the other, closed her eyes to slits, then opened them wide. "That painting is marvelous. It looks mysterious. It has so much depth. You can almost hear the sound of the ocean. When I first looked at it I thought it was all gray, but when you look close, it's got all kinds of color in it." She tilted her head again.

"What about handcuffs?" Ben demanded.

"He came up the steps into the kitchen swinging a pair of handcuffs."

Ben sat on the couch across from her chair, shaking his head. "It's hard to tell with these obsessive guys what they'll do. He might stalk you for years, until some other obsessive interest takes over. If he meets someone else, his obsession might shift to her." Ben drank his tea, looking steadily at Elizabeth over the rim of the mug.

"I wouldn't wish him on another woman, Ben, but it would be nice to have someone else take over."

"I'll ask Casey to bring you a change of clothes. Victoria will know what you need, won't she?"

Elizabeth nodded.

They sat quietly looking out at the rain, sipping tea. Low clouds drifted across the view, partially obscuring the dunes and the sea beyond. Then the clouds lifted and Elizabeth could see breakers. She could feel the surf, almost hear the hiss as the swash moved back down the beach to meet the next oncoming wave. Rain beat against the window, eased up, hit again with force. The clouds moved in, lifted, moved back.

"All you need to do is look out at that, Ben, and troubles drop into perspective. Think how long that surf has been beating on the shore, exactly like that. Our great-grandparents and their great-grandparents felt it, just the way we do…. Thanks."

Ben grunted, a faint smile on his leathery face.

SIXTEEN

ANGELO CLATTERED DOWN the attic stairs. Victoria, two floors below, could feel the house shake. When he entered the cookroom he was carrying two brown bottles and a bag of potato chips.

"Want a beer, Victoria?" he said.

Victoria looked at her watch. "It's only ten o'clock in the morning."

"Live it up, Victoria." Angelo put the two bottles on the table. "It's a good day to drink beer."

"All right, a half glass." Victoria looked out the window at the cedar trees across the field, their tops bending with the wind and rain. "Wind's still nor'east. We'll probably have another day or so of this." She looked at Angelo's jeans. "Lovely colors."

"You're a real card, Victoria." Angelo grinned, showing large, white, slightly crooked teeth. "When I'm famous, I'll give you an autographed copy of my jeans." He put the potato chips on the table and scratched McCavity's head. McCavity closed his eyes and purred. Angelo poured Victoria a half glass of beer.

"Hey, Victoria, where's Elizabeth? Didn't see her last night."

"Staying with a friend. You missed the excitement yesterday."

"What happened?" Angelo sat at the table. "Winthrop and I went to Boston. The art museum. Got the last boat back."

"Lockwood, Elizabeth's ex-husband, showed up." Victoria wasn't sure how much to tell Angelo. "Casey asked him, rather firmly, to leave. He's been parked on New Lane for several weeks, watching her, apparently."

"Does he drive that old Jeep?"

"Yes." Victoria lifted her half glass of beer in a salute.

"I wondered." Angelo sat across from her, opened his own beer, and tipped the bottle up to drink. He put it back on the table and wiped his mouth with the back of his hand, leaving a mustache of orange and red. "He's a creepy guy. I've walked past a couple of times. Wondered what he was up to." He opened the potato chip bag and offered it to Victoria, who took a handful.

A blue car splashed through the puddles in the drive and pulled up under the Norway maple. Victoria saw Maddy Hutchinson get out. She was wearing a blue slicker, the same color as the car, and was carrying a covered dish. She came up the steps and opened the kitchen door.

"Hello! Anybody home?"

"Come in," Victoria called out.

Maddy shut the door behind her and set her dish on the kitchen table. Angelo stood up. Maddy glanced at Victoria's half-finished beer and lifted her eyebrows slightly.

"Good morning," Victoria said, raising her glass to Maddy. "You've met Angelo, my artist-in-residence, haven't you?"

Maddy nodded politely.

"Angelo, this is Mrs. Hutchinson, our retired minister's wife."

Angelo grinned, his teeth white against the orange and red smear he'd extended almost to his left ear.

"Something smells good." Victoria indicated the dish Maddy had put on the table.

"I made it this morning. I hope you like it." Maddy slipped off her blue slicker and laid it on the back of her chair.

"Thank you." Victoria's dark eyes met Maddy's blue and green ones. "You've always been such a good cook."

Maddy smiled.

"Gotta go now, Victoria," said Angelo. "Pick up some paints I ordered from DaRosa's. Nice to see you, Mrs. H. Regards to the Reverend Jack." The door slammed behind him.

Victoria turned to watch him leave. "Look at this, Maddy."

Angelo's car was parked so it pointed out into the driveway. He opened the driver's door and with his right hand on the steering wheel, left hand on the door frame, started to push the car. As it picked up speed, he leaped into it and Victoria heard the engine catch.

Maddy laughed. "The people you attract!"

Victoria started to get up. "I don't suppose you'd like to share my beer. Would you like a cup of tea?"

"I'll get the tea. After all this time, I know my way around your kitchen."

Maddy filled the teakettle, opened the cupboard above it, selected a blue mug, and found a tea bag.

Victoria wondered why she was always so bothered by the way Maddy, her friend of twenty years, made herself at home. Perhaps the feeling came from her New England upbringing, with its respect for privacy.

The teakettle whistled and Maddy unplugged it, poured hot water over the tea bag, and returned to the cookroom. She pulled out the chair Angelo had left. Victoria wondered if she should mention the likelihood of wet oil paint on the seat, but before she could, Maddy sat, smoothly lifting the fabric of her beige silk slacks over her knees. Victoria noticed Maddy was wearing sleek nylons and looked down at her own woolly socks and heavy shoes, the one with its hole cut out on top for her sore toe. Maddy patted the silk scarf she had tucked into her beige silk shirt, pulled down the sleeves of her matching cashmere blazer.

The only time Victoria ever thought about clothes was when she was around Maddy. Then she always felt dumpy, as if matching clothing was important.

Maddy fished the tea bag out of her cup with her spoon, wrapped the string around the bag to squeeze out the last of the water, and set it on the side of her saucer.

After they talked about the weather and recent problems with the Steamship Authority and the hospital, Victoria asked, "How is Jack?"

"I'm worried sick about him. And I'm furious with Jack Jackson." She sat forward and clutched the blue mug tightly. "He wouldn't dream of calling on Jack. Wouldn't think of making Jack feel his ministry had been worthwhile, something he, Jack Jackson, could build on. Oh no!" Maddy's cheeks were coloring a hectic pink. "All his talk about beneficences for the church. The church doesn't need beneficences, certainly not the way he's going about getting them."

Victoria was silent.

Maddy extracted a lacy hankie from her blazer pocket and dabbed her eyes. "I'm so sorry, Victoria. You're the only person in town I feel I can talk to."

"We go back a long way." Victoria prudently changed the subject. "What did you bring that smells so good?"

Maddy refolded her hankie and Victoria caught a whiff of the light scent Maddy always wore. "Jack doesn't have much appetite these days. I thought you might like it. It's a quiche."

"How nice," Victoria said. "I haven't had quiche in a long time. Did you make it with Swiss cheese and bacon?"

"I made several." Maddy patted her hair and smiled. "Swiss

cheese, bacon, and mushrooms. I put in lots of mushrooms. It's actually a mushroom quiche."

"Mushrooms." Victoria stopped stroking McCavity. "Mushrooms," she repeated. The wrinkles on her face formed into a frown. "Did you pick them yourself?"

"No," Maddy said. "Hal Greene, before he died, gave me a jar of his mushrooms, preserved in olive oil and garlic. I haven't tried any yet; Jack has no appetite for anything, but they smell wonderful. I set aside two slices for our lunch, in case I can tempt him."

Maddy finished her tea and put on her blue rain jacket. "I've got to be on my way. I have a couple of calls I want to make to some elderly people who don't get out often." Maddy opened the kitchen door. "Enjoy! Sorry I had that little outburst."

After Maddy left, Victoria picked up the phone and dialed Casey. She got the answering machine at the station. "I need to take some mushrooms to Jessica's, immediately," she said into the machine. "Can you give me a ride there? Right away!"

JACK JACKSON WAS in his upstairs study above the kitchen, where he could hear the rain drumming on the roof and look over the Mill Pond and police station. He heard someone drive up to the house, knock on the door. Heard Betty answer, could hear little oohs and aahs of recognition, a woman, obviously, but he couldn't hear what she was saying. He then heard Betty say, "This is certainly important enough for us to interrupt him."

It had better be important, Jack thought with annoyance. Betty knows I'm not to be disturbed, ever, when I'm working on my sermon. He composed his face so that when Betty opened the door he would appear to be deep in the throes of writing. Actually, he had been paging through a copy of *Hus-*

tler someone had left on a seat on the Bonanza bus last time he'd gone to Boston. He shoved the magazine in a drawer, went back to his word processor. The left-alone screen was dancing with cartoon-strip rabbits who bounced erratically from the lower left corner of the screen to the right, and occasionally piped out in a mechanical voice, "What's up, Doc?" Someday he would find a more fitting screen saver. In the meantime, while he was reading or doing research or simply daydreaming, he would occasionally hit the space bar and the screen would reemerge with white words on a blue background.

"Jack, dearie," Betty said on the other side of his closed door. "I hate to be a bother, but there's someone here who wants to talk to you."

"You can come in. You know the door's not locked."

Betty opened the door halfway and peered around it. Jack looked up with a scowl. "I hope this is important."

"I do think so. Would you want to come downstairs, or shall I have her come up?"

"Her?" Jack's scowl deepened. "Who's 'her'?"

"Shhh! Not so loud."

"Who's 'her'?" Jack said even louder.

Betty came into his study and closed the door.

"You remember when Jack Hutchinson and Maddy Steinbeck left the Arlington church?"

"Yes, of course. Come to the point, Betty. You know I'm busy."

"You remember Jack's wife, Lydia? The wife he left for Maddy?"

"The point, Betty. Come to the point."

"I am, dearie. Don't rush me. You get me all nervous."

"Dammit!" Jack slapped his hand on his desk.

"Lydia's here."

"Here? In West Tisbury?"

"Yes. At our house. In the kitchen."

"What for?" Jack's scowl faded.

"She wants to talk to you, she said."

"Did she say why?"

"No, but she seems disturbed," Betty said softly. "I think it would be a good idea for you to see her."

"I'll be right down, Betty. Give me a few minutes."

Betty shut the door, and Jack could hear her hands squeak as they slid along the polished stair railing. The sound was irritating, like fingernails on chalkboard. She did it on purpose to annoy him, he thought, when she wanted to make a point, get even for some imagined wrong. As the squeak tapered off, he heard the clucking and twittering of women meeting again after years and years.

This was an interesting development. Lydia Hutchinson. What was she doing here, and why did she want to talk with him? The unfortunate affair, as he and Betty called it, had happened more than twenty years ago. As far as he knew, Lydia had no connection to the Island other than Jack Hutchinson. Well, he would find out soon enough.

He opened the drawer into which he'd hastily shoved the copy of *Hustler,* and turned the magazine over so the liquor ad on the back faced up, piled a stack of Bible lessons on top of it, and closed the drawer again. He pushed his swivel chair away from the desk and stood, looked at himself in the mirror to the left of the door, smoothed his scanty hair over the top of his pink scalp, pulled his sweater over his stomach— which bulged only slightly—closed the study door behind him, and followed Betty downstairs, his right hand holding the banister, deliberately sliding it along so it made a long loud squeak as he went down the carpeted stairs.

Betty and Lydia were in the seldom-used parlor, Betty sitting on the couch, Lydia in the armchair Betty had reupholstered in a golden yellow velvet. She probably hadn't even heard his banister squeak, Jack thought, mildly disappointed. The teakettle whistled as he entered the parlor. Betty scurried out to the kitchen.

In his most ministerial voice, Jack said, "Lydia, good to see you, my dear." He held his hand out to her to shake. She half turned in the chair, took his hand with the moist fingertips of hers. "So good to see you." He pulled up a chair so it made the third point of a triangle with the couch and Lydia's chair, the coffee table in the middle. Betty would bring tea and banana bread he had baked yesterday, thin-sliced and spread with cream cheese.

"How can I help you? I assume this is not a social call. What brings you to the Vineyard—and to me?"

Lydia had aged gracefully, Jack was glad to see. The twenty years had been good to her. Her once mousy brown hair had turned a most attractive white with wings of darker hair flaring out from her forehead on either side of a central part. She had always dressed nicely, nothing chic like Maddy, but in quiet good taste, and he noticed that the same quiet good taste was now expensive quiet good taste. Her face had a few more lines in it, but they were peaceful, happy lines.

Lydia smoothed her skirt over her thighs. "This is most awkward. I'm not sure quite how to begin."

Betty returned with the black lacquer tray, teapot, three dainty cups and three saucers, sugar bowl, cream pitcher, lemon slices, dainty flower-printed napkins, and his banana bread, sliced thin and spread with cream cheese, as he had supposed.

"When did you arrive, Lydia?" Betty asked.

"I've been here a little over a month. I'm staying with friends in Edgartown."

"A lovely time of year to be on the Island," Betty said.

"I needed to think through a few things."

"Yes, of course," Jack said.

"Would you like me to leave?" Betty asked. "Let you have some privacy?"

Jack turned to Lydia, raised his eyebrows in a question.

"No, I'd like you both to be here." Jack had forgotten how musical Lydia's voice was. He wondered again, as he had repeatedly over the years, what Jack Hutchinson had seen in Maddy, with her strange eyes, that had torn him away from this lovely woman? It certainly told you something about Jack, he thought.

Betty poured tea, and the three discussed cream, sugar, and lemon. Murmured pleasantries about Jack's banana bread. Talked about the nasty weather they'd been having. Jack had crossed his right leg over his left, and he began to move his right foot, shaking it with ill-concealed impatience.

Lydia said again, "I'm not sure where to begin."

"Why don't you begin at the beginning?" Jack felt a bit clownish as he said the cliché. "Always a good place to start."

"Yes. Well. As you know, Maddy Steinbeck and Jack," she paused, put her teacup in its saucer, and put them both on the coffee table. She left her sentence unfinished.

"Most unfortunate." Jack moved his foot, up and down, from side to side. He held his saucer in his left hand, the fragile handle of the teacup in his right. While he was waiting for Lydia to get to the point, he thought how easy it would be to crush the teacup. He hated those damned violet-printed eggshell-thin teacups.

"When Jack left me," Lydia finally continued, "I always

assumed he would come to his senses. I was sure he would eventually return to me. Our marriage had been a good one. I understood the temptations he faced, and I was willing to wait for him, understand him, forgive him."

She unfolded her paper napkin on her lap, on the blue skirt that echoed the dark blue of her eyes, the color of the sea in a thunderstorm. Jack had not known Lydia well enough to realize how much force those deep blue eyes conveyed.

"People kept telling me to get on with my life, but I was. I had enough to keep me occupied." She smoothed her napkin and picked up her cup and saucer, took a sip of tea. Betty lifted her own cup and saucer.

"I stayed active in the church, you know."

Jack hadn't known, but he nodded.

"The children, of course."

"Of course," Betty said.

"So the years passed. Phil Steinbeck, Maddy's former husband, and I found ourselves in the same church groups, the same hiking club, the same bird-watching group. We discovered we had a great deal in common."

Jack's right foot moved up and down, back and forth. He uncrossed his legs, shifted in his chair, and crossed his left leg over his right.

"We decided recently we had so much in common, we would like to spend what we have left of our lives together."

"How nice, Lydia. Isn't it, dearie? What a sweet ending to an unfortunate affair."

"And why are you here now?" Jack wiggled his left foot.

Lydia looked at him with her large dark blue metallic eyes, the two sweeping wings of dark hair against the white, looking, Jack thought, like satyr's horns.

"Jack and I were never divorced. I refused."

Betty put her teacup and saucer on the coffee table with a rattle.

Jack's foot twitched once and stopped.

"You mean, Maddy and Jack aren't married?" Betty stared at the other woman.

Lydia looked intently at Betty and nodded.

"He preached here for twenty years, morals, ethics, readings from philosophers on leading a decent life, all that sort of thing, and they were never married?" Betty continued to stare at Lydia.

"That's right."

"Well," Jack said. "Well, well."

There was a stunned silence between Jack and Betty. Lydia sipped her tea and looked at Jack over the rim of the translucent teacup.

"Now that Phil and I are thinking about marriage, I suppose I should think about divorce."

"Yes," Jack said. "Yes, indeed." He uncrossed his legs and set both feet flat on the floor. "Have you talked to him, to Jack, about this?"

"No. I've been out of touch with him ever since he left."

"Twenty years," said Betty.

Lydia turned her head with its white hair and satyr's horns to Betty. "Twenty years." She turned to Jack.

"I was hoping you might talk to him on my behalf."

VICTORIA PACED back and forth in the kitchen, looking at the wall clock, then at her watch. Jessica had told her that the kitchen laboratory would be ready and waiting.

Where was Casey?

Who else could take her to Jessica's with the suspect quiche? That miserable Manny Smith. If he hadn't parked the

Meals on Wheels van so she couldn't move her car without touching his, she would still be driving. She needed her car now. It had really not been her fault. She still couldn't believe how that soft-spoken man could use such bad language.

She paced. She missed Elizabeth. Casey had told Elizabeth to stay at Ben's another couple of days. Elizabeth's car was parked in the drive under the maple tree. Victoria considered driving the car herself. This certainly qualified as an emergency. Elizabeth's car had a gearshift, the kind of car Victoria preferred. In fact, the car that had touched the Meals on Wheels van had been automatic. That had been the trouble.

She was about to dial the police station for the fourth time, when the phone rang.

Casey was on the line. "What's up, Victoria?"

"Maddy Hutchinson gave me a mushroom quiche, and I think she may be delivering mushroom quiches all over town. We've got to get to Jessica's right away and have the one she gave me analyzed."

"Who's she taking them to?"

"She said only that she was visiting elderly people. She didn't tell me she was taking them quiches. But I'm sure she is."

"I'll be right there."

Within five minutes, the Bronco pulled up next to the kitchen steps. Victoria was waiting, quiche in hand.

Casey looked over at Victoria, and when they were on the main road, she turned on her siren.

SEVENTEEN

"DEFINITELY AMANITA," Jessica said. "A slice of this would do a pretty good job on whoever ate it, especially an elderly or ill person."

"We've got to stop Maddy," Victoria said.

"I'll get Junior and the two patrolmen on it right away." Casey keyed her radio. Junior came on. "An emergency, Junior. Take both cruisers, you and Josh and Elmer, find Maddy Hutchinson, and pull her over."

Junior's voice came over the radio. "She driving that blue BMW?"

Casey looked at Victoria, who nodded.

"Find out if she's given away any mushroom quiches."

"What?" Junior said.

"If she has, find out who she gave them to, go pick them up right away."

"Roger," Junior said.

"Victoria and I are leaving Oak Bluffs. We'll look for her along State Road. Get the Tisbury police to look for her too."

"Roger," Junior said.

Junior immediately contacted the Vineyard Haven cops. He had no idea what was going on, but he figured he could find Maddy Hutchinson without too much trouble. He asked the Vineyard Haven cops to check on their side of the town line, the Chilmark cops to check on their side, and sent Josh and

Elmer along North Road and Middle Road. He knew South Road and the maze of sand roads that led off it better than anyone else, so he took that area.

He remembered how Maddy and Jack Hutchinson visited with parishioners all over hell and gone. They went first to the most fragile people, even if it meant backtracking. Maddy probably was delivering her quiches the same way, he figured, to the neediest first. She must have had about an hour lead time, Junior thought, considering the time it took to identify the mushrooms. She probably had finished her errands and gone home. He decided to check there first.

The Hutchinsons' house was over the West Tisbury town line in Chilmark, strictly speaking not his turf, but he thought under the circumstances he could break the territorial code.

He went past Alley's store, blue lights flashing, no siren. The usual gang was assembled on the porch. He passed Maley's Gallery on the left, the dancing white statues forlorn in the drizzling rain, passed the church, passed the gas station. He crossed the brook and the town line, drove up the hill on the other side. All the time, he looked for the blue BMW.

"WHERE'S HE GOING in such a hurry?" Joe Hanover said as Junior sped past Alley's, blue lights flashing. The cruiser's tires kicked up a rooster tail of spray.

"Who knows?" Donald Schwartz shrugged. "What's up, Sarah?"

"You won't believe what I just heard." Sarah Germaine had got off work at the Wampanoag Tribal Headquarters in Aquinnah. Rainwater overflowed the gutters in steady streams where leaves blocked the flow.

"Looks like we'll have another day of this." Lincoln Sibert

stood with his back against the shingled front of the building, looking out at the rain.

Sarah went on. "Remember the scandal involving the Reverend Jack Hutchinson and his wife Maddy?"

"Yeah, I remember." Donald was drinking coffee out of a Black Dog paper cup. "I was about twenty at the time."

"You was just a kid then." Joe jabbed an elbow into Donald's ribs. "That was some to-do, let me tell you. If it wasn't for the Trumbulls, the church probably wouldn't of hired him."

Lincoln was standing next to the rusty red Coca-Cola dispenser, an artifact from the 1940s. "Times have changed. Nowadays nobody gives a damn what people do."

"What brought that old bygone up?" Donald lifted the plastic lid of his cup and took another sip of coffee.

Sarah put her mail on the bench. The three men continued to stand.

"The first Mrs. Hutchinson is in town," said Sarah.

"Yeah?" Joe spit out what was left of his Red Man chewing tobacco. "So what?" He took his hands out of his pockets long enough to adjust his baseball cap.

"Wouldn't know her if I saw her." Lincoln scratched his shoulders on the shingled front of the building.

"I never met the lady." Donald watched the streams of rainwater coming off the roof.

"The first Mrs. Hutchinson says there is no second Mrs. Hutchinson." Sarah paused to see if the news registered on the porch gang. "Maddy and Jack Hutchinson are not married."

"They ain't, hunh?" Joe rocked onto his toes.

"Where'd you hear that?" Donald drained his coffee, mashed the cup, and tossed it across the porch toward the trash can. The cup rolled in a semicircle where it fell.

"That can't be right." Lincoln stopped moving his shoulders. "He's a minister. Ministers don't do that."

"Well," said Sarah, "this one did. For twenty years, we all thought Maddy was the perfect minister's wife, thought what a nice couple they were. And they weren't even married."

"To tell you the truth," Joe muttered, "I never trusted that woman. Didja ever see anyone with eyes like that? Two different colors." He turned his back on Sarah, looked out at the rain, and rocked back and forth on his feet. A car went by, swishing on the wet road, windshield wipers going.

"I don't suppose that means much," said Lincoln. "They must be common-law or something after all this time."

"They would be if…" Sarah paused. "If his first wife had divorced him." Sarah stopped and smiled knowingly. "She didn't."

"I'll be," said Donald. "You never can tell, can you?"

Lincoln shifted slightly. "She's in West Tisbury now?"

"She went to see the Reverend Jack Jackson."

"Is that right. How'd you find all this out?" Joe said.

"I have my sources. She wants a divorce now because—get this—she wants to marry Maddy's ex-husband."

"You don't say?" said Donald.

"Twenty years later?" said Lincoln.

"Ain't love grand," said Joe.

"She wants help from the Reverend Jack Jackson in getting the divorce."

"Bet Jack Jackson's having a happy hissy fit over this," said Joe. Taffy, in the front seat of Joe's truck, barked twice, grinned at Joe. "Jack Jackson don't think much of Jack Hutchinson. Can't stand his wife, Maddy. Only she ain't his wife, you say? Wait till my wife hears this."

THE NEWS SPREAD like a grass fire throughout West Tisbury. In a short time, everyone knew. Mrs. Jack Hutchinson—the only Mrs. Jack Hutchinson—was in town, seeking a divorce from the Reverend Jack Hutchinson after twenty years so she could marry Maddy's (what's her last name now?) ex-husband.

JUNIOR PASSED open meadows and plunged into the oak and beech woods beyond, looking in driveways, down roads, wherever a car might park. No blue BMW. The road curved, bounded by lichen-covered stone walls. He passed the sheep farm, where sheep grazed in pastures that rolled gently down to the gray Atlantic.

He turned right through an opening in the stone wall, and started up a steep winding hill. On either side, wild viburnum blocked his view. The Hutchinsons' house was at the end of the road, and with relief he saw the blue BMW parked on a gravel pad, bounded by railroad ties, neatly weeded chrysan- themums and marigolds, spots of sun in this gloomy day. He knocked on the door, opened it.

"Anyone home?"

"It's Junior!" Maddy said. "What a surprise. What brings you here?"

"This is an emergency. I need to find the mushroom dishes you gave to people today."

"Why? What's wrong?" Maddy put one hand to her throat, the other on the door frame. "I think I've just tempted Jack to have a little bite."

"No! Don't touch it!" Junior could see into the living room. The Reverend Jack Hutchinson had a tray in his lap and was cutting into the pointed end of the pie-shaped slice of quiche. Junior pushed past Maddy and snatched the quiche away from Jack.

"I'll need to take both pieces, sir."

Jack recoiled.

"I'm really sorry, sir. I'll explain as soon as I can," Junior said.

Jack looked at him in astonishment over the top of his rimless bifocals, the fork poised in his hand. His easy chair was in front of the large picture window that framed a view of the ocean, gray and threatening in the rain.

"What are you doing?" Maddy said, alarmed.

"Who else has them?"

"I took one to Victoria…"

"Yes, yes," Junior said. "The rest. How many were there? Who has the other ones?"

"Molly Bettencourt's mother." Maddy's hand was still on her throat. "Molly's maiden name was Ferreira."

"Where does Mrs. Ferreira live?"

"Off Barnes Road." Maddy shut the door and moved away from it into the living room. "What is this all about?"

Junior made a note in his spiral-bound book. "Who else did you take the quiches to?"

"I took two to Windemere's long-term-care unit. I thought it might cheer them up." Maddy had stepped into the living room where she was silhouetted in front of the gray Atlantic. "What is going on, Junior?"

"I'll explain later. Let me use your phone."

The Reverend Hutchinson was sitting in his easy chair, the empty tray still in his lap. He looked questioningly at Junior.

"We've got an emergency here, sir."

Maddy took the tray from Jack's lap and carried it into the kitchen. Junior went to the kitchen phone, looked up the number for Windemere in *The Island Book*, got Susan Fisher, one of the nurses on the desk, and ordered her to get the quiches back. He told her someone from the police department would pick them up.

"It's easy to chew and digest and I thought they might like to share them," Maddy said in a whiny voice that set Junior's teeth on edge. "And Mrs. Ferreira has been so depressed since Molly's death."

"I need Mrs. Ferreira's phone number. There are about two dozen Ferreiras in the phone book. Which one is she?"

"I've got her number in my address book." Maddy fumbled with the book, hands shaking .

The line was busy. Junior wrote out a receipt for Maddy's quiche, tore the page out of his notebook, and handed it to Maddy, who took it without looking at it. He dialed again. Busy.

"Mrs. Hutchinson, keep trying to reach her, will you? Tell her not to eat the quiche. Someone will be by to pick it up." Maddy had wrapped the two slices of quiche in foil, and he took them with him.

"What's this all about, Sergeant?" The Reverend Jack got to his feet slowly.

"Something apparently is wrong with the quiche, sir. We'll give you the details when we can."

"Anything we can do besides call?" the Reverend Jack asked.

"Thank you, sir. We've got to get through to Mrs. Ferreira, keep her from eating any of that quiche."

He brushed past Maddy, who was standing, her crownlike arrangement of white braids, usually so perfect, slightly askew. As soon as he got into his cruiser, he called Casey on his radio.

"We need to get through to Molly's mother, Mrs. Ferreira. Mrs. Hutchinson took a quiche to her. Her line's been busy. Two at Windemere. Nurse Susan Fisher is holding them for us."

"NOT ALL OF THESE are made with amanitas," Jessica said, after Casey and Victoria had delivered the quiches to her, two slices from the Hutchinsons, an entire quiche from Mrs. Ferreira, and two from Windemere. Jessica had run her tests immediately.

"Which ones?" Casey asked.

"Mrs. Ferreira's were common edible field mushrooms, as was one of the two Windemere quiches. Victoria's was made with amanitas. So was the Reverend Hutchinson's."

"Jack's?" Victoria said. "Jack Hutchinson's? Are you positive?"

"Yes. I've labeled everything," Jessica said. "Look at this." She stood aside so Victoria could see the specimens on glass slides, neatly labeled in Jessica's tidy printing.

"Where did the rest of the Hutchinsons' quiche go? We retrieved only two slices," Victoria said.

"You're right," Casey said. "What's Maddy's number?"

Maddy must have been close to the phone, because almost immediately after she dialed, Casey said, "Mrs. Hutchinson, where is the rest of the quiche you and Reverend Hutchinson kept aside for your lunch?" She nodded. Made notes. "Yes, ma'am. Sorry we haven't explained. We will as soon as we possibly can. Yes, ma'am." She hung the phone back on its wall bracket. Victoria looked at her questioningly.

"She said she'd forgotten. She took a piece to Edna Coffin, left the rest at the Reverend Jack Jackson's. A peace offering, she told me."

"Humpf," Victoria said. "Hardly."

"She said she left it on his kitchen table."

They got no answer at Edna's. Casey called Junior on the radio, told him to retrieve Edna's quiche slice. "Yes, ma'am," said Junior.

Next, she called the Reverend Jackson. He said that, since he didn't care for mushrooms, he'd taken his half of the quiche to the poor homeless man in the battered Jeep that was always parked on New Lane. He hadn't realized it had come from Maddy Hutchinson. Why on earth would she think he would eat any food she brought him?

Casey radioed Junior, told him to get the quiche from Lockwood. "That's not exactly the way we intended to solve Elizabeth's problem." Casey laughed and put her handheld radio back in its case on her belt.

"Let me know if you need an analysis of anything else," Jessica said. "I'll keep things set up, in case."

ONCE THEY WERE back in the Bronco, they drove slowly away from Jessica's, dodging puddles in the rutted road. The rain was beginning to let up. The windshield wipers worked intermittently to clear the droplets.

The two were silent. Casey concentrated on the puddles, and Victoria looked out the window at the field bordered by goldenrod and purple asters, at Sengekontacket beyond the field, and the sound misted over by the pearly rain.

"I can't believe she would deliberately go around poisoning people. Unless she's cracked up."

"Who knows," Casey said.

"When Maddy came by with the quiche this morning, I asked her if she picked the mushrooms. She said she got them from Hal Greene. Mushrooms in oil and garlic."

"Hal Greene, eh?" Casey said.

"It's curious that some quiches were made with edible mushrooms, some poisonous," Victoria said.

"The whole thing is weird." Casey swerved around a large puddle. "I meant to tell you, Victoria, Doc Erickson has agreed to an exhumation of Molly's corpse. He believes we have probable cause." Casey turned left onto the pavement.

"Depending on what Doc Erickson finds out about Molly's death, maybe we should think about exhuming Hal Greene," Casey said. "His death didn't exactly fit the pattern of a heart attack. Wonder if he ate his own mushrooms?"

Victoria noticed that Casey was using "we" more often, and she smiled.

LOCKWOOD HAD BEEN listening to an organ concerto by Bach on his Jeep's radio, the volume turned up high. A battered red Volvo stopped next to his Jeep, and a short, pudgy man in a green jacket and blue baseball cap got out and came over, a foil-covered dish in his hand.

Lockwood rolled down his window and lowered the volume on Bach's organ concerto.

"I've noticed you here for some time, and thought I'd introduce myself," the man said. The baseball cap had *USNS Shark* printed in gold letters across the front. "I'm Reverend Milton Jackson, minister of the Congregational church."

"How do you do." Lockwood extended his hand through the open Jeep window. "I'm Lockwood Wolfrich. I thought Jack Hutchinson was minister."

"He retired about a year ago," the Reverend Jackson said, his mouth working in an expression Lockwood didn't understand. "By the way, you can call me Jack, everyone else does."

"Fine." Lockwood wondered where all this was leading.

"I'd like to invite you to join us at church next Sunday. Everyone is welcome. You don't need to dress up."

"Thanks." Lockwood waited.

"I didn't know whether you'd had lunch or not, but thought you might enjoy some of this mushroom quiche one of my parishioners left me."

"That's mighty nice of you." Quiche sounded good, and Lockwood hadn't thought about lunch. "Appreciate it, Reverend."

"Jack," Jack said. "See you Sunday?"

Lockwood made a noncommittal sound, thanked Jack, and held his hand out for him to shake again before he got into his Volvo and drove away. Lockwood took the foil off the aluminum pan. The quiche looked good, golden brown, mushrooms liberally sprinkled on top, and mushrooms showing through the custardy filling. West Tisbury had its share of good cooks, he recalled. He thought about his own cooking. He hadn't made quiche for a long time. He told himself that when Elizabeth came back, he might make something like this for her as a treat.

He decided to wait a bit before he ate the quiche. Something to look forward to in the long afternoon.

He was still puzzled about Elizabeth's whereabouts. He hadn't seen her for at least two days, not since she'd played that game of hide-and-seek with him before he'd had that encounter with the smart-ass police chief.

A half hour after the Reverend Jack Jackson had brought him his lunch, the police cruiser pulled up and parked in front of his Jeep, Junior Norton at the helm. This was beginning to constitute police harassment, Lockwood thought with annoyance. What did they want now?

WFCC was playing something Wagnerian. Lockwood decided not to lower the volume. Let Junior talk over the French horns and hunting calls. He wound down his window. The kid was sauntering toward the Jeep from the cruiser, hiking up his gun belt as he walked, his feet splayed out. Toes pointed out like a duck, Lockwood thought. He grinned at the idea, bared his teeth, waited to see what the next cop move was going to be.

"Anything wrong, Officer?" Lockwood used just enough falsetto to be obnoxious without being downright insulting.

"Mr. Wolfrich, sir, I understand Reverend Jackson brought you a covered dish of some kind."

This took Lockwood by surprise, and he was at a momentary loss. "Yes?" he said, a question, not an answer.

"I'll need to get that dish from you, sir."

"Is this an order?" Lockwood recovered quickly.

"No, sir, a request. I would like to take that quiche, sir." He held out his hand.

"I think not," Lockwood said. "No, I think not."

"Sir, I can't order you to give it to me, but we have reason to believe there is something wrong with the food, sir."

"Is that right?" Lockwood grinned. "You think this new minister is poisoning people, is that it?"

"Sir, we would like your cooperation on this. I must ask you again to give me that quiche." Junior held out his hand.

"If you want it, you'll need to bring me something in writing, an official document. By then, I may have eaten this poisonous manna."

"Sir, for the last time, I must take that quiche."

"Sorry, boy, get me something in writing." Lockwood wound up the window between Wagner and himself on the inside, Junior on the outside, grinned his yellow-toothed grin through the closed window, and started up the Jeep. Driving away from Junior, he turned his head toward the fragrant quiche opened on the seat next to him. He didn't choose to watch Junior waddle back to the cruiser.

Something wrong with it, eh? A dish brought to him by the

minister, cooked by a parishioner? Sure. He'd file a harass-ment complaint against the West Tisbury cops. What kind of one-horse operation was it anyway that it had to resort to this kid stuff?

The encounter had taken his appetite away. When he stopped at the main road, he put the foil cover on the dispos-able pan again and drove back to his campsite, where he poured himself a stiff bourbon.

EIGHTEEN

THE ENCOUNTER HAD TAKEN Junior's appetite away, too. He almost hoped Lockwood would eat the damned quiche. Serve him right. He got back into the cruiser, turned left at the main road, parked in front of the police station, and, hitching up his belt, strode in.

"He wants a court order."

Casey looked up questioningly from her computer monitor. "We're probably both thinking the same thing, Junior. Namely, we warned him, and now it's his problem. But if Wolfrich needs a court order, we'll have to get a court order. I'll call the magistrate." She looked at her watch. "The courthouse is closed now." She picked up the phone. "I'll send one of the other guys to reason with Wolfrich. You head on home."

"Thanks, Chief." Junior cleared the papers from his desk, stood up, and stretched. He looked forward to getting back to his camp on the Great Pond. Junior's great-grandfather had built the camp for duck hunting a century before and the place hadn't changed much. It was still primitive, lighted with kerosene lamps, and heated by the stone fireplace. Junior's only concession to modern living was his battery-powered police scanner, which occasionally crackled a message for the chief or the fire department, or something for emergency techs in one of the other Island towns.

"Need me to do anything before I leave, Chief?"

Casey turned from her computer. "No thanks, Junior. Have a good evening. See you in the morning."

After he left the station house he turned onto the Quansoo Road, which ran down a narrow neck of land between Tisbury Great Pond and Black Point Pond. A network of roads formed an unmarked maze on the neck. Only someone familiar with the area could negotiate it, a *terra incognita* that baffled his boss, Casey. As he got closer to his place the trees became salt-shorn scrub, gnarled by the wind, branches bent away from the influence of the sea. He turned onto a smaller rutted road between two large, stumpy wolf trees. He didn't know how they got the name "wolf trees," but the name fitted them, somehow—large, spreading, twisted oaks, covered with lichen and festooned with the pewter-colored moss called old man's beard. As he approached his shack, the trees gave way to wild rose, bayberry, and poison ivy.

On the other side of the pond he could make out his father's house, dim in the gathering dusk. The rain was a steady drizzle now. He saw someone in yellow foul-weather gear moving around outside his father's place. The only person who might be there was Elizabeth, and that meant only one thing. She was hiding out from that freak ex-husband, Lockwood.

The more Junior thought about Lockwood, the more he began to recall images from years ago. Lockwood had worked for Junior's grandfather one summer. Junior had been eight or nine at the time, and Lockwood had been a college student. "Woody," that's what his grandfather had called Lockwood.

Junior opened the door of his shack and stepped inside, out of the rain. On his right was a smoke-darkened fireplace. Above it his duck decoys were lined up on the mantelpiece. He had carved the decoys. Junior didn't tell many people where he lived, didn't talk about his carving. He was like his father, a private person.

A couple of months ago, right after the bluefish started running, Junior had met a surf caster when he was fishing at the opening. She was using a type of lure he had never seen before. Every time she cast, she hooked a fish. The half-dozen other regulars at the opening were watching with awe. The surf caster's name was Barbara Pulaski, and she had a four-year-old daughter, Ashley, who was always with her. When Junior met them, late one afternoon at the turn of high tide, Ashley was building a sand castle near the swash line where the sand was damp.

Surf casting led to breakfasts or suppers at Junior's shack after the blues moved away with the tide. He'd fry up bacon and bluefish and eggs on his kerosene stove.

One evening a couple of weeks after they'd met, Barbara and Ashley had stayed for supper, and Ashley picked up one of Junior's half-finished decoys. Her mother took it from her. "That's not a toy, honey."

Ashley's eyes filled.

"She can have it," Junior said. "That one didn't turn out right." He laughed. "Some kind of metaphor, I guess."

After supper, Ashley curled up in her Winnie-the-Pooh sleeping bag next to Junior's smoky fire, her arms around the black duck decoy. She hummed to her duck and fell asleep in the middle of her song.

From then on, for the first time in his life, Junior talked, really talked. He told Barbara about the mother who'd left him. About life with his father, fishing and hunting and foraging. About his life as a cop, how disappointed he was not to get the chief's job. He told her about his growing respect for Casey, and his relief, now, at not having the responsibility. He wasn't sure he was ready to handle it yet, he told her.

Now, weeks later, as Junior lighted the fire to take the chill off the damp afternoon, he couldn't get his mind off Lockwood. He wanted to hear Barbara's reaction to the story of Lockwood and the quiche. He was so preoccupied, he was startled when his door banged open and Ashley, clad in a rain-wet blue slicker, grabbed him around his knees.

"Mama and I caught a huge fish—a striped bass."

"Great!" Junior lifted her up in his arms. "Wish I'd been there to see. How shall we cook it?"

"With mushrooms?" Barbara asked, coming up behind him in her own rain-wet slicker.

Junior laughed and set Ashley down. "Speaking of mushrooms…" He told Barbara about Lockwood and the mushroom quiche while they made supper together.

"He's a bully," Junior said, after they'd finished and had cleaned up the dishes. "A guy six and a half feet tall, two hundred sixty pounds."

Barbara settled on the couch in front of the fire and Junior sat next to her.

"I've taken enough psychology courses to understand why spouses stay with those sickos," Junior said. "Look at you."

"Five years," Barbara murmured.

Ashley played on the braided rug next to the fire. Junior and Barbara talked.

"The guy's superconfident, so damned sure of himself," Junior said. "Figures he can control everything and everyone. He's goddamned invulnerable."

"He's got a weakness, I guarantee. Wife beaters often do. He's covering up something he doesn't like about himself."

"What, though? I wish I knew."

Barbara tucked her bare feet under her on the couch. "Do you remember what he was like when you were children?"

Junior shook his head. "Not much. He was tall and skinny with broad shoulders. He was strong, really strong. My grandfather liked him, but I seem to recall we kids were scared of him."

The fire sizzled comfortably. Ashley had found a book on Junior's bookshelf about Island wildlife and was lying on her stomach, reading out loud.

"What's this?" She looked up at her mother and pointed to a picture of a snake.

Barbara leaned down to look. "A garter snake, honey."

"And this?" Ashley pointed.

"That's a milk snake."

"I know what a milk snake is," Ashley said. "Junior showed me a snakeskin. It's pretty."

Junior sat up straight.

Barbara turned a page for her daughter. "And this little green one is a grass snake. And here's a corn snake."

Junior stood up. "That's it!"

Barbara sat back. "What is?"

"That summer, when Woody—Lockwood, you know?"

Barbara nodded.

"Woody was working for my grandfather. I must have been eight or so. I was over at Victoria and Jonathan Trumbulls with my cousin Jared, playing on the bulkhead doors that opened into the Trumbulls' cellar." Junior had gone over to the fireplace and was leaning against the mantelpiece. "When Mr. Trumbull wasn't looking, we'd climb to the top of the slanting doors and run down, or we'd sit down and slide."

Barbara smiled.

"Once I got a splinter doing that, and my father had to take it out with a needle sterilized in a match flame."

"Served you right," Barbara said.

"There was this one time when Jared opened the bulkhead door. I don't think you've seen Mrs. Trumbull's cellar."

Barbara shook her head.

"It's got stone steps that lead down under the house. When the sun's out, the steps get nice and warm under the bulkhead doors." Junior shoved a log to the back of the fireplace. "I can see it so clearly, now." He laughed. "On the top step there were two corn snakes, coiled together, knotted up so you couldn't tell whether it was one snake or a half dozen. Jared and I knelt by the doors and watched those snakes for several minutes."

Barbara shuddered. "I'm not wild about snakes."

Junior laughed again. "Well, Jared said to me, 'Want to see Woody go crazy?' and I said, 'Sure.' Of course I wanted to see Woody go crazy. He was talking grown-up talk with my grandfather on the other side of the driveway, and I was watching those snakes writhe, muscles moving down the lengths of their bodies, but all knotted up. You couldn't tell which snake was which."

Ashley looked up from her book. "Snakes eat mice."

"You're right, honey, they do." Barbara turned back to Junior. "Then what happened?"

"Jared called over to Woody. He had this real, sweet, innocent-sounding voice, almost like a girl. Still does. He sings tenor in the church choir these days."

"Yes, yes," said Barbara. "What happened next?"

"Jared called out, 'Come see what we found, Woody!' and then he looked at me and laughed, a mean sort of laugh…. It's all coming back, now."

"I think I know what's next," said Barbara.

"Lockwood had been talking to my grandfather and Mr. Trumbull. He strolled over to see what us kids wanted to show him. I even remember how he had his hands in his pockets. And what he was wearing." Junior laughed again. "Tan chinos and a yellow short-sleeved shirt. The guy seemed like such an adult to us. He was almost as tall as my grandfather."

"Mama?" said Ashley, getting up from the floor. "Would you read to me?"

"In a minute, honey. Junior's telling me a story about when he was a boy. Sit next to me and listen."

"I wasn't much older than you, Ashley," Junior said, once Ashley had squirmed into the space beside Barbara. "Woody sauntered over, looking real relaxed and grown-up. He leaned over to see what Jared and I had to show him. He looked down at the cellar stairs, and suddenly, he straightened up as if he'd been stung by a bee." Junior stood up straight. "He screamed. A high-pitched, scary scream, loud and warbling, like the siren at the firehouse."

Ashley's eyes were wide as she stared at Junior. She popped her thumb into her mouth and twisted her hair with the fingers of her other hand.

Lockwood's reaction had made a huge impression on Junior. The scream had been spooky, Junior recalled. Woody's expression had frozen into one of terror, the kind of expression Junior had seen only in vampire movies. His mouth had opened, and his face turned purple; his eyes bulged, and veins in his forehead and his neck throbbed so Junior could see blood pounding into this apparition of a grown-up. Saliva flew out of his mouth, and he shouted at the kids in a high-pitched hysterical voice to shut the goddamned cellar door, twitching as he backed away from the snakes on the cellar stones.

Ashley took her thumb out of her mouth. "Tell me some more about when you were little."

Junior looked down at her. "I thought I'd never forget.

Woody staggered back to my grandfather's truck, opened the door on the passenger side, sat down, and gasped for breath."

"What about Jared?" Barbara asked.

"Jared looked at me with that innocent expression of his and said, 'You see? It works every time.'"

"Didn't Woody like snakes?" Ashley asked.

"I guess not," said Junior.

Junior had been amazed, astonished at the reaction of this college man. Hardly a monster. He looked like one but acted like *he'd* been *attacked* by a monster.

Barbara read a story to Ashley and settled her in her sleeping bag by the fire, and Junior and Barbara talked about Lockwood and the quiche.

"It's comical, in a way. Big guy like him—it probably won't kill him. But it'll make him sick, for sure." Junior watched Ashley cuddle her black duck, stick her thumb back into her mouth, and close her eyes. "Trouble is," he continued, "I'm a cop, and we gotta go through due process. I've been wishing I could find some way to get to that bastard, and I think I just may have an idea, thanks to Ashley."

As far as getting back at Lockwood as a cop, Junior's hands were tied. Lockwood was probably ready to accuse him of harassment. He would have to "yes, sir" and "no, sir" Lockwood, take his insults and insinuations, when he would like to kick him someplace where it would damage the creep. But now that Elizabeth was safely with his father, he would be able to shake the guy up some other way, and he thought he knew how. He'd like to see what a city-raised bully would do when a real stalker went after him.

For the past couple of days he had been wondering how he could get at the guy and still be within legal bounds. He had thought about immobilizing the Jeep—he could think of several ways of doing that, but what would he accomplish? Anyway, that was hardly legal. He wanted the guy to understand what fear was like, the fear he instilled in Elizabeth. If the Jeep was immobilized, Lockwood would simply get it fixed. He'd be angry, probably, but not frightened. He'd go after the perpetrator in a direct way. No, Junior had decided, that wouldn't work.

He'd thought about leaving something in Lockwood's trailer that would indicate someone had been there, a note of some kind? A bunch of flowers? Deer ticks in his bedding? No, none of those ideas seemed appropriate. Might puzzle the guy but not frighten him.

After tonight, he knew what he could do.

The beauty of his plan, Junior decided, was that he was doing nothing illegal. He would start by laying an old snakeskin in the path between where Lockwood parked his car and the trailer, in a natural-seeming place. No one would see him, and even if they did, no one would care. Even if they cared and stopped him, he wasn't doing anything wrong. Depending on Lockwood's reaction, he would decide what to do next.

He would have no problem finding an old snakeskin. They were all over the place and he'd collected a few of them. The Island didn't have any poisonous snakes, but it had plenty of other kinds. Snakes liked to crawl up on rough sun-warmed rocks not far from his camp, where they could wriggle out of their too-small skins, the stone's roughness holding the old skin, like a hand helping you out of your coat. He kept the perfect skins he found; he liked the iridescence of the scales, the papery thinness of the skin. He let Ashley play with the skins the snakes had discarded.

He looked on top of his bookcase, where he kept treasures like pieces of wampum shell, feathers, and arrowheads. There were also several perfect snakeskins.

Shame to sacrifice them, Junior thought. However, it's a good cause.

The next day he folded one of the skins into an old copy of the *Island Enquirer* and took it with him when he went to work. Rain was still coming down, the third day of the nor'easter. Clouds were thinning, and the sky looked as if it might clear later in the day.

He decided to leave the snakeskin at Lockwood's campsite after he got off work, before Lockwood returned from his stakeout on New Lane. That would be easy enough.

After work, he changed into jeans, plaid shirt, and his boots with the lug soles. That way, no one would report to Lockwood that there'd been a uniformed policeman around his place. He drove up, openly, to Lockwood's campsite, as if he were planning to visit. He stayed only long enough to drop the snakeskin in the path between Lockwood's parking spot and his trailer.

Junior was curious to know how this first small step would go over with Lockwood, so he parked his truck farther along the campground road and walked back along the edge of a small pond behind the campsites until he was between Lockwood's trailer and the pond.

He seated himself on a rock and prepared to wait. The rain had tapered off shortly after noon, and the air was moist and muggy. A mist was rising in tendrils from the surface of the pond. The trees dripped when a breeze went through them. The smell of warm, moist pine perfumed the air around him. He had done enough stakeouts when he was in training that he didn't mind waiting. He had plenty to think about. Barbara and her magic lure, Ashley clutching the black duck decoy in her sleep.

He looked out at the pond, heard chickadees calling, heard

towhees rustling in the soggy leaves, heard an osprey's plain-tive cry. Heard Lockwood's Jeep pull up to its usual spot, ex-actly so. Gads, the guy was methodical. Even the oil drops from his engine lined up in the exact same place on the ground. Junior had noted that when he dropped the snakeskin in the path.

Junior could see Lockwood from where he sat on the stone, could see him start up the path, heard him let out a muffled cry, a gasp, heard him stop. Lockwood turned back down the path, practically leaped the three or four steps to his Jeep, opened the passenger door and got in that side. What the hell was he going to do? Junior wondered. Looks as if the snake plan might just work.

After a full five minutes, Lockwood got out of the Jeep again, a small hatchet in his hand. He crossed the camp road to a thicket, and Junior heard him hack at something. Lock-wood returned with a long branch, walked slowly up the path to the snakeskin. Junior could see him as he picked up the skin on the end of the long branch. He carried it back across the camp road and hurled branch and snakeskin into the shrubbery.

Junior laughed to himself. I've got your number, Lock-wood Wolfrich. You ain't seen nothin' yet.

CASEY AND VICTORIA had taken Elizabeth's clothes, the book she was reading, and the Sunday crossword puzzle she had abandoned, to Ben's place.

"Stay away from home another couple of days, if Ben doesn't mind," Casey said. The sky was beginning to clear. A breeze riffled Victoria's hair and swayed the tall grasses at the side of Ben's yard. Victoria tugged at one of the grass heads and nibbled the sweet end. The sound of the ocean was a gen-tle throb.

After Casey and Victoria left, Ben found two pairs of olive-green waders in the shed behind his house, and he and Elizabeth went down to the shore to gather oysters for their supper.

The sun had come out. Mist curled from the calm surface of the Great Pond. Occasionally Elizabeth could see a fish leap out of the water leaving expanding circles of wavelets, one where it came out of the water, one where it went back in. An osprey circled, its mournful, piping cry floated down to her. She could hear the muted drumming of surf. The surf and the osprey and the splash of fish were the only sounds in the warm afternoon.

After they had gathered enough oysters, Elizabeth took off the heavy waders. She felt light and damp, a newly emerged butterfly. She wanted to run along the shore of the cove with this new lightness, a lightness she hadn't felt for years, spreading her arms like wings.

CHRIST, LOCKWOOD THOUGHT, that snakeskin shook him up more than he would have expected. He didn't think they shed like that, right in a path. He shuddered. This horror of snakes went back so far, he couldn't remember ever accepting them as fellow passengers on Earth. His was a primordial revulsion, a fear he had never been able to conquer.

He had planned to have that quiche for supper, that parishioner's "poisonous quiche," as he called it in his mind, but he'd lost his appetite after the snakeskin incident. It would keep another day in his ice chest. He would go into Oak Bluffs, maybe get a bowl of chowder at Linda Jean's. Maybe walk around some. A bit of exercise would wipe away the incident. It would be good to stroll up and down Circuit Avenue, do some people watching.

His mind slithered onto the snakeskin again. This is irrational, he told himself. He had to work on this phobia. It was like people terrified of flying or of mice. He couldn't understand either fear, but he supposed it was something like what he felt about snakes.

He turned his mind deliberately to Elizabeth. Where could she be? Obviously, she was hiding somewhere, playing games with him. But where? He had cruised past the houses of her childhood friends and found no sign of her.

Cousin Edna might know. He would call her from the pay phone at the campground before he drove into Oak Bluffs.

"Lockwood!" she said, sounding pleased. "It's always nice to hear from you, darling."

"If you're not busy, I'd like to stop by and see you." Lockwood made a wry face into the mouthpiece of the pay phone.

Cousin Edna made a sympathetic clucking sound. "Do come to call, darling, I have some lovely sherry," she said. "I believe Victoria is out riding with the police chief, or I'd invite her, too. This afternoon, dear boy?"

It hadn't occurred to Lockwood that Cousin Edna might invite Victoria. After the police encounter of two days ago, he did not want to be in the same house with Victoria, at least not yet.

"What a shame." Lockwood tried to keep the relief out of his voice. "This afternoon, then, around five."

He hadn't wanted to talk about Elizabeth over the phone; he wasn't sure how much Victoria and the bitch had poisoned Cousin Edna's mind against him. He wanted to see her face, so he could adjust his conversation accordingly.

Before he went to Cousin Edna's he had some errands he needed to do. He would get some groceries in Oak Bluffs, watch Victoria's house for a half hour or so—where in hell could Elizabeth have gone?—then go to Cousin Edna's. He ought to take her something. A box of Chilmark Chocolates. She'd like that. He could picture her picking out a plump chocolate and popping it into her mouth. Cousin Edna might be useful. He would put up with her company in exchange for her gossip.

NINETEEN

WHEN LOCKWOOD PULLED INTO Cousin Edna's drive, a white van was parked by the rhododendron bushes. He could see the right side, black letters highlighted with gold leaf, MEALS ON WHEELS, and, underneath, FOOD FIT FOR AN ANGEL. The print glittered in the afternoon sun. Below the print and off to one side was a stripe of mismatched paint about two feet long and a foot wide.

Cousin Edna had told him about Victoria's run-in with the driver and Lockwood had laughed. Victoria had a lot of guts, he thought. Why shouldn't other people watch out for her driving? That female cop and Elizabeth, in a tizzy over a mere fender-bender. Probably overexcited by hormones.

He stifled his familiar irritation, squashed the feeling into its mental compartment, and snapped a lid on it. Too bad Victoria had to lose her license over a two-by-one-foot scratch. He looked closer and emended "scratch" to "gouge." Still, anyone could have done that. You had to admire the way Victoria refused to give in to some stereotypical old-age slow-driving behavior.

Cousin Edna was dressed in a rose-colored sweater that matched her lipstick and accented her large bosom. A cardigan, the same rose color, was slung over her shoulders. She wore a pleated gray skirt and low-heeled black shoes with bows in front.

"Lockwood, darling!" she said, embracing him. Lockwood stiffened at her touch and held his breath to keep from taking in any more Chanel No. 5. "So good to see you. Come in!" She looked up at him. "You've grown a beard. How distinguished!"

Lockwood bared his teeth in a smile and followed Cousin Edna into her living room. A pale young man rose from the easy chair next to the picture window that looked over the grassy lawn. The man had a pale mustache and pale hair the color of hay. The stranger clasped his hands in front of him protectively.

"I don't believe you know Mandred Smith, do you, Lockwood? He works at the hospital's nursing home, and he drives the Meals on Wheels van."

Lockwood extended his hand. "Nice vehicle."

"It was, once." Manny looked up at Lockwood. "You're a big son of a gun. How's the air up there?"

"Rare." Lockwood gritted his teeth. He never had a riposte ready at the right time. Later he would come up with a half-dozen put-downs. He looked down on Manny's head, could see pink freckled scalp showing through his thin hair. He told himself to forget it and shook Manny's hand.

"Mandred's father was Brewster Harrington-Smith," Cousin Edna said, fluttering her hands from one to the other of the two men. "He died a little over a week ago, wasn't it, Mandred?"

"Something like that." Manny unclasped and reclasped his hands. He looked down at his blue-and-white Nikes.

"My condolences," Lockwood said civilly. "Must be a difficult time for you." Now that Manny had tilted his head, Lockwood could see a large mole between tufts of hair.

"It was a blessing, really. I don't know whether you knew my father or not." Lockwood grunted. "He had Alzheimer's," Manny continued. "He wandered off into the woods."

"So I understand," Lockwood said.

An uncomfortable silence followed. Lockwood couldn't think of anything to say. Cousin Edna had bustled into the kitchen, and Lockwood could hear water running, the clink of glasses. He and Manny sat in silence until Cousin Edna returned with a silver tray, glasses, and a sherry decanter.

Lockwood got quickly to his feet. "Let me help you. I'll pour, if you'd like."

"Lovely, darling." Cousin Edna relinquished the tray to Lockwood and sat in a rocker between the two men. "Mandred often stops by on his way to work, don't you, Mandred?" Cousin Edna straightened the pleats of her gray skirt over her knees and looked down coyly. Lockwood passed the tray to her and to Manny, set it on the table beside Cousin Edna, and sat down again.

"Cousin Edna said you work at the hospital."

"I work at the nursing home. I'm the chef." Manny held his glass up to the light. "Very fine, Mrs. Coffin. Amontillado."

Cousin Edna simpered. "It's lovely to have such appreciative, handsome young men visit. My friends will be simply green!"

Manny's expression made Lockwood feel, for the first time, that there might be something behind that pale facade. He grinned conspiratorially at Manny over Cousin Edna's blue coiffure, but Manny looked back at him stonily.

"Do you like your work?" Lockwood asked.

"Very much."

"Manfred also works with Meals on Wheels," said Cousin Edna.

"Many of the elderly have no family, and nothing to look forward to," said Manny. "I bring them some pleasure with my meals."

"You certainly do," Cousin Edna said. "'Food Fit for an Angel.' How appropriate. I know so many people who look forward to your noon visits." She sipped her sherry. "You drive the van as a volunteer, don't you, Manfred?"

"Yes. The Reverend Jackson thought it would give me a chance to circulate. And it has. My clients have become my friends."

"They are fortunate to have you," Cousin Edna said. "Jeremiah Silvia was one of your clients, wasn't he?" She rocked gently.

"Yes. I was at the hospital when he was admitted." Manny gazed at Cousin Edna. She shifted her feet so both were flat on the floor. "The doctors found nothing wrong with him, discharged him the next day. That afternoon he was dead." Manny had become almost animated, Lockwood noted. Maybe not animated, but at least his face showed some life. "You'd think the doctors would be more careful in their diagnoses. Obviously, something was not right."

Lockwood thought about Cousin Edna's dead seagull and felt a laugh welling up. He quickly covered it with a cough. Murder, he thought. Murder! He reached into his pocket for his red bandanna handkerchief and held it over his mouth. He put his half-finished drink on the floor, took off his glasses, and dabbed his eyes.

"Are you all right, Lockwood?" Cousin Edna started out of her chair.

"No, no, please." Lockwood held his hand to indicate she needn't get up. He laughed harder and covered his face with his bandanna. "Swallowed something the wrong way," he sputtered.

Manny stared at Lockwood over the rim of his glass, set the glass back on the tray, and stood. "Thank you, Mrs. Coffin." He bowed slightly. "I've got to finish my deliveries. Don't get up."

"Lovely man," Cousin Edna said after Manny had left.

"Does he deliver meals to Victoria?" Lockwood asked.

"I don't believe so. Why?"

"I happened to go past Victoria's house the other day," Lockwood said, not caring to go into details about his stake-out, "and saw his van in the drive." He put his handkerchief back in his pocket. He speculated on how much he could learn from Cousin Edna without telling her any more than necessary. "It's not the first time I've seen his van there. Per-haps he delivers meals when Elizabeth is away?"

"I didn't know she was away." Cousin Edna rocked gently.

"I'm not sure she is. Her car is there." Lockwood wondered if he would be giving away more than he would learn but de-cided to barge ahead. "I haven't seen her around for a few days."

Cousin Edna looked appraisingly at him, and he was afraid he had gone too far. Despite appearances, she was not stupid, he told himself. She stopped rocking and looked at Lockwood. "I'll have to talk to Victoria."

"Don't tell her I said anything," Lockwood said hastily. He had a queasy feeling, as if he were in a funhouse hall of mir-rors that reflected and distorted everything endlessly. Cousin Edna did that to him, and he could feel the lid lift slightly on his pent-up irritation. "As you can imagine, things are still awkward."

"Of course, I understand totally." Cousin Edna rocked again.

Oh, but she doesn't, Lockwood thought to himself. She doesn't know the half of it.

On the way back to his campsite, he realized he was hun-gry and thought about the Parishioner's Poisonous Quiche. His appetite had returned, and he looked forward to eating the

quiche with a cold bottle of beer. He'd light a campfire in front
of his tent trailer, sit back in one of his folding chairs, and relax, watch the light fade over the pond, the Canada geese settle for the night, hear the night noises come up, the crickets
and cicadas. Maybe he would heat the quiche in a pan next
to the fire. The thought of it made his mouth water.

Decent of the minister to approach him, invite him to
church. Little did the Reverend Jackson know how familiar
he was with that church from all the years he had been here
with the bitch. Fat chance he would show up at church service. Still, it was decent of Jackson to bring him the quiche.
What was with that kid who was playing policeman? What a
stupid fool thing to do, tell him something was wrong with
the quiche. He would file a police harassment report with
whatever authority oversaw him, for sure.

As he eased into the parking space at his campsite, he
lined up the rearview mirror with the stunted oak, and moved
forward until the left fender just touched the bayberry bush.
As he pulled on the brake and turned off the ignition, he
thought again about his visit with Cousin Edna and Manny.

Meals on Wheels, indeed, he thought. Maybe he could
convince Victoria that was the perfect cover for a mass-mur-
derer. How ironic. He got out of the Jeep, laughing out loud.
He wiped tears from under his glasses with his red bandanna. He started up the now familiar path and was about
to step up into his tent trailer when he saw it. He had almost
put his foot on it. Another snakeskin. It glistened on the step
of his trailer. Twinkled with iridescent rainbows as if it still
clothed a living snake. He shrieked. He jumped at the sight
of the snakeskin, winding up in a thorny wild rose. Edging
away from the rosebush he moved toward his Jeep and
backed into the passenger seat, his breathing coming in air-

less gasps. He hoped no one had heard him yell. He tried to think rationally, but his mind kept slipping. Why the hell would two snakes shed their skins right there? He had to get rid of the skin. He couldn't bear the thought of going near that ghastly thing. Were there dozens of snakes around, and he just happened upon two of them? Was this the time of year they shed skins? Were they litter mates or whatever snakes are, he wondered, born around here, and returning to shed skins at the same time? Lockwood considered moving out of the campground. Then he told himself that two snakes were no more than an unfortunate coincidence. He reminded himself that there were no poisonous snakes on Martha's Vineyard. He told himself that snakes were not slimy. He said to himself that snakes formed an important part of the food chain.

He began to shudder. He had to get hold of himself, get that thing off his step before it got to him worse than it already had. He wondered if snakes smelled fear and played on it, like dogs.

He took his hatchet out of his tool kit in the Jeep, crossed the road, cut a six-foot-long sapling, and went back to the skin. He told himself not to think about it. But he was shivering so violently he had to make a couple of thrusts with the end of the sapling before he could lift up the snakeskin, carry it across the camp road, and hurl sapling and skin into the brush. He had a sudden reassuring thought. Maybe a skunk or raccoon had retrieved the skin that he'd thrown into the undergrowth the night before. Maybe it was one skin, the same one.

So much for his evening campfire plans. The quiche would keep until breakfast. By then he'd have recovered, things would be in better perspective. He would go to Linda Jean's in Oak Bluffs for supper. Maybe he would even strike up a conversation with someone, a touch of reality.

He got into his Jeep, backed out of his parking spot, and went out through the camp road.

He turned right onto Barnes Road. As he drove into Oak Bluffs, he passed the upper end of Lagoon Pond on his left. He saw a green-and-black-hulled sailboat riding peacefully at its mooring, the hull and masts doubled by their reflection in the still waters of Lagoon Pond. The scene looked idyllic.

He thought again how this was his home, too. Why should he have to camp out in a nest of snakes while that bitch was living in luxury. Maybe not luxury, exactly, but living the way he had planned to live with her in his declining years. He thought again about the snakeskins. Was it possible that someone who knew of his phobia over snakes was setting him up?

Elizabeth? This wasn't how she would behave. She would be direct, not play on a phobia. She would never pull this kind of trick. The more he thought, the more it seemed possible that a person was doing this. But who? Thinking that someone might be watching gave him an eerie feeling. But maybe it was a simple coincidence. Two snakes shedding their skins in the same place.

By the next morning, Lockwood was convinced that what he'd experienced had been a natural phenomenon. The morning was bright. He started a small campfire, decided to have bacon and eggs, rather than the quiche. It would keep, he thought, at least another day. His mission was to figure out where Elizabeth was keeping herself. He would take his place by the side of New Lane again and wait. Eventually, something was bound to happen.

"THE GUY MUST BE a Rasputin," Junior said to Casey. "If he ate that quiche, he must have the constitution of—I don't know what. He refused to give it up, laughed when I said we believed something was wrong with the food. I didn't go into detail." Junior shifted a pile of papers from the In box on the corner of his desk to the empty space he had cleared in front of him.

"I hope he hasn't eaten it yet," Casey said. "Josh went to the courthouse this morning to get the order for Wolfrich to give up the quiche, but he hasn't come back yet. If anything happens to Wolfrich…"

"By now, I should think it would be spoiled. It's made with eggs and cream." Junior toyed with the pencils on his desk. "Probably smell bad, so if he hasn't eaten it yet, he probably won't. He must have an ice chest for refrigeration. Not real effective."

Casey had turned from her computer screen to listen to Junior.

"If he ate a couple of pieces," Junior mused, "at the very least, he would be violently sick, according to Jessica. Sick enough to make him head for the emergency room. Might not kill him, but there's a fifty-fifty chance it would."

"Wolfrich wasn't there when Elmer went by his campsite to reason with him. Yet there he is, parked in the same old spot on the lane as though nothing happened." Casey turned back to her computer. "I hope Josh gets back soon." She pecked at a couple of keys. "I hope the guy has thrown out that quiche. But if he hasn't, we've got to get it."

Junior put both hands on top of the stack of papers in front of him, then began to sort the papers into smaller piles on his desk and the table behind him. "Damn this paperwork."

"I'm telling Elizabeth to stay at Ben's until we get Lockwood out of the way. Victoria is okay. She's got those two guys mothering her, Winthrop and Angelo, although she doesn't exactly need mothering." She typed several words, moved her mouse, clicked, and her screen changed.

Junior laughed. "You're not matchmaking, are you, Chief? My dad is old enough to be Elizabeth's father."

"This is serious." Casey worked the screen symbols with her mouse, her back to Junior. "Nothing funny about it." She looked at her watch. "Almost noon," she said. "See you tomorrow."

This was a short day for Junior. He changed into his flannel shirt, his jeans, and his hiking boots at the police station.

"Got great plans for this afternoon?" Casey asked when he reappeared in his civvies.

"Oh yes." Junior grinned.

"Looks as if you and your surf-casting friend and her daughter might be having a picnic, right?" Casey indicated the covered basket Junior had brought into the station house that morning. "Great day for it. Bring me a fish, will you? I love bluefish."

"Hmmm." Junior eyed the basket with an amused look.

He backed his truck out of the small parking area in front of the police station, turned right toward New Lane, the direction of his father's house. He passed Lockwood and lifted the fingers of his left hand, as usual, in a kind of greeting. Lockwood did the same and bared his teeth.

Junior went only as far as the bend in the road, where Lockwood could no longer see the truck. He parked in a grove of oak trees, well hidden, even if Lockwood should decide to drive this way. He left the key in the ignition, lifted the basket off the seat next to him, and shut both doors without locking them. Casey would be bullshit, he thought. She wants everything locked up tight. Even Lockwood didn't lock his car. Junior walked back along the lane, but before he came within sight of Lockwood's Jeep, he doubled back onto Victoria's land, behind the viburnum and wild cherry and euonymus, until he could see the vehicle. He wriggled under the shrubbery, the basket against his chest, and lay down where he could keep an eye on Lockwood.

He heard the mournful cry of a hawk, hunting. Crickets chirped in the dry grasses. Something small rustled, a field mouse, probably. The autumn breeze drifted over him, bringing the scent of newly washed grasses and autumn leaves, the pungent smell of wild cherry, the whisper of tall moving grasses, the lulling murmur of surf on the south shore. Junior could see blue sky above, see the grasses in the meadow next to him undulate as the breeze passed over the fluffy seed stalks. Not a bad place for a stakeout, he thought.

He didn't have to wait long.

Lockwood got out of the driver's side of the Jeep, stretched, yawned, shut the door. He swung his arms from side to side in a kind of loosening-up exercise and walked past Junior's hideout without seeing him, down a road Junior knew led to a sheltered place where Lockwood could take a leak without being seen.

Junior held the basket close to him and ran quietly to the passenger side of the Jeep, glanced to make sure there was no sign of Lockwood, opened the door, no noise, and placed the basket on the passenger seat, smoothing the red-checked Black Dog napkin over the basket. He shut the door quietly, held the handle until the door was lined up, then let it go with a faint click that latched the door. He could see Lockwood coming out of the side road, zipping his fly. Junior dropped down to all fours and slithered under the shrubbery ahead of the Jeep. He couldn't chance going back where he'd been. Lockwood would pass right next to him and he would not have time to settle down. He slid on his stomach under the wild cherry. He noticed he was squirming through a patch of lush poison ivy. If this works, he figured, it was worth a week of running, itching pustules.

Lockwood walked down the middle of the lane to his Jeep. Junior could see him from the new hiding place. Christ, the guy was whistling "Dixie," of all things, moving easily despite his weight. He was an imposing figure with that great height. The noonday sun glinted off his glasses. He was hatless and the breeze ruffled his shaggy hair, his beard. He had both hands in the pockets of his jeans. He was wearing a long-sleeved white shirt, with the sleeves rolled up. The breeze lifted his collar. He whistled. Junior watched.

Lockwood was next to the Jeep. He looked both ways, up and down the lane, opened the door and got in, first sitting on the seat, then swinging his legs in. He shut the door. While Junior watched, he wished he wasn't so sensitive to poison ivy. Maybe he could clean up in time once he got home. A dip in sea water should neutralize the stuff. He watched the Jeep.

He heard Lockwood say, out loud, "Well, now, what's this?" And he heard Lockwood say, out loud, "Another poison dish from the minister," and Lockwood laughed, a mellow, happy laugh, which ended in the most horrendous scream Junior had ever heard.

The Jeep door burst open. Lockwood slammed it shut and tore across the lane without looking. He leaped over the four-foot shrubbery on the other side of the road as if he were competing in a track meet. He tore across Doane's pasture as if every fiend in hell was after him, which he probably thought was exactly the case. Junior stood up. No need to hide any longer. Lockwood was a disappearing image. Where the hell is he going? Junior wondered.

He opened the passenger door and picked up the basket.

Lockwood had taken off the red-checked napkin. Below it was a plastic container from Cronig's salad bar, and in the container, nicely held in by its closed lid, were a dozen baby garter snakes, five inches long at least, writhing and wriggling in an entirely snakelike manner. Junior grinned. He took the basket of snakes, closed the passenger side door, carried the basket to the poison ivy patch where he'd lain, lifted the lid of the plastic container, and released the snakes, who wriggled and sidled and uncoiled in their entirely snakelike manner and disappeared under the poison ivy.

"Thanks, fellas," said Junior. "And girls."

"WHAT'N HELL IS his trouble?" Joe said to Lincoln, who was leaning on the driver's side window of Joe's truck. Taffy was in back, tongue out, ears up, tail wagging, grinning at Lincoln, who ruffled her silky blond ears.

"Who knows. You never can tell with these off-Islanders."

"Who's he calling?" Joe nodded to the public phone on the outside wall of Alley's. "Christ, he looks as if hell and damnation is after him."

"A cab." Lincoln looked at the obviously distraught man. "He's ordering a cab from Dietrich's."

"That the one with the worms?"

"They got a fumigator," Lincoln said.

"Won't hurt to see what it's all about, I guess."

Lincoln moved aside so Joe could get out of his truck. They looked both ways and waited for the ComElectric truck to pass. The driver waved.

"Who's that?" asked Lincoln.

"How'm I supposed to know?"

Sarah was sitting on the bench with her usual smug look, her head cocked to one side.

"Yeah, yeah, Sarah. What's up?" Joe stood in front of her.

"Shhh!" said Sarah. "I'm listening."

"Nothing more to hear. He called Dietrich's," said Joe.

Lincoln had one foot on the porch step, and nodded to the side of the store. "He's gone around back and he's muttering to himself."

Just then Donald arrived from the parking lot. "Who's the big guy?" He jerked his thumb toward Lockwood, who was around the corner.

"He's the one who's been sittin' in the Jeep on New Lane," said Joe.

"What's his trouble?" Donald sat down heavily next to Sarah.

"Who knows?" said Lincoln.

"Shhh!" Sarah held her index finger to her lips.

They could hear the big guy mumbling something to himself. His incoherent words ran on and on, rising and falling.

"'Ass'?" Joe said, puzzled.

"Not 'ass,'" said Sarah. "'Asp.'"

They could make out "moccasin," in the gibberish, "Rattlers."

They looked at one another and shrugged. A black van marked DIETRICH'S pulled up, and the guy practically leaped into it. They heard him say, louder than he needed to, "Steamship Authority! Quick!" and the cab pulled away.

"Not the fastest way I'd choose to make a quick getaway," Joe said. "The Steamship Authority?"

TWENTY

COUSIN EDNA COULD scarcely wait until Lockwood left before she dialed Victoria. Was Victoria actually getting Meals on Wheels and not telling her? Was Elizabeth away? Had the two of them had an argument and Elizabeth left home? Cousin Edna could smell juicy gossip, ripe and waiting to be plucked.

However, Victoria didn't answer the phone, and a full day passed before Cousin Edna finally got through. In the meantime, fantastic theories bubbled and brewed in her mind to explain the facts she had gleaned from Lockwood.

The following day Victoria finally answered.

"I haven't spoken to you for a while, Victoria," Cousin Edna said, trying with difficulty to hold back her eagerness. "I wanted to remind you that the Kippers' meeting is at my house this time. Come early, so I can show you where you'll be seated as speaker, and you can test your voice to see if it carries properly."

"I know how to project my voice."

"How is Elizabeth?" Cousin Edna sidled into the subject she wanted to discuss. "I haven't seen her or you for some time."

"Fine, she's absolutely fine, busy, productive, creative." Victoria's voice was bland.

"Is she there right now?" Edna said. "I'd love to say hello to her."

"Not right now, but I'll tell her you called."

"And my dear," Edna said quickly, before Victoria could hang up the phone. "What's this about your getting Meals on Wheels these days? I had no idea."

"Meals on Wheels?" Victoria asked blankly.

"Yes. Someone I know saw the van there the other day."

"I'm not getting Meals on Wheels." Victoria thought of the plastic container of cream of mushroom soup that had been left on her kitchen table. She and Casey had taken the soup to Jessica. Amanitas.

"Are you sure your memory isn't slipping, my dear? At our age…"

"For heaven's sake, Edna. What is your trouble?"

"This wasn't the first time my informant saw the Meals on Wheels van deliver food to your house. It's nothing to be ashamed of, Victoria. If I didn't enjoy cooking so much myself, I'd sign up for the service, too. Manny is a wonderful chef. In fact, he'll be catering refreshments for the Kippers' meeting."

"What *are* you talking about?" But Victoria was beginning to get an idea.

JUNIOR NORTON had discovered the joy of bragging to someone who understood him.

Ashley was tucked into her sleeping bag, her small arms wrapped around Donald, the black duck. The fire was burning well for a change. The wind was from the southwest, which meant fine weather for the next several days and also meant the right kind of draft in the old chimney.

Junior and Barbara sat on the battered couch in front of the fire, holding hands, sipping red wine Barbara had bought in Oak Bluffs.

She snuggled against him and sighed. "I hope you got the poison ivy washed off in time. Has anyone heard from Lockwood?"

"Casey contacted him in Virginia, asked him what he wanted to do about the Jeep." Junior's left arm tightened around Barbara's shoulders. He put his wineglass on the table next to the couch and scratched his neck with his right hand. "He told Casey he'd sign a release for her to sell the Jeep. He didn't want it, apparently. Said he would pay whatever charges or fines there were. He was quite civil about the whole thing."

"What about his tent trailer at the campground?" Barbara put her hand on Junior's thigh. "Did he simply leave it there?"

"I checked with the campground," Junior said, distracted by Barbara's hand. "Lockwood called them, said he would be back one of these days, said he'd pay whatever storage bills accrued for keeping the trailer there, said he was putting a check in the mail."

Ashley made a soft, contented sound in her sleep. The fire hummed. The lamps flickered. The surf drummed. Junior lifted his sweater and scratched his chest.

WHEN BEN PULLED INTO Victoria's drive, she was standing on the steps waiting. Elizabeth embraced her as if she hadn't seen her grandmother for weeks, although Victoria and Casey had stopped at Ben's every day.

Ben carried Elizabeth's belongings into the house. "I'll leave you for now." He put an arm around her shoulders. "See you soon." He got back into his pickup truck, drove around the circle, and waved. They watched his truck turn onto New Lane, where it was hidden, briefly, by undergrowth, then saw it again through an opening in the shrubbery.

Victoria and Elizabeth went into the house, arm in arm. Victoria had made fresh coffee, and the two sat in the cookroom, catching up on news. Victoria's typewriter was on the table, an almost-full page of writing flopping over the top of the machine.

"So Lockwood's really, really gone?" Elizabeth lifted the chipped blue mug to her mouth. "I can really relax?"

"Apparently." Victoria sipped from her yellow mug.

McCavity appeared from some hideaway in the main house and looked up at Victoria, who patted her lap in invitation. He crouched and sprang into Elizabeth's lap instead and curled around to face Victoria.

"How's this week's column coming?" Elizabeth asked, stroking the cat.

"I had lots of news. I said you were back from a visit with a friend on the Great Pond," Victoria said.

"That's only two miles away," Elizabeth said. "Not exactly news."

"People are interested in what our family does." Victoria moved the notes for her column to one side.

"Here's some news." Elizabeth stroked McCavity. The tip of his tail twitched as her hand moved down his back. "Ben has asked me to go with him to the Corkscrew Swamp in Florida to bird-watch." Elizabeth watched her grandmother's face as the wrinkles formed disappointment, then immediately reformed into delight for Elizabeth's sake.

"When are you going?" Victoria said brightly. "I hope not right away." She moved her chair closer to the table. "When do you plan to leave?" She shifted the notes that were spread out in front of her. "That will be a nice break for you," she said.

Elizabeth laughed. "I'm not playing fair, Gram," she said. "There's nothing between Ben and me. He's invited both of us, you and me." She watched the transformation of her grandmother's expression into one of pure joy.

"When do we leave?" Victoria asked.

"Not right away. Ben suggested early February." She took the two coffee mugs into the kitchen and washed them. "I found something before I ran off to Ben's," she said over her shoulder. "Before Lockwood showed up, when I was putting the books away, I came across a letter that had never been opened, addressed to your grandfather. I'll get it."

She returned a few moments later from the library with the thin envelope. Victoria took an ivory letter opener out of a cup on the windowsill and gave it to her.

"Don't you want to open it?" Elizabeth asked.

"No, you do it."

Elizabeth worked the blade of the letter opener under the flap so she wouldn't have to slit the envelope. The flap separated easily. Inside was another sealed envelope, this one addressed to Victoria's mother in handwriting Elizabeth didn't recognize. She held it out to Victoria, who turned over the envelope.

"I don't recognize the handwriting, either."

Inside was a letter, written on both sides of the paper. The writing bled through so it was difficult to read. Elizabeth turned over the page. It was signed, "William Barrett."

"My great-grandfather," Elizabeth said, gazing at the signature. "Your father. A real letter from your own father. How about that!"

"Go ahead and read it." Victoria moved her chair closer to Elizabeth's so she could read the letter with her.

"It starts out, 'My dearest wife.' That must be your mother? My great-grandmother. You were only three when it was written." She turned her head to look at Victoria. "You said in your autobiography you remembered him from then, didn't you?" Elizabeth held the letter closer to her grandmother, who nodded.

"It says, 'I write this letter with great pain, both physical and mental.'" Elizabeth looked at her grandmother, whose head was down, reading ahead. "'I addressed this to your father because I don't have the courage to face you or to think of you reading it alone. I pray he will be with you when you read this.' She never got the letter," Elizabeth said. "How sad."

"Go on," Victoria said, leaning forward.

"'I do not know how much you suspect, my dearest. On my last trip to the Orient I found I was becoming easily fatigued. I saw a Japanese physician. He found a cancer. My body is hopelessly riddled with the disease. He told me I have only a short time to live, a few months at most. He gave me a supply of opiates. With the short time I have left, the opiates will keep the pain at bay. I want to say good-bye to you, my dearest. I do not want to waste away in front of you, nor do I want to be a burden to you. I want you to remember the virile husband you married. I sense, in my drugged state, I have behaved in an unconscionable manner. I can only tell you how horrified I am at my own actions.

"'I leave for San Francisco tomorrow, as you know. I shall not return. I intend to end my life with the opiates the physician advised me to use when the time came.

"'I do not want you and our daughters to live in indecision about my fate. It is for the best.

"'In order to ensure you do not suffer financially, I enclose my will, made out to your benefit, and notarized.'"

Victoria reached for the envelope and drew out a second piece of thin paper. "Go on," she said, softly, turning the second paper over and over in her hands.

"'I have loved you more with each passing year. I trust you will understand and remember me kindly as I once was.'"

"Wow," Elizabeth said, and put the letter on the table. Victoria sat back in her chair and stared out the window.

"Did you have any idea? Did your mother know he intended to commit suicide?"

"No," Victoria said softly. "How sad. My poor, poor mother, Things might have been so different."

"*That* is hard to take," Elizabeth said.

Victoria went on as if Elizabeth had not spoken. "My father's behavior, according to my sisters, had changed remarkably from the time he returned from Japan until he left again. He had become surly, violent, nasty, quite unlike himself, according to them." Victoria stopped.

"The effect of the drugs, probably," Elizabeth said.

"My sisters remembered our father well. I didn't," Victoria went on. "He had become so ugly that when he disappeared, there were rumors in town that my mother had killed him."

"My God!" Elizabeth put her hand on her throat.

"The rumor was that she poisoned him," Victoria said. "She had told everyone he'd gone to San Francisco. No one believed her."

"This letter would have vindicated her. It's awful enough, but not as bad as what she went through." Elizabeth moved her chair closer to her grandmother.

Victoria continued. "She had no money. No one knew whether Father was alive or murdered or what." Victoria paused and moved the papers on the table absently, without looking at them. "We had no evidence that he had died, no will. She couldn't use his money."

"How awful."

"My mother tried to earn a living as a governess. No one would hire her. She tried to run a boardinghouse. No one would come." Victoria's face was pained. "Finally, in desperation, she left me with my grandparents here in this house and went to New York to start a new life. This letter would have made all the difference in the world."

"Why do you suppose your grandfather never opened the letter?"

"Probably because it was addressed to him, and he was upset with my father for his behavior in the months before he disappeared." Elizabeth could feel the sag in her grandmother's shoulders. "He wanted to have nothing to do with his son-in-law. He probably put the letter aside to open at some later time when he wasn't quite so angry, and then forgot it."

"Your grandparents never talked to you about your father?"

"Never." Victoria refocused on her granddaughter. "His name was never mentioned in my presence."

THE DAY AFTER Victoria had read the letter, Casey stopped by to see how Victoria's paper on law enforcement was coming along.

"Elizabeth can't take me to the hospital to read to the elderly today, Casey. Can you?"

"Sure, Victoria. I need to go to Oak Bluffs anyway. I have to pick up some papers at the town hall." Casey looked at her watch. "Eleven-thirty okay? That gives you about an hour."

"I'll be ready," Victoria said.

When Casey pulled up in the Bronco, Victoria was waiting with her string bag of books in one hand, her pocketbook in the other. She climbed up into her usual seat.

Casey turned toward Edgartown, the back way into Oak Bluffs and the hospital.

"You're kind of quiet today," Casey said. "Is anything the matter?"

Victoria shook her head.

The southwest wind brought the smells of autumn through

the open Bronco windows, of earth fullness, of ripening acorns, drying crops, of wild grapes on the tangled vines along the road.

"Are those grapes good for anything?" Casey asked as they passed a section where vines twined among the shrubs and they could see clusters of grapes, ripe and dusky purple.

"Next time you have a day off, you and Patrick and Elizabeth and I can gather some and make jelly."

"I've never done that. Might be fun for Zorba."

"'Zorba'?" Victoria looked questioningly at Casey.

"That's what Patrick now calls himself, 'Zorba.' He and Angelo play ectoplasmic sci-fi games on my computer. Angelo is 'Xerxes.' He's ended up being a good friend to both of us."

The back way took them past the airport and the campground, where Lockwood's tent-trailer was still set up. They turned in at the hospital's emergency entrance. The surgeon's bright yellow Jeep truck stood out in the crowded hospital lot.

"Pick you up in about an hour?" Casey stopped at the entrance and set the brake.

"I'll wait for you by the front door. On the bench," Victoria said. "You don't need to hurry, I've got my crossword puzzle book." She unfastened her seat belt.

"Don't get out just yet. I've got to pull up a little, let Manny get by with his van."

The van parked beside them. Manny opened the driver's side door and stepped out. The sun sparkled on the identification on the van, MEALS ON WHEELS: FOOD FIT FOR AN ANGEL.

"You can get out now, Victoria."

Victoria remained in her seat, staring from Manny to the sign on the van. She held the buckle of the seat belt in her hand.

Manny nodded to Casey, scowled at Victoria, and went

around to the back of the van. He twisted the silver handle that opened the back door and reached into the van.

"Victoria?" Casey said.

Victoria watched Manny as he slid a large tray of food containers out of the back of the van.

"Victoria!" Casey said. "What's the matter?"

Manny turned at the sound of the police chief's voice, shoved the trays of food back into the van, and slammed the rear door shut. He ran around to the driver's side and leaped in. He swung the van around in a wide arc, shifted into reverse, backed up, slammed into the passenger side of the police Bronco, and sped off through the parking lot into the road and out of sight.

"Go after him!" Victoria shouted.

"Lord, Victoria. Are you hurt?"

"Of course not. Go after him."

"He did some serious damage to the vehicle, Victoria. I'll radio Oak Bluffs, have them pick him up."

Victoria tried to open her side door and couldn't budge it. The entire panel was mashed in. Bent metal touched her seat.

Casey radioed Oak Bluffs. "The white Meals on Wheels van. Can't miss it."

She hustled out of the Bronco and around to Victoria's side to inspect the damage.

"Lord!" she said again.

"What does it look like?" Victoria asked.

"The right fender is against the wheel. I won't be able to drive."

"Your nice clean car," Victoria said.

"I'm not worried about the car, it's you. I'm getting them to bring out a wheelchair, check you out, Victoria. He might have hurt you."

"Absolutely not. I don't need a wheelchair."

"Get out my side. Your door is wiped out. If that creep had been going any faster…" Casey's hands were in fists by her side.

Victoria gathered up her coat under her, slid across the gearshift, under the radio wires that hung below the dashboard, under the steering wheel. She swiveled around so she would land on her feet, held on to the sides of the Bronco, slid off the seat, and collapsed in Casey's arms.

"This is ridiculous," Victoria said as the orderly helped her into a wheelchair. "It's no more than a twisted ankle. A couple of aspirins and I'll be fine."

Two hours later, after Victoria's ankle was X-rayed and bandaged, Casey returned in the police department's old Crown Victoria.

"It's not broken," Victoria said. "Just sprained."

"Thank goodness." Casey pushed the wheelchair to the police vehicle and helped Victoria into the passenger seat. "That bastard," she muttered. "The Oak Bluffs cops stopped him at the blinker. He's in big trouble."

Victoria's lips formed a wicked smile. "Are you going to take his license away?"

TWENTY-ONE

"ALMOST READY, VICTORIA?" Casey had come to pick up Victoria for the Kippers' meeting. "You look great. The ladies will be impressed."

Casey was wearing her full uniform, freshly pressed, navy wool blouse with emblems and patches, wool trousers with a wide, pale blue stripe, shiny black boots.

Victoria smoothed the skirt of her new dark green suit and patted the bow of her new white blouse. Spread out in front of her on the cookroom table was a heap of papers, some typewritten, some scribbled over with her backhand writing. She put the papers in a manila folder, thumped the edge of it on the table to straighten out the contents, and put it next to her pocketbook.

"Which earrings do you think I should wear?" She held out two sets for Casey's inspection.

Casey examined them with great seriousness. "The black ones. They'll match the trim on your suit."

Victoria limped into the bathroom off the cookroom to look in the mirror. She left the door open so she could confer with Casey. She clipped on the earrings and turned her head first one way then the other, looking at her reflection. Casey watched with admiration.

"Lipstick." Victoria reached into the cabinet over the washing machine, where she kept her rarely used cosmetics, and rummaged around until she found a lipstick that pleased her, smoothed it on, pressed her lips together.

Casey was holding a square white box, about the size of a shoe box, tied with blue ribbon. "I have something for you, but I'll wait until we get to Mrs. Coffin's to give it to you."

Elizabeth came in from the garden carrying a sprig of white clematis that she pinned to her grandmother's suit jacket. She kissed Victoria on both cheeks. "Break a leg!"

"I tried."

Ben Norton showed up and held his arm out for Victoria, who took it and limped slowly down the stone steps. Casey carried the folder of papers. Victoria had to hike up her tight new skirt to get up into her seat in the Bronco.

"Great legs for a fifty-year-old, Victoria." Ben winked at her. "See you in a bit."

Casey drove past the bayberry bushes and forsythia, now turned a mellow dark red, between the two stone posts that used to support a gate in the days of horses.

"Are you nervous, Victoria?" Casey noted the look of pleasure on the wrinkled face.

"No. I've rehearsed my talk pretty well."

Casey turned into Edna's driveway. "Looks as if we're the first ones here."

She opened the passenger door, replaced since Manny had backed into it.

"What's going to happen to Manny?" Victoria asked.

"He's got a court hearing next week. You won't need to go to that—unless you want to, of course."

Victoria smiled and slid out of her seat. The two walked slowly to Cousin Edna's door so Victoria could favor her ankle.

Edna greeted them, dressed in billowy pink gauze. "Chief O'Neill, Victoria, you both look so chic!" She twittered over

Victoria's ankle before she ushered them into the living room, where they could look out over the pond, the bird feeder, and the lawn, freshly cut by Ricky Rezendes.

Two dozen golden rental chairs were arranged in rows in front of a wooden music stand at the end of the large room. Three chairs were set up behind the stand, in front of an immaculate brick fireplace in which there were three unburned birch logs.

"One chair for you, Victoria, one for Chief O'Neill, and one for Connie Rowen, who'll introduce the police chief." Edna adjusted her floating pink scarf, and gave a slight quick turn that set her diaphanous skirt swirling around her plump legs.

Casey put Victoria's folder on the music stand and turned to Edna. "Do you need any help, Mrs. Coffin?"

"I think everything is under control, thank you, Chief O'Neill. Manny Smith is catering, you know."

Victoria held her hand up to her mouth and whispered to Casey, "He ought to be in jail." Casey avoided Victoria's eyes.

Cousin Edna clasped her hands together, setting her skirt in motion again. "You do look marvelous in that uniform, Chief O'Neill." She scuttled around Victoria, trying to help her, getting a cushion Victoria could rest her foot on.

Victoria frowned. "Edna, I'm fine. Don't fuss so."

Edna fluttered some more, complimented Victoria on her new suit, and flounced to the door in answer to a knock, leaving a wispy trail of perfume.

"You came together, how nice, dear."

"Yes. Maddy and I came together."

More voices. "So glad you could come." "How nice to see you." "Delighted you could make it." "Darling, how sweet!"

Victoria could sort out comments above the growing din: "Don't your refreshments look elegant!" "Too pretty to eat."

"How charming your garden looks." "You've gone to so much effort!" "The chairs are such a nice touch." "I must ask Manny for his recipe." "I'm sure these are low calorie!"

The golden chairs began to fill with Kippers. The twittering and clucking increased.

Suddenly, the entry, which had been increasingly noisy, got quiet. The quiet spread to the living room. There was a rustle as women turned to look.

"Why Betty Jackson!" Edna said in her throaty voice. "How sweet of you to come." Victoria knew Edna well enough to know she was caught off guard. "How delightful to have you as our guest today. You know most of the other girls, I believe." She put her hand on Betty's arm and turned to the women nearest her. "You know our minister's wife, of course." Edna and Betty entered the living room together, holding hands.

Heads turned toward Maddy, who stood next to the wide windows that looked out onto the lawn, talking with Sally Snyder. As the room grew quiet, Maddy looked up. Her blue and green paisley-printed dress picked up the colors of her eyes. She walked to the entry, between the chairs and the music stand. Her taffeta slip swished with each step. Her scent trailed behind her. The silence grew.

Maddy held out both hands to Betty, who hesitated only a brief instant, let go of Edna's hand, then took Maddy's in hers. "I'm glad you were able to accept my invitation," Maddy said.

There was an almost audible intake of breath from the women who had trickled into the living room and established places on the chairs. The chatter level rose again. Members greeted Victoria. Casey stood to one side, hands clasped behind her back. Victoria, seated, introduced Casey to the few women who didn't know her.

Connie Rowen, in a pale yellow dress topped with a matching pale yellow cardigan, stepped up to the music stand and waited a few minutes for members to notice her. Finally, she rapped on the stand with the Kippers' mahogany gavel. The twittering eased off and finally stopped. Connie smiled at the group, looked from one to another of the members.

"We're dispensing with business today because we have an unusually interesting program by Mrs. Trumbull, who will speak on law enforcement in West Tisbury. Mrs. Trumbull has invited as her special guest, West Tisbury's Chief of Police, Mary Kathleen O'Neill, also known as Casey."

The ladies applauded politely.

"Chief O'Neill has graciously agreed to answer questions after the lecture." Connie Rowen paused and gazed at her audience. She looked from right to left, as, Victoria, sitting behind her, knew she had learned at the Speaking Out group. "I also asked Chief O'Neill if she would introduce our speaker, whom we all know and love." Connie Rowen started the applause, a light patting of her right fingers on the palm of her left hand. She stepped back from the music stand.

Polite applause, gentle murmurs. Ladies turned to their right or left, made soft comments to one another, heads nodded, pink and coral lips smiled at Casey, who marched the two steps to the music stand. Connie Rowen stepped back from the podium and sat in the still-warm seat Casey had vacated.

"It has been almost a year since I became West Tisbury's police chief," Casey said, clutching the sides of the music stand with both hands. The stand shook slightly. "I came here, where everyone knows everybody or is related to them, from a big-city police force. Chief Ben Norton was a tough act to follow. My most important challenge, I thought, was to turn the police department into a professional force that would be the pride of the Island." Casey took her hands off the stand and put them behind her back. Victoria could see they were trembling.

"First," Casey said, "I made a list of what the town needed. On my list were things like 'road signs,' 'locks on the police station door,' 'get rid of ducks, geese, and swans at the police station.' Not exactly the kind of list I kept in Brockton." The women laughed politely.

"Next, I had to learn who my townspeople were, who lived where, and who was related to whom." She told them about making a mildly insulting joke about someone only to learn he was related to her sergeant. Her audience responded with soft laughter.

"Then," Casey said, "I had the good sense to invite Mrs. Trumbull to ride with me." Victoria looked out over the sherbet-colored dresses.

"Mrs. Trumbull knows everyone in town, she knows where everyone lives, and most of all, she has been working with me to try to unravel a mystery she will tell you about today." Casey shifted her weight from one foot to the other and put her hands back on the music stand.

"Now then," she said. "It goes against every regulation in the police manuals to have a ninety-two-year-old civilian riding shotgun in the chief's vehicle." Casey looked around at the faces in front of her. "I'm trying to establish a professional force."

Casey stopped there. She stepped away from the music stand and went over to her chair. Connie moved both legs smoothly to one side so Casey could bring out the square white box tied with gold ribbon from under the chair.

"I finally figured out a solution," Casey said when she returned to the music stand.

The ladies leaned forward in their chairs.

"Mrs. Trumbull, would you please step up to the podium."

Victoria hoisted herself out of her chair and limped to the music stand.

"I hereby appoint Victoria Trumbull my deputy," Casey said. She took a small jewelry box out of the pocket of her blouse, opened it, and pinned onto Victoria's new jacket a blue-and-gold enameled police badge that read, "Deputy, West Tisbury Police Department." The ladies applauded vigorously.

"This goes with the badge," Casey said, handing the square white box to Victoria, who undid the ribbon, lifted the lid, and took out a navy blue baseball cap, which she promptly set on her newly barbered white hair. On it, gold letters read, "West Tisbury Police, Deputy."

There was a scuffling of chairs, and, one after another, the ladies rose to their feet, applauding. A dozen different scents mingled on the stirred air. The applause went on and on.

"And now," Casey said, as members sat down again, "I introduce our speaker, Deputy Victoria Trumbull of the West Tisbury Police Department."

Victoria took her place at the podium. "My lecture was originally titled, 'Law Enforcement in West Tisbury, Then and Now,'" she said, when things had quieted. "But when I came up with the title, we didn't have a series of murders to solve."

She adjusted her new cap the way she'd seen Junior adjust his, and there were smiles from her audience.

"During the past two months, four people died, all from apparently natural causes," she said. "Hal Greene had a weak heart, Molly Bettencourt had a severe case of flu, Jeremiah Silvia had various complaints, and Brewster Harrington-Smith had Alzheimer's and wandered off into the woods. All of them, except Molly, were elderly, and all of these, except Molly, had left sizable bequests to the West Tisbury church."

Not a mascaraed eyelash fluttered. No papers rustled. The birds at the feeder chirped.

"West Tisbury hasn't had that many deaths over a six-week period since the flu epidemic of 1918. So I was suspicious." She looked behind her at Casey, who was sitting in Connie's chair. Connie was in Casey's. "Chief O'Neill's hands were tied. Nothing was overtly wrong, no reason to investigate the four deaths."

Victoria glanced at Edna, who sat at the back of the room, where, Victoria reasoned, she could help Manny with the refreshments as soon as the lecture was over.

"Molly Bettencourt's was the only death that didn't fit, even though Doc Erickson had labeled it a natural death, caused by flu complications." Victoria grasped the music stand with both hands and leaned forward. "However, Molly died only after I had taken a tuna-noodle-mushroom casserole to her that was left on my table. The casserole was meant for me."

The women gasped, one sharp intake of breath. All eyes were on Victoria.

"I had made no secret of the fact I was leaving a paper worth quite a bit of money to the church."

Betty Jackson stared at Victoria.

"Then, Frederick, Edna's pet seagull, died after eating a stuffed bluefish fillet the Reverend Milton Jackson had given her. Edna doesn't care for bluefish, and she fed it to the gull."

Heads turned toward Betty, who stared at Victoria, her face pale.

"I knew Chief O'Neill had no reason to disinter any of the bodies of the four people who had died, but the seagull was different." Victoria looked out over the two dozen women. "I asked my granddaughter to dig up the gull she had buried next to Edna's bird feeder." Heads turned toward the window and the feeder outside, where two cardinals were scattering seeds onto the freshly disturbed ground.

"I performed an autopsy on the gull, and we took the gull's innards to Jessica Dell. For those of you who don't know her, she is the Island's mushroom expert." Victoria moved away from the music stand and, limping, paced the way she had seen some lawyer pace on television. "Jessica identified the material from the gull as amanita, a deadly mushroom found all over the Vineyard. It's sometimes called 'death's angel.'"

Manicured hands went to pink and coral mouths. Victoria continued. "It looked as though Edna Coffin was another intended victim. Edna occasionally tells more than she should." In the back row, Edna made a low choking sound. Heads turned to look. "She had said to anyone who would listen that she was leaving a large sum of money to the church."

Betty looked at Victoria, unblinking. "Had I eaten the tuna noodle casserole left on my table, and had Edna eaten the stuffed bluefish Jack Jackson brought her, we'd have been victims four and five, the church would have been considerably richer in beneficences, and Molly Bettencourt would still be alive."

Absolute silence. Not a single rustle or audible breath.

"The seagull's death from amanita was enough to give Chief O'Neill probable cause to disinter Molly, and, sure enough, Molly's death was due to amanita poisoning." Victoria stopped at the music stand and folded her hands on the papers spread out on it. "After that, we found that Hal Greene, Brewster Harrington-Smith, and Jeremiah Silvia all died of amanita poisoning."

Victoria put her hands in the pockets of her skirt.

"Who had the motive? That was a question Casey and I have discussed over and over for the past week. And who had the opportunity?"

A slight gust of wind eddied leaves around the base of the feeder; the cardinals' feathers lifted in the breeze.

"My immediate suspicion was that Jack Jackson was responsible." Betty made a slight sound and started to get to her feet. Victoria said, "Sit down, Betty."

Betty sat.

Victoria went on. "The Reverend Jackson is a good cook, he'd given the bluefish to Edna, he'd stuffed it with a mushroom mixture himself, he had been actively promoting beneficences for the church, and he could easily have given any of the five intended victims a poisoned dish. If Edna had died, we never would have known where the bluefish came from."

In the back of the room Edna got up with an expression Victoria recognized as a signal to her that she had said quite enough. Victoria went on as if she had not noticed. "It seemed implausible for the Reverend Jackson to kill off his parishioners. After all, they had made commitments to leave beneficences to the church. All were elderly, assuming the tuna noodle casserole was meant for me. Jack Jackson had nothing to gain by speeding up their deaths." She turned to Betty, who was now rigid, her arms crossed over her grandmotherly bosom, her legs in their shiny stockings crossed tightly. "I have to admit, I could almost see Jack as a murderer." Betty stared at her, head held so stiffly it almost quivered.

"I even saw you as a suspect, Betty," Victoria continued. "You had the same motives, Jack would look good if you could help get beneficences a year or two sooner. You, of course, are not a cook, and that would seem to deflect suspicion from you. But, as minister's wife, you call on neighbors, bring them dishes your husband has prepared."

Edna stood in the doorway, holding a piece of aluminum foil she evidently had taken off a plate of snacks. She mouthed something at Victoria. Except for a few whispers, the rest of the audience sat like stones in the Indian cemetery.

"While this was going on, we had some unpleasantness with Elizabeth's ex-husband, Lockwood. I became suspicious of him. He has trouble, sometimes, distinguishing between right and wrong. He is quite amoral. But the only motive I could assign to Lockwood was trying to frighten Elizabeth." She turned from the stand. "It was possible that, if she refused to return to him, he might attempt to kill her."

For the hundredth time in the past weeks, Victoria realized how badly shaken she was by Lockwood. He had seemed almost like her real grandson during the years he had been married to Elizabeth. She thought how she had taken Elizabeth too much for granted.

She continued, subdued. "If he couldn't have her, no one else could. In fact, I learned that Lockwood had taken a basket of mine, filled it with amanitas, and left it where he was fairly sure someone would find it and return it to me." She looked around at her audience. All were watching her. "He didn't care what happened with the basket of mushrooms. If someone took them home and ate them and died, suspicion would fall on me—or, he supposed, Elizabeth. If the basket were to come back to me, which it did, he was probably amused by imagining the puzzlement it would cause, which it certainly did.

"Lockwood is a good cook," Victoria said. "He spent many summers here on the Vineyard. He knows doors are open and knows people take covered dishes to neighbors." She paused and took a sip of water from the glass set up on a small table next to the music stand. "But that he would kill only elderly people who were leaving money to the church didn't seem plausible. That didn't fit."

Edna stared glassy-eyed at Victoria.

"I went through a list of everyone I could think of who might possibly have a motive. Then Lydia, who turned out to be the Reverend Jack Hutchinson's real wife, showed up at the Reverend Jack Jackson's house." Maddy coughed discreetly. "She had been on-Island throughout the time of the murders. Her motive? Well, I thought about that for a while." Victoria limped a couple of steps toward the window and returned to her notes.

"Lydia Hutchinson refused to divorce Jack because she fantasized that he would return to her someday. A bit like Lockwood in some ways." Victoria looked up. The audience sat motionless. "We all know the saying about hatred and the spurned woman. It's true." Victoria shuffled her notes.

"It was difficult to imagine her taking dishes around to various houses, but not impossible.

"Now, we come to Maddy," Victoria said.

"My dear!" Maddy put a white hand to her throat. "My dear!"

Faces turned to Maddy. Edna fanned herself with a Lyme disease brochure.

"Maddy has been a friend of mine for twenty years," Victoria continued. "I had no suspicion, whatsoever, of Maddy until the mushroom quiche she delivered to me proved to be almost solid amanitas in a luscious egg custard."

Maddy cried out and rose to her feet.

"Please sit down, Maddy. I haven't finished. I was sure it was you when I found that you had taken the poisonous mushroom quiches not only to me but to the nursing home, to

Molly's elderly mother, and to Jack Jackson." She paused. "And to your own husband. Jack."

Maddy cried out, a desolate wail.

The ladies shifted nervously, looked at one another, at Betty, at Maddy.

Victoria grasped the music stand with both hands. "Maddy was understandably upset with Jack Jackson and had even been overheard threatening him."

"I was frustrated!" Maddy cried.

"There was no doubt that the quiches you were taking around the Island were made with poisonous mushrooms. You admitted to making them." Victoria left the podium again and paced, hands clasped behind her back under her jacket, the way a TV lawyer would do this scene. She turned back to her audience. "But I thought it strange that Maddy would want to poison me. We have been friends for years. And it seemed strange that she would think of killing her husband. But the idea made an odd kind of sense. Her husband no longer had the power that had attracted Maddy to him in the first place." Maddy looked out the window, avoiding eye contact with Victoria, hands held together in her lap. "Jack was so ill she might have felt his death was the only way out."

The muffled sound from the audience was a mixture of shock and ghoulishness.

"What puzzled me was why she had made some with poisonous mushrooms and some with common field mushrooms. That didn't seem to fit any part of the picture. Then in talking to her, we learned she had used a jar of preserved mushrooms Hal Greene had given her before he died and supplemented them with field mushrooms."

Betty gasped. "Hal gave my Jack a jar of mushrooms, too."

Victoria turned to her. "Did he cook with them? Did you eat any of Hal Greene's mushrooms?" She leaned over the music stand.

"No," Betty almost sobbed. "Jack doesn't care for mushrooms. He used them to stuff the bluefish he gave to Edna."

Edna emitted a shrill birdlike cry.

"That," Victoria said, "gives us the final puzzle piece. None of the people I mentioned, Jack Jackson, Betty, Maddy, Lockwood, or Lydia could have been the killer."

The ladies shifted in their seats. A faint whiff of perfume wafted over the room, a mingle of fruity, floral, spicy, exotic, musky fragrances.

"Let's take a break now," Victoria said. She felt a heady, theatrical power.

"No!" "Oh, my dear!" "Certainly not!" "Please finish!" "Don't stop!"

"I need to rest my voice," Victoria murmured and turned to Casey, who scowled at her. "I'll continue after the refreshments, Edna. You might ask Manny to serve now."

Edna's blue hair was slightly ruffled. Her pink dress was awry. She stood and went into the kitchen. The ladies began to stand at their places and the level of talk rose again. Someone said, "Why did she stop at that point?"

Casey got to her feet and stood behind Victoria. "What do you think you're doing, Victoria? Are you crazy?"

"Don't move," Victoria whispered. "Do you have your gun?"

"Of course, but…"

"Refreshments, ladies!" Edna jingled a small silver hand bell. During the brief time she had left the room she had fixed her hair and straightened her dress. "Let's all show Manny our appreciation."

As Manny entered the room carrying a tray of canapés,

Edna started a light applause. Manny, dressed in a starched white coat, nodded slightly, avoiding Victoria's gaze.

Victoria turned to Casey. "Are you ready?"

"What are you talking about?"

Victoria waited until Manny was surrounded by the ladies, then pointed straight at him and called to Casey, "Arrest that man!"

"Victoria…" Casey started to say.

Manny looked into Victoria's face with an expression of disgust. He turned quickly, knocking Sally Snyder into one of the chairs. He dropped the tray, spilling canapés over Cousin Edna's newly cleaned carpet, and pushed his way through the knot of women toward the door. Someone screamed. Casey was after Manny instantly. He had almost reached the back door when he suddenly grabbed Edna's arm and yanked her toward him. He twisted and pulled a razor-sharp boning knife out from under his white jacket and held it against Edna's throat. "Stay away. She's coming with me."

Casey skidded to a stop in front of him, her gun drawn. He kicked the door open and backed out, shielding himself with Edna, whose face was doughlike.

The ladies stood frozen in place. Victoria looked out through the open door behind Manny and smiled.

"Drop it, Manny." Ben Norton, who was waiting with Junior on the step behind Manny, seized the small man's thin arms in his big hands and squeezed until his knuckles were white. Manny screamed and his knife clattered to the floor. Cousin Edna swooned. Casey whipped Manny's hands behind him and clipped handcuffs onto his wrists. Quickly, almost before anyone had time to react, Casey and Ben and Junior hustled Manny into the Crown Victoria that was parked in front of the Bronco and, siren wailing, took off.

Victoria was the first to speak. "Someone get Edna a glass of cold water and get her to bed."

"No, no," Edna said, struggling to her feet. "The meeting must go on."

Maddy and Betty hurried to Edna's side. Someone cleaned up the spilled canapés from the carpet.

"Well," Maddy said when the ladies were seated again. "Did you have to put us through all that, Victoria? Couldn't you have used fewer theatrics? How did you know the killer was Manny?"

"Lockwood was the one who came up with the final clue," Victoria said, once the audience had settled down and attention was focused on her again. "He had kept in touch with Edna. He counted on the fact that," Victoria hesitated, "Edna likes to, ah, chat with her friends."

Edna, now sitting in one of the front seats, was fanning herself with the brochure she'd picked up again, opened out so sketches of deer ticks faced Victoria. "Lockwood asked Edna why I was getting meals delivered to my house."

Victoria looked at her audience. "I, of course, don't get meals delivered to me. That's something for the elderly or infirm. Edna, naturally, reported back to me what Lockwood had said. She mentioned that Lockwood, who had been watching my house from New Lane for some time, said the Meals on Wheels van had come to my house at least twice during that time."

Victoria leaned over the podium. "Recently, I had the misfortune of backing into the van."

Edna stopped fanning herself for a moment.

"I don't know how many of you realize Manny is, or was, Brewster Harrington-Smith's son." Victoria looked up and saw a sea of blank expressions. "Manny dropped the Harring-

ton and the hyphen and was known simply as 'Manny Smith.'
Most people didn't even know the two were related. Brewster often dropped the hyphen and the Smith and went simply by 'Harrington.'" Nods from the audience. "Brewster was what we used to call 'difficult,' a man who made life miserable for his family.

"Manny himself is more than a trifle unstable, possibly as a result of childhood experiences with his father. He worked as a chef at the nursing home as well as a volunteer delivering meals to shut-ins." Victoria paced, hands behind her. "When I backed into his van, he went into a paroxysm of rage. I had trouble believing that such a seemingly gentle person could say the things he did."

Victoria adjusted her new cap. "Edna told me Manny's father planned to change his will to give his sizable fortune to the church." Victoria took another sip of water. "Manny undoubtedly heard about it. So Manny decided to kill several birds with one stone, I suppose you could say. He wanted to stop his father before he changed his will, not realizing it was too late. He wanted to get even with me for, as he called it, 'destroying' his van." Victoria looked around at her rapt audience .

"But Manny had other reasons. He quite sincerely imagined that elderly people were all desperately unhappy," Victoria said. "Working at the nursing home and driving the Meals on Wheels van, he began to think he could do his elderly friends a favor by easing them out of this life." She looked out the window and saw a squirrel in the center of the feeder, its fluffy tail held up for balance. "Remember the sign on his van says, FOOD FIT FOR AN ANGEL. I don't know whether his recognition of death's angel mushrooms as an instrument of murder inspired him or not. The amanitas were certainly an easy-to-obtain murder weapon. He was a chef, and he had the delivery system to take dishes around to unsuspecting people.

"Hal Greene was his first victim. We learned this afternoon that Manny had given Hal several jars of mushrooms preserved in oil and garlic. Not all were amanita, Manny was playing a kind of Russian roulette.

"Casey was troubled by Hal's symptoms." Victoria looked around at Casey's empty seat. "She said his symptoms didn't seem typical of a heart attack. But since Doc Erickson was treating Hal for a heart condition, it seemed logical for him to put Hal's death down to natural causes.

"I had no idea who had brought me the tuna noodle casserole I gave to Molly." Victoria's hooded eyes lost some of their glitter briefly. "Then when Edna told me Lockwood had seen the van come to my house, not once but twice, I began to suspect Manny.

"At that point, everything came together. First Hal Greene, himself—who'd shared the jars of preserved mushrooms Manny had given him with Jack Jackson and Maddy—dined on the mushrooms. We saw what happened." The ladies watched Victoria, unmoving.

"According to Jessica, amanitas, or death's angels, are fatal only about fifty percent of the time for normal healthy people," Victoria said. "But for someone who is elderly or ill, they are invariably fatal. It was not much of a gamble.

"It all fits together." Victoria gazed out of the window. "Manny gave jars of preserved mushrooms to Hal Greene. Hal gave mushrooms to Jack Jackson, and that's what killed Edna's gull." Victoria was quiet for a brief moment. She clasped her hands on the music stand. "Fortunately, we identified the mushrooms in Maddy's quiche and retrieved all the quiches Maddy so generously gave away." Maddy looked at Victoria with an enigmatic smile.

"That explains Hal's death. Manny imagined he was doing Hal a kindness. And Molly's death. Manny intended that for me." Victoria paused again. "Manny delivered his angels of death to Jeremiah Silvia, and again, he felt it was an act of kindness. Jeremiah was always complaining about how awful he felt. And Manny delivered a deadly meal to Brewster, his father, for a complex of reasons. His last and final attempt was on me again, a container of mushroom soup. But by this time, I had become wary of food left on my kitchen table. Those mushrooms, too, were amanitas." Victoria limped away from the music stand toward Edna. She bent slightly and touched Edna's shoulder. "It is Edna who deserves credit for giving us the final clue, the key that unlocked the mystery. That clue stopped a serial killer before he could put any more people out of their misery."

Edna's expression was difficult to decipher. There was an element of fury at seeing her meeting turn into a debacle on the day when she was hostess. In her expression there was also a flicker of respect for her cousin-in-law.

"Questions?" Victoria said brightly.

TWENTY-TWO

"GRAM, YOU CAN'T wear that cap to church. It won't do." Elizabeth stood in the cookroom door, hands on her hips.

Victoria had set her blue police cap on her head at an angle. Elizabeth had noticed lately that, when Victoria was not wearing the cap, her hair had a crease in back, and her face had become two-toned, pale above her eyes, where the cap shaded her face, tanned below.

"I don't know why not," Victoria clipped on her gold earrings and turned her head slightly so she could see herself in the bathroom mirror. "When I was a child, we always wore hats to church."

"Not police caps."

"We've gotten out of the habit," Victoria went on as if she hadn't heard. "I think we should go back to the custom again."

"But a baseball cap with 'West Tisbury Police, Deputy' on it?" Elizabeth stood watching her at the bathroom door.

"It's a nice hat." Victoria's jaw set stubbornly in a way Elizabeth recognized. "It matches my plaid suit and my earrings." She turned her head first one way then the other.

When her grandmother came out of the bathroom, Elizabeth knew she'd lost the battle. Victoria looked stylishly put together, even with the baseball cap. She had a certain chic that kids today, with their baggy trousers and backward-facing baseball caps, yearned for. Elizabeth held the blue quilted coat, and Victoria slipped her arms into the sleeves.

"The hat matches my coat, too. It's not as if it's a regular Sunday church service." She picked up her pocketbook from the chair under the spider plant. "Jessica will probably come to the wedding. I know she was invited." Victoria lifted a pile of papers from the bookshelf where she kept the notes for her column. "I wonder where her mushroom book can be? I ought to return it to her."

"It's under the dining room table. I'll get it." Elizabeth retrieved the volume from the top of a pile of books.

"Things have taken a strange turn," Elizabeth said. "Here we are, going to Maddy and Jack's wedding, with Jack Jackson performing the ceremony. And Lockwood has disappeared. I wonder why he gave up?"

"We'll probably never know." Victoria shrugged.

Once they were outdoors, Victoria got into the passenger side of the convertible while Elizabeth brushed off the yellow leaves that had covered the windshield.

"And then you figured out who the killer was. I'm impressed." She looked over at her grandmother, the beaklike nose, hooded eyes. "Who would have guessed the guilty party was Manny Smith, the guy driving the van you demolished."

"I did not…" Victoria started to say, then stopped when she saw the mischievous look on Elizabeth's face.

"I heard you disrupted the Kippers' meeting, too. The ladies will never be the same."

"My lecture had a unifying effect," Victoria said. "The Kippers are all speaking to one another for the first time in years. They've temporarily buried the hatchet."

"What hatchet?" Elizabeth had reached the end of the drive, where she had stopped for a car to pass, and looked at Victoria.

"For wearing the same color dress to meetings or serving the same sandwiches. Being upset over something significant will do them good."

"Exactly what did you say that bothered them so much?" Elizabeth turned onto the main road. "Even the gang on the steps of Alley's is buzzing about it."

"I did a denouement, like Nero Wolfe."

"I suppose you accused each one in turn of the murders, and each one gasped with outrage?"

Victoria nodded.

Elizabeth glanced to her left as they passed New Lane. Grass on the side of the road where the Jeep had parked was beginning to grow back.

"Lydia Hutchinson got her divorce from Jack, thanks to Jack Jackson's help," Victoria said. "Both Jacks are now speaking to each other. Jack Hutchinson's depression seems to be clearing up, and I hear Cousin Edna's Jack is making an effort to conquer his jealousy. He's forming a twelve-step program, JEANS, for 'Jealousy Anonymous.'"

"Someone told me Jack Jackson has asked Jack Hutchinson to serve as sexton." Elizabeth glanced at her grandmother. "And as sexton he'll ring the church bell on Sunday mornings when Jack is in the pulpit."

Elizabeth slowed as they neared the Mill Pond.

"Maddy has invited Betty to come to Kippers' meetings as guest, until one of us drops out or dies."

"Is Casey reconciled to the fact that Angelo is more interested in Winthrop than he is in her?" Elizabeth asked.

"Angelo and Casey and her son are great buddies. Angelo's teaching Casey to play computer games. They've been going on picnics with Winthrop."

They passed the police station. Ducks and geese squatted

on the front steps. Elizabeth stopped to let the swans waddle across the road, their long necks stretched ahead of them. A car coming from the opposite direction stopped, too.

Elizabeth started up again, slowly, because a turtle was beginning to cross the road on the other side of the mill. Brakes squealed as a car coming down Brandy Brow stopped.

"Going too fast," Victoria remarked. She pulled down the visor and looked at herself in the tiny mirror.

"If we don't hit any more traffic, we'll be right on time. You'll want to show off your chapeau."

A WEEK AFTER the wedding, Victoria and Elizabeth were working in the kitchen. "I made some soup this morning from the carcass of last Sunday's chicken," Elizabeth said. "Shall we take some to Casey?"

"That would be nice." Victoria gathered her notes together and put them in the gray folder she used for her weekly column.

Elizabeth ladled the warm chicken soup into an empty cottage cheese container and snapped on the lid. "This is probably more than enough."

Once Victoria had settled herself in the passenger seat, Elizabeth handed her the soup container and they headed out the drive.

"I didn't think there was a bug around that could touch Casey. She's usually so healthy."

Victoria started to answer her granddaughter, but snickered instead. Elizabeth glanced sharply at her. They drove past New Lane, past Old County Road, past the police station and the old mill and the duck pond. They drove past Brandy Brow, past Alley's. The gang on the porch waved. Victoria waved back with her left hand. She was trying to hold back gales of laughter. They drove past Maley's statues of dancing nudes.

Elizabeth looked at Victoria with irritation. "There's nothing funny about being sick. You never did get your flu shot, and you should."

Victoria wiped away tears of laughter with her free hand. They drove past the church, past the gas station. Elizabeth found herself joining in despite her annoyance, not knowing why she was laughing.

"Okay, Gram. What's so funny?"

Victoria, between peals of merry laughter, said, "Casey got her flu shot three days ago."

Elizabeth looked at her grandmother, puzzled. "We'd better control ourselves before we get to Casey's sickbed. What's wrong with her, anyway?"

Victoria's large brown eyes were magnified by her tears. "Reaction to flu shot," she said.

HARLEQUIN®
INTRIGUE®

WE'LL LEAVE YOU BREATHLESS!

If you've been looking for thrilling tales of
contemporary passion and sensuous love stories
with taut, edge-of-the-seat suspense—then
you'll love Harlequin Intrigue!

Every month, you'll meet six new heroes
who are guaranteed to make your spine tingle
and your pulse pound. With them you'll enter
into the exciting world of Harlequin Intrigue—
where your life is on the line
and so is your heart!

THAT'S INTRIGUE—
ROMANTIC SUSPENSE
AT ITS BEST!

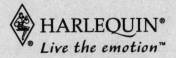

HARLEQUIN®
Live the emotion™

HARLEQUIN®
Presents

The world's bestselling romance series...
The series that brings you your favorite authors,
month after month:

Helen Bianchin...Emma Darcy
Lynne Graham...Penny Jordan
Miranda Lee...Sandra Marton
Anne Mather...Carole Mortimer
Susan Napier...Michelle Reid

and many more uniquely talented authors!

Wealthy, powerful, gorgeous men...
Women who have feelings just like your own...
The stories you love, set in exotic, glamorous locations...

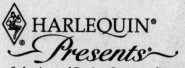

HARLEQUIN®
Presents

Seduction and Passion Guaranteed!

HPDIR104

V *Silhouette*

SPECIAL EDITION™

Emotional, compelling stories that capture the intensity of living, loving and creating a family in today's world.

Special Edition features bestselling authors such as Nora Roberts, Susan Mallery, Sherryl Woods, Christine Rimmer, Joan Elliott Pickart— and many more!

For a romantic, complex and emotional read, choose Silhouette Special Edition.

V *Silhouette*®

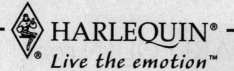

xxx 12-24-05

eHARLEQUIN.com

The Ultimate Destination for Women's Fiction

For **FREE online reading,** visit
www.eHarlequin.com now and enjoy:

Online Reads
Read **Daily** and **Weekly** chapters from
our Internet-exclusive stories by your
favorite authors.

Interactive Novels
Cast your vote to help decide how these
stories unfold…then stay tuned!

Quick Reads
For shorter romantic reads, try our
collection of Poems, Toasts, & More!

Online Read Library
Miss one of our online reads?
Come here to catch up!

Reading Groups
Discuss, share and rave with other
community members!

— For great reading online, —
visit www.eHarlequin.com today!